COPENHAGEN NOIR

COPENHAGEN NOIR

EDITED BY BO TAO MICHAËLIS

Translated by Mark Kline

This collection is comprised of works of fiction. All names, characters, places, and incidents are the product of the authors' imaginations. Any resemblance to real events or persons, living or dead, is entirely coincidental.

The translation of this volume is supported by the Danish National Arts Council's Literature Committee.

Published by Akashic Books
©2011 Akashic Books

Series concept by Tim McLoughlin and Johnny Temple
Copenhagen map by Aaron Petrovich

ISBN-13: 978-1-936070-66-4
Library of Congress Control Number: 2010922712

First printing

Akashic Books
PO Box 1456
New York, NY 10009
info@akashicbooks.com
www.akashicbooks.com

Printed in Canada

Also in the Akashic Noir Series:

Forthcoming:

COPENHAGEN

ØRESUND

NORTHWEST

VANLØSE

NØRREBRO

ØRSTEDSPARKEN
CITY CENTER

FREDERIKSBERG

FREDERIKSBERG ALLÉ

CENTRAL STATION

VESTERBRO

ISTEDGADE

VALBY

ØRESTAD

AMAGER

MALMÖ, SWEDEN

KALVEBODERNE

KØGE BUGT

TABLE OF CONTENTS

PART III: CORPSES

Copenhagen demands time.
—Dan Turèll

INTRODUCTION
THE SEAMY SIDE OF MODERNISM

The French word for *black* is currently an often (mis) used trendy word for irrational and uncontrollable crime, a melodramatic, spectacular, and thrilling intrigue in an entertaining story that begins well but ends badly. The word gained this interpretation in the postwar world of the 1940s, after the launch of a French series of hard-boiled books, "Série Noire," written by American, English, and French authors, from Dashiell Hammett to Cornell Woolrich and Raymond Chandler, to Georges Simenon and Léo Malet. Black on black, death never gives credit and life is short and dirty, like a kid's shirt. Yet, what does *noir* mean nowadays with regards to concept, style, and genre?

Noir is the story of the fateful coincidence, the precarious absurdity and bitter nonchalance of life. It speaks of loss of control and lack of insight, of irrationality's impact on what seems to make sense—the throw of the dice that didn't win, to put it simply. The style is minimalistic, open, and terse. It attempts to describe an unpredictable calamity rather than any act of clear rationality. Capturing the murderer is neither what's necessary nor important. Because noir is seldom interested in illuminating a valid truth or forming clarity, it rarely seeks a transparent understanding that it doesn't believe in anyway. Noir is the crime genre's bleak nostalgia and, at the same time, its unsentimental vision of modern times; without degenerating into cheap puritanism or bigoted abstinence, it often includes sexuality, and more in the light of being used destructively than as any romantic idealism. A noir story seldom has a happy ending. When it does happen, such as in Chandler's Philip Marlowe books, it is with a bittersweet taste of compromise or bargaining. Life goes on with a wounded soul, and only that which is lost is eternal. Past, present, and future melt into one synchronous now, which cancels out every hope that times change and things will be better. As a famous title from a noir writer, Horace McCoy, puts it: kiss tomorrow goodbye, because nothing will be there at daybreak.

Noir is disillusionment and melancholy in relation to the big city, the melting pot of modernism. Some classic noir stories do take place in the country, but the metropolis appears either as modernism's revenge or as temptations fallen for in the past that now must be paid for; it often involves cold revenge, heated confrontation, old love, or as all three at the same time and place.

The most archetypical noir short story is Ernest Hemingway's "The Killers," originally published in *Scribner's* in 1927. Two hit men arrive in a country town to shoot a newcomer with a big-city past. It doesn't happen, they don't find him that day, but as the narration progresses, we readers know from reading between the lines that it is only a question of time before the killing takes place. Such is life in noir—you can't avoid your fate; at the most you can delay it and hope that death comes quickly and relatively painlessly as the long sleep that we all must enter at some given point in our lives.

Noir loves flight, ill-fated love, the cold avenger. You could say that Alexander Dumas's classic novel of revenge from 1844, *The Count of Monte Cristo*, is the first noir novel, with its lengthy and cold-blooded reprisal that can be traced back to the main character's disadvantaged, unfair, and virtually psychopathic past. Others identify Greek tragedy, with its gruesome destinies and lack of redeeming Providence, as the oldest forerunner of the genre.

No matter. The important point is that noir only *seems* to operate within the crime genre. There is noir that merely touches occasionally on an actual crime story; Paul Auster's novels about New York come to mind, but authors from other genres and other parts of the globe can also be included. Japan's Haruki Murakami, England's Ian McEwan, and Sweden's Karin Alvtegen all can be said to create works resembling noir. The dark style does not require bodies, pathetic sex, or cover-to-cover violence. More a clear literary, late-modernist, and existential sense that in the evil streets of the big city and dark suburbs is found the consummate experience of shock—the confrontation with the seamy side of modernism.

Europe's End and the Gateway to Scandinavia:
Copenhagen As Noir

Copenhagen: the Little Mermaid, H.C. Andersen, Søren Kierkegaard, and Karen Blixen, a big city that perhaps more than any other is the absolute capital, origin, and center of northern European romanticism of the 1800s. Denmark's Copenhagen, with its ramparts and moats forming the shell of the city and suburbs, has retained a glint of back then, that world of yesterday. To be exact, the city's archaic Middle Ages center, with the beautiful buildings, squares, and streets that tourists meet from their hotels, a comfortable inner circle with Tivoli as its midpoint and King's Square its end. At one point our metropolis was presented as an idyllic, modest-sized big city, where police stopped traffic when a mother duck guided her ugly ducklings across the street populated by cars, bicycles, and streetcars. But naturally, and quite unfortunately, such is the case no longer.

Copenhagen long ago abandoned its Sleeping Beauty slumber for a cosmopolitan night and day that never sleeps, neither in a good nor bad way. Four-wheel drive vehicles, limos, and expensive sports cars now sail down the boulevards and avenues that were once characterized by girls bicycling on dirt paths and healthy boys briskly walking to work or to girlfriends. Those times are gone forever.

The main character of Naja Marie Aidt's noir story, "Women in Copenhagen," returns to the city after seventeen years and realizes that the place has become more multicultural, turbulent, and global than the Brooklyn where he lives. Everything is in flux, in a variety of colors. Gone is the provincial city appointed as capital; instead, one is confronted with a metropolis where the food is from the Middle East, the wine from California, the women from Africa, and the mafia from Russia. Mafia! A new word at these latitudes, where crime formerly took place among bands identified with city neighborhoods and regions. Beatings were bloody noses from a few punches, not like now with knifings and shotgun blasts in the gut and an unmarked grave out in the sticks or under the deep blue sea. Between the wars, in the 1930s, we in Denmark spoke of "white slavery," poor women kidnapped to a life of prostitution in foreign brothels—today it's called trafficking, and now we speak of the vile import of East European women. And moreover, we are indeed the last country in Scandinavia to criminalize the customer of such activity, the buying of a hooker.

The short stories in *Copenhagen Noir* deal often with this phenomenon, the introduction of women from the outside—often the third world—to our own little den of capitalist lust, to abuse them. Our northern nation, where Europe ends and Scandinavia begins, and which time and again boasts of its romantic lifestyle and puritanical decency in song, in verses concerning our mellow nature, our hale and hearty men and gentle women. This anthology articulates with skill and resolve the dark side of our romantic identity depicted by our nineteenth-century golden-age literature and contemporary hits on radio and TV, rhyming on love and pain. Here we see the modernist noir, linked to organized prostitution run by criminals from outside our borders. This is a different Copenhagen from what the still lifes suggest in tourist brochures.

But Copenhagen is also something other than the medium-sized capital of the Danes. The Øresundsbro was finished June 1, 2000, connecting Denmark with Sweden—or perhaps more significantly, from a historic perspective, with the Swedish province of Skåne, the former Danish province lost in the mid-1600s after a number of catastrophic wars. We also lost the region's capital city, Malmø, which was largely Danish and which, in the period after the Swedish annexation, still attempted to preserve its Danish character. The bridge to Malmø has not only stirred a renaissance for this "freedom movement"; it has also connected southern Sweden more closely to Copenhagen than to the country's actual capital, beautiful Stockholm. Nowadays, Swedes/Skånings work in Copenhagen and Danes live in Malmø. The bridge has transformed Malmø into a large suburb of Copenhagen; generally speaking, our capital could be seen as a Manhattan to a Malmø that, via one of Europe's longest bridges, has become a northern European Brooklyn! Therefore, it is natural that the Swedish author Kristian Lundberg, who lives in Malmø, is included in this anthology, with a story about his hero, the alcoholic Catholic policeman Nils Forsberg. Lundberg sees Copenhagen as the end of the rainbow, on the other side of the bridge, a big city that in many ways has put Malmø in a different perspective, different from its status as a big Swedish city.

But Copenhagen was once not only the Danish capital. The city was, in fact, the capital of Norway for four hundred years, much longer than Norway's present one, Oslo. Norway justifiably wrested its independence from Denmark in 1814, but long afterward, even to the present day, Norwegians have held a nostalgic and "metropolitan" love for Copenhagen, Europe's end and the gateway to Scandinavia. But for Norwegians it must actually be the opposite: for them Copenhagen must still be the gateway to Europe, for the cultural bonds are strong and persistent via history, the royalty, and, in particular, language, culture, and literature. Danes and Norwegians are like close relatives who meet affectionately after a happy divorce, who get along very well. Norway's greatest crime writer, Gunnar Staalesen from Bergen, naturally sends his hero detective, the sensitive yet hard-boiled Varg Veum, on a mission to Copenhagen. As far back as in one of his first detective novels, *Sleeping Beauty* from 1980, Varg Veum is at work in the center of Copenhagen, in the district that is more or less red-light, stretching from Central Station toward the "mean streets" where gangsters find their apprentices and hookers their customers. Therefore, it is fitting that this Norwegian author has a place in an anthology about crime and punishment in Norway's old capital, where Scandinavia begins and ends in a metropolis for the entire region.

All the short stories in *Copenhagen Noir* are about meaninglessness, violence, and murder in various districts of the city. Written for the most part by Copenhageners, but also by authors— Helle Helle, Susanne Staun, and Gretelise Holm—who now live in the provinces but have spent a part of their lives in the Queen's city, having absorbed the city and never completely abandoned it. Denmark's celebrated author from the island of Amager (where the Øresundsbro begins), Klaus Rifbjerg, is of course included, with a historical noir story from that great island, an assimilated part of the capital. But the collection also includes inhabitants of ethnic backgrounds from outside the shadow of the Danish flag. Common for all the writers is a love for Copenhagen and for the dark story of coincidence and necessity, the good and bad luck of humans. In a metropolis that both has a style of its own yet also resembles the other black pearls of cities across the globe: New York, Los Angeles, London, Paris, and Berlin. Enjoy.

Bo Tao Michaëlis
Copenhagen, Denmark
October 2010

PART I

(MEN AND) WOMEN

WOMEN IN COPENHAGEN

BY NAJA MARIE AIDT

Ørstedsparken

I f you ever come to Copenhagen and ride into town from the airport on a rainy, dark November evening, the taxi driver will doubtless take the harbor road and you will travel through residential neighborhoods and abandoned areas with old factories where the wind rattles the windows, and you will see the lights from across the sound in Sweden and be puzzled at how quiet and deserted it is here. You have arrived in Scandinavia. You have just entered a long, bitter winter. Here there are no free rides. Here you are left to your own fate. The taxi driver listens to Arabian pop music and talks on the phone. The taxi meter ticks. You get a glimpse of a young woman with blond hair down her back, standing alone on a street corner, apparently wondering which way to go. You see black water sloshing in the canals and lights from bars and pubs. Noisy groups of drunk kids popping out of the dark with beer in plastic bags; their glowing cigarettes. And suddenly you've arrived. The driver runs your credit card through the machine and sends you out in the rain. You're here.

That's how it was for me when I arrived in Copenhagen to clear up a painful situation. November. Rain. Wind. The low sky. A sense of desolation. I had lived in Brooklyn so long that I felt like a stranger. My Danish was rusty. My parents long dead and gone. But Lucille was there. Or was she? That was the question.

* * *

The night clerk glances at me and hands me a heavy key. I say that I don't know how long I'm staying; he doesn't raise an eyebrow but sends me up to the third floor, and I walk through a hallway that has seen better days and let myself into room 304. A bed, a desk, a chair. A bathroom with a leaky faucet. The raw, damp cold that characterizes Denmark in the winter. I push the curtain open and look down at the back courtyard. Trash cans, overturned bicycles. A glimpse of night sky, a full, misty moon. But no stars. I hang my shirts in the closet. Wash my hands and take a drink of cold water from the faucet. I need a shave. I lie down on the bed, float around a moment in the confused but weightless condition just before sleep—and then darkness; it's been a long time since I've had any sleep and I desperately need it. I see Lucille clearly in my dreams. Her narrow, freckled face, her sparkling blue eyes. The birthmark on her forehead. The smooth, light-colored hair, lying like a helmet on her head. She smiles. She is missing one of her front teeth. I see Lucille as the child she was a long time ago. And I wake up bathed in sweat and grope around for the clock. It's three a.m. A feeling of guilt, and something vague, unpleasant. I turn over. But I can't sleep. I switch on the bedside lamp and sit up. Light a cigarette. And then it sweeps through me, as it so often has. The memories from this city. Isabel, Lucille's mother, her warm breath in my ear. Her breasts and silky, meaty thighs. The unmistakable French accent that enhanced whatever she said, turned it into something special. The image of her, there in the doorway with Lucille standing behind like a shadow, that day I left her. That day I left them. We'd had soup and drunk some wine. Isabel grabbed my hand under the table. But I had already made up my mind. Now it's hard for me to understand why. Because that little bit of happiness we truly did find now and then, I never captured again; there's been nothing but quick stopovers in sleazy rooms with burned-out, sad women, the brief physical satisfaction that kind of sex provides, a bad taste in my mouth. I wanted to be free and see the world, instead I prowled around like a caged animal; the world isn't big enough for someone so restless that he searches relentlessly, without a clue to what he is looking for.

I see Lucille, like a shadow behind her mother. I hear the front door slam behind me. I haven't seen her since. At one point I heard in a roundabout way that Isabel had died, but I didn't write Lucille, didn't even send a funeral wreath. Suddenly I got an e-mail from her in September, and that's when I knew I had to find her. If she's still alive. I listen to the wind, a few cats hissing and howling in the courtyard, the faint sound of groaning intercourse from somewhere in the building. *If she's still alive.*

I spend the next few days sniffing around the neighborhood: Vendersgade, Farimagsgade, the other street leading to the lakes. The old hospital the university has taken over, the Botanical Gardens and its hothouses and meticulously laid beds and paths. The weather improves, clear and cold, the light is fantastic around four, five o'clock when the sun sets at the end of Nørrebrogade. I eat at the wine bar on Nansensgade. Tapas and a bottle of intense, full-bodied Bordeaux. Lurch back to the room at midnight, half-drunk. On Tuesday I catch sight of a surprisingly pretty face in the bakery. It turns out to be Lucille's childhood friend Kirsten. She recognizes me. And I recognize her from her smile and thick, copper-colored hair. She gives me a hug. "How are you? How's Lucille doing?" she asks. "I was just about to ask you the same question. I'm trying to get hold of her." "I haven't seen her for several months. She was living with that guy Dmitrij down on Turesensgade. But I'm sure you know that." "Dmitrij?" "Yeah. But I think she moved out. He's Russian. He speaks Russian, anyway. I think." She remembers their street number. I scratch it down on the bakery receipt. We chat for a while, she says she still lives here in her old neighborhood, I give her a short version of my life in New York, make it sound more glamorous than it is. I say that I'm here to see Lucille. That I've come to see her again after all these years. She says that they are still friends. That she had been really happy when Lucille suddenly showed up. And she talks about this Dmitrij: "He seemed to be a little . . . rough," she says, "or . . . it surprised me, Lucille picking that kind of boyfriend. She's a totally different type." I don't know what type Lucille is. I don't tell her that. Kirsten goes on: "He wasn't exactly a friendly person, or how should I say it? I was actually a little afraid of him, that sounds crazy, but I was. I only visited them once." I nod. We walk toward Ørstedsparken, she has to pick her daughter up at daycare. "You look almost the same," she says, with a sudden tenderness in her voice, "it must be nearly . . . eighteen years since I last saw you." We look into each other's eyes a moment. "You spilled something red on your shirt," she says, pointing at my chest, "is it wine?" She laughs at me. I follow her with greedy eyes until she turns a corner, and I'm ashamed of the desire rising up in me; her gait is light and feathery, she wears a short jacket that fits snugly across her back. I look down at myself, the large wine stain. My shirt is crookedly buttoned too.

Lucille wrote: *I think I'm in danger. Don't know where to hide. Can't go to the police. Can you help me?* I read her e-mail again. I wrote back immediately after it came. She never answered. I slip on my jacket and walk down to meet Dmitrij on Turesensgade.

* * *

A woman with two small children lets herself out, I stick my foot in before the door closes. The hallway has recently been renovated, like most of this city. Everything has changed since I lived in the neighborhood with Isabel: the façades have been repaired, roses and trees planted, buildings in rear courtyards torn down in favor of "common-area environments." It no longer looks like a city, but more like a residential district; the bars, the butcher, the tobacco shops have disappeared, replaced by stores with organic chocolate and expensive children's clothing. It's clean and orderly. But you can still get a tattoo, I see, and even though that shop also has an attractive, exclusive look, it seems they mostly do piercing. *Andreev* is the name on the door. I knock. And knock again. Just as I turn to walk away the door is flung open. A man in a crewcut, midthirties, stares at me. Narrow, steel-gray eyes, pale skin. "What do you want?" he asks. He nearly spits the words out. "I'd like to talk to Lucille." "She doesn't live here anymore." "Where does she live?" He shrugs his shoulders. "How should I know? She's gone." "Gone? Where to? Out of the country?" "Don't know." I hear muffled voices in the apartment, chairs scraping. Russian is spoken. I get a glimpse of a long-haired, dark-skinned man, he lights a cigarette. The door slams shut.

In the evening I go for a walk in Ørstedsparken. The homosexuals' park. A young guy comes up to me when I sit down on a bench by the public bathrooms. I politely turn down his offer. Two panting men walk out of the bushes. There is a lot going on here. Men of all ages circulate, stop, eye each other from head to toe, ask for a light, talk for a while, move further inside the park, or use the little houses on the playground behind me. Everything seems very straightforward and efficient. Yellow lights shine over the bridge, giving the lake a dreamlike, foggy look, the wind whips the last leaves off the trees. The night air is cold. I stand up and head toward Israels Plads, the square where the hash dealers hang out. That's also something new: in the old days you had to go out to Christiania to buy the stuff. The Free Town, which nowadays is also being "normalized." Everything has to be "cozy," a terrible idea for a city. A group of nearly grown boys with Mideastern roots shiver under a streetlight, talking and playfully shoving each other. While I smoke a cigarette, several customers approach them and buy whatever they are looking for. Wonder if it's only hash. The boys aren't a day over seventeen. A police car drives by and the boys scatter quickly into the dark. I buy a cup of coffee in the 7-Eleven and wait for a half hour on a bench with a good view of the square. Then I recognize the dark, long-haired Russian. It looks like he's collecting from the boys. But evidently there is a problem, one of the boys raises his voice, wants to discuss something, the longhair starts shouting, threatening, his fist right under the boy's chin. Everything is quiet. They look at the ground. I decide to follow him. He walks up to Nørreport Station and hails a cab. I hop in a second cab and tell the driver to follow them. I can see him counting money in the backseat. Running his fingers through his hair. We head toward Sydhavnen. Out here the wind whips up. The car stops at an empty lot down by the harbor. I ride farther on and get out behind the cover of a wooden fence. It's icy cold, below freezing. I breathe white clouds. I check my watch: one-thirty. From here I can see the Russian pacing back and forth, talking loudly on the phone, gesturing. Then they appear out of the dark. Five—seven—nine girls. Young and black. He collects again. One of the girls stays in the background. He calls her over. She backs away. But then she walks over to him anyway, and he keeps her there while the others head back toward the harbor in their thin clothes. I've read about these girls, especially the ones from Gambia, in the Danish paper I still get. They are held as prostitutes here, often under threat and against their will. They are promised a life of luxury in cozy little Copenhagen. And end up as slaves. The Russian slaps the girl. Slaps her again. Hisses something or other in her face while clenching her chin. Then he brutally shoves her away; she stumbles and falls, he turns and walks quickly back to the street. I want to help the girl up. But I plod after the Russian. For a long time, through deserted streets. We're almost up to Enghave Station before he finally flags a taxi.

It doesn't surprise me that he returns to Turesensgade and Dmitrij. So Lucille has had a boyfriend who not only runs a hash operation but is also a pimp, maybe a sex trafficker. Apparently the longhair does the dirty work. I'm beginning to get an idea of what might have happened; I feel my pulse beating in my temples.

The next morning I meet Kirsten again in the bakery. She looks sweet, a bit puffy in the face from sleep, with clear eyes and an arched red mouth. She holds her daughter's hand. I ask her if Lucille had a job the last time she saw her. She says that she is in teacher's college. She looks at me. "Haven't you found her yet?" I shake my head. "I think I have her phone number, wait just a second." She pays and hands a pastry to her daughter. And sends Lucille's number to my phone. "I remember your apartment so well, back when I was a kid," Kirsten says, and smiles. "That long creepy hallway, the dining room table we built caves under. And Lucille's mother." "Isabel," I say. "Yeah. Isabel." She grabs her bag. "Call me," she whispers, and she's out the door, I watch her lift her daughter up on her bike seat. I'm left with my coffee and my paper and suddenly I feel wide awake.

Across from the building on Turesensgade is a large courtyard passageway—it's possible to stand hidden in there and still see the second-floor apartment's windows. I can also keep an eye on the front door. I brace myself for a long lookout. I end up standing there four hours. My legs and lower back are sore. I give up. Nothing happens. I do see Dmitrij drive up in a red car together with a tall, well-tanned man. I also see the long-hair run down the stairs and return a few minutes later. With cigarettes. Just a trip to the kiosk. That's it. I don't know what I imagined would happen. I call Lucille's number several times, but there doesn't seem to be any connection. I send a text, ask her to call. I get no answer. I wander up to Funch's Wine Bar on Farimagsgade for a sandwich with beer and aquavit. Roast pork and round sausage. The red cabbage melts in my mouth, the pickles are crunchy. It must be over fifteen years since I've had a Danish lunch. And whether it is the taste exploding in my mouth, or how I'm haunted by the thought of Kirsten's red lips, I suddenly start crying. I bawl my eyes out. Over the time that has gone by, the years in Brooklyn, Isabel now dead, Lucille disappeared—Lucille, the closest I ever came to having my own child. All the missed opportunities, everything I've run away from. But also this strange pleasure at coming back to Copenhagen, where I was born. I'm sentimental. I blow my nose and order another aquavit. Then my phone rings. Frantically I snatch it out of my pocket, thinking it's Lucille. But no, it's Kirsten. She hears me sniffling. "Have you picked up a cold since this morning?" My voice is hoarse: "No, no." Silence. "What is it? You're not sitting there crying, are you?" Pause. "No." "Did you get hold of Lucille?" "Unfortunately no." "Honestly, is something wrong? I mean, is she . . . do you think she's disappeared, seriously, or what?" "I don't know," I say, and that is the truth. Kirsten says she will call later, which thoroughly pleases me.

I go to the police in the afternoon, but Lucille has not been reported as missing. They're visibly annoyed by my request. They're on coffee break, it looks like. The policeman sighs loudly and stirs his coffee. "And what makes you think she's disappeared? Have you talked to her boss? Her family?" I stand up and walk out in the middle of this conversation. I call the teacher's college that, according to Kirsten, she attends. They haven't seen her in six weeks and have been wondering why she hasn't called in sick. They wrote to the address on Ture-sensgade but Lucille hasn't contacted them. They have also tried her cell phone. "I'm glad you called," the secretary says, "I didn't know who to contact. Lucille didn't specify a contact person on her information card. Are you her father?" I hesitate a moment. "Yes," I lie, "I'm her father."

I rest for a while at the hotel. It's already twilight. Deep-blue late afternoon. I close my eyes and feel a pang of homesickness. See Brooklyn in my head, the corner of Flatbush and Bergen where I live in a small, badly heated apartment. The eternal noise of traffic, howling ambulances, horns, and shouting, the rumble of underground trains. Suddenly I miss Joe, who serves me coffee and asks about my bronchitis every morning when I sit down in my regular window seat at his diner. The subway trip to the West Village, to the modest office where I write my mediocre poems, job applications, and the few ad copy assignments I get that put bread on the table; the sounds, smells, the people I see every day and make polite conversation with, all the strange faces gliding past me on the street for the first and only time. The sea of humanity, the loneliness. But also that sense of being a part of something, of belonging. That's my life. A beer at the bar when the Giants are on TV. The weekly stroll to the laundromat. Mrs. Rabinowitz, my next-door neighbor, who once tried to get me in the sack when we were both younger, and who has now focused all her love on a small fat dog named Ozzie, whose barking keeps me up half the night. I see her painted face, her blinking, near-sighted eyes: "How are you today, Mr. Thomsen? Going out?" It occurs to me that she must have Russian blood with that name, a thought that makes me sit up with a start because now I see Dmitrij in my mind's eye, strangling Lucille with his bare hands, the longhair and the suntanned guy in the background; it looks like they're in a summer house, I glimpse an orchard and a gray sea in the distance. I get up, badly shaken, and reach for the bottle of gin. Shortly after, I hear the telephone ring, but I'm unable to speak. I read the display: Kirsten's number, lit up in green.

Much later that night, stumbling out of Jagtstuen, a bar on Israels Plads where I've been drinking heavily for several hours and playing all the oldies on the jukebox, my first impulse is to wake Kirsten up. I want to kiss her. I want to touch her white, matte skin. Then I tell myself: *No, no, don't do it, don't you dare do it.* I manage to turn around and stagger down the hushed street toward the hotel. A rat scurries under a car. I fish around in my pockets for my cigarettes. It starts to rain, a light drizzle. Suddenly, a car roars up the street at high speed. I'm startled, automatically I step back. Whining brakes as it turns the corner at Turesensgade. The car is red. And slowly, through my foggy head, it dawns on me that it's Dmitrij's car. I try to get a grip on myself, to walk straight, I'm swaying from being so drunk. I hold onto a building and edge over to the corner. Back against the wall and carefully turn my head to see what's going on. What's going on is that Dmitrij and his dark-skinned helper are lifting something out of the trunk. It looks heavy. My heart skips a beat. Obviously they are in a rush, they act harried and nervous, constantly checking up and down the street. Dmitrij apparently tells his helper to hold the door; he lurches while carrying his heavy load into the hallway. The door slams. But his helper comes out again, they forgot to lock the car. He grabs something from the glove compartment. Holds it up, studies it intently for a moment. Dmitrij half-stifles his cry from an open hallway window: "Maks! Maks!" And then a bunch of Russian I don't understand.

Maks puts the object in his pocket, and he whistles as he disappears into the building.

Silence. My head is buzzing. The rain is pouring down. I slide to a crouch and feel my stomach turn. Then I throw up and once more splatter myself. It takes me forever to stand up. After I finally find the hotel and my bed, I sleep in my clothes, a heavy, dreamless sleep. And wake up late Thursday morning with a remarkable headache and pain in my stomach. The usual thoughts: *Where am I? Who am I?*

So his name is Maks, the dark-skinned guy. That's the first real thought I have after doubting if what I thought happened actually happened, being so wasted, and what *did* happen? Maksim, that's what. I know that familial variation of the name from Brooklyn. Maksim. With the gun. I'm sure it was a gun he was staring at. Then I remember everything clearly. I stink of vomit. Oh God, I'd forgotten about that. I get up, take a shower, pick a clean shirt from the closet, find a plastic bag and stuff my dirty clothes inside. On my way out I drop it off at the reception desk to be washed.

After standing in the passageway on Turesensgade for almost two hours (freezing with a rumbling stomach), Dmitrij, Maks, and the suntanned man come outside and get in the red car. A Mazda. They take off and turn right at Nansensgade. I realize this is my chance. After a few minutes, and just as before, a mother with a baby on her arm opens the front door and I duck inside. It's one o'clock. People are at work, the hallway is quiet. The door is not hard to open. I use my pocketknife. I'm inside.

Empty vodka and beer bottles, full ashtrays. A horribly sweet, nauseating smell. Bedroom, living room, a tiny bathroom. An unmade double bed and a few mattresses on the floor. In the kitchen, a pile of dirty dishes, banana flies, pizza boxes, overflowing trash bags. I walk through the hall. I catch sight of myself in the mirror. I look like hell. I notice a kid's drawing behind me, in a frame. I turn around. *Lucille, 9 years old*, written in a clumsy child's hand. The drawing is a house with father, mother, and girl standing in front on the steps. Beside the house, a big lion, mouth wide open. Meticulously drawn flowers and butterflies. A shining sun, a cloud, a bird. In the lower left-hand corner, an odd little troll-like figure with fangs and horns. The drawing hangs crooked on the wall. A lump rises in my throat. Into the living room again. Behind some stacked chairs is the bundle they carried up last night. Packed in black sacks and heavily taped. I take a deep breath and kneel down. I manage to carefully strip off the tape in one spot. I peel the plastic sacks apart from each other, a small opening appears. A dead hand. A woman's hand, already stiff and blue. A cheap ring with a fake stone of green glass on her ring finger. But it's not Lucille's hand. The skin is dark. I try to think quickly and clearly. I hear my teeth chattering. It must be one of the girls from Sydhavnen. Maybe even the one Maks smacked around. The stench is now unbearable. My hands shake as I tape it back up again, glance behind me, and see that I left the pocketknife on the floor beside the sacks; I pick it up and get out of there. My back is wet from a cold sweat. I wrestle with the door. Drop the pocketknife, finally tumble down the stairs. Four black men are waiting in the hallway, one is sitting on the steps. He doesn't move as I pass by. I feign indifference. Say hello. One of the men standing there nods, but his expression doesn't change. And when I reach the street and hurry off toward Ørstedsparken, the red Mazda returns. I crouch behind a street workers' tent. The three Russians jump out of the car and are met by the four black men stepping out onto the street. Before I know it, the suntanned man has been knifed in the gut. He gets stabbed again and again. He slides down to the sidewalk. Dmitrij hammers his fist into the jaw of one of the four, Maks is fighting another one and kicks him in the groin, the man doubles over. No one makes a sound. Blood flows on the sidewalk, down into the gutter, the gray asphalt turns black. The knife is knocked out of the hand of the man who stabbed the Russian. Maks pulls out a gun. But Dmitrij gestures to him: don't shoot. The knifer and his three partners jump into a black car with tinted windows and drive away. Dmitrij picks the knife up, pockets it, he and Maks carry the suntanned man, possibly dead, to the car and into the backseat, they take off—and they're gone. Only now I hear myself, my breath, fluty, mournful, raspy. I'm paralyzed from fright and have no idea what to do to get myself up and out of here, away from this crime scene. I think: *What would have happened if the four men had barged in on me in the apartment?* I swallow. They could just as well have. Why didn't they?

Later I sit on a doorstep and drink coffee, while doing my best to consume a pitifully dry sandwich, turkey and mayonnaise. All I think about now is the hand in the sack. The body lying by itself back in the apartment, what will they do with that? Why haven't they gotten rid of it? The relief that it wasn't Lucille doesn't hit me until late in the day. At that moment I grieve for the unknown dead girl. And it is clear to me that it must be some sort of mafia war going on here. The Russians versus the Gambian slavers. The Russians are presumably fighting for a share of the market. And now they've shown their muscle by killing one of the enemy's girls. That's my conclusion. At midnight something finally shows up on Internet news. A paragraph about an unidentified white male, dumped on the ground outside the emergency room at Bispebjerg Hospital, catches my attention. He has suffered multiple stab wounds and is in critical condition. Police are searching for family or others who know him. They are also requesting any information, if anyone has seen or heard anything, that could aid in clearing up this case. A description of the man. I turn the computer off. Lie on the bed. The water pipes sigh. Someone nearby is listening to Lou Reed. And then I think: *It wasn't her. It wasn't Lucille.* I nod off; all night long I'm tormented by troubled dreams and I wake at daybreak with a start, my body tense and stiff. I get up and drink some water. Get dressed and go out in the sleeping, dusk-gray city. It's now Friday.

Isabel was no beauty queen, but she had a warmth that was special. Something open, generous, overwhelmingly loving. That's what I fell for. And that's what later on I punished her for. She was so easily hurt, she was innocent, she didn't *understand* my moodiness. Which in a way came about because I felt I was a worse, less giving person than she was. Which also happens to be true. I confused her, I played funny games, as Joe would say. When I met Isabel, Lucille had just turned three. She was trusting and her speech wasn't yet fully developed—she could say *idiot* in Danish, and *Salut* and *Je suis une très très grande fille.* In the beginning I left her to Isabel. But that changed. I was the one who took her to school on her first day. Who biked with her across the commons on weekends, who taught her how to drink soda without getting it up her nose. And who told her stories at night when she lay in her bed. About small creatures with horns and fangs. I was also the one who in the end failed her and disappeared. The sense of Isabel's sleeping body close to mine is sometimes so strong and real that I wake up in the night thinking she is there, though I still don't believe she was the love of my life. Which has yet to happen for me. But her presence. Her being there and her ability to create—life, a kind of safeness, safe and sound. I wonder if Lucille looks like her. If her laughter is as bright as her mother's. Not that there is much to laugh about just now, when I'm not even sure that she *can* laugh. I walk along the lakes toward Vesterbro. Past Hoved-banegården, the main station, where the pushers hang out, and down Istedgade, the porn street. An addict has just shot up in a basement stairwell. He falls forward. The last drunks stagger noisily down the street. In the gray dawn I see a group of young black women. They are huddled together on a corner, they laugh and talk loudly to each other in their native language. They look young and healthy, they don't look like whores. But they are at the bottom of the pecking order and come out only after the other prostitutes have gone home. They get the worst customers. All the scum. The violent, the drunk, the sick. A car pulls up to the group and stops. Negotiations take place through the front windshield. A fat hand points at the girl it wants. She gets in the backseat. For a moment the group is silent. Then I recognize one of the four men from the fight last night on Turesensgade, he shows up all of a sudden. His jaw is swollen and cut. He speaks harshly to the girls and apparently orders them to spread out, and so they do, immediately. It looks sad: now each one of them is alone on this miserable November

morning in a foreign country. I walk on up toward Halmtor-
vet and shuffle past Tivoli and Rådhuspladsen, the town hall
square, cut through Ørstedsparken where there is still some action, then up Gothersgade and Bartholinsgade. I stop at the
front lawn of the Kommunehospital, the old district hospital.
I've bought coffee and warm croissants, I find a bench and rest.
Moisture drips from the trees. Windows gradually begin to light
up, people awaken; I notice that the rosebuds have been ruined by frost, that a fox sneaks through the bushes, I hear birds
chirping and the wind rustling shriveled leaves. I came here
often with Lucille, we played ball. I taught her how to catch
and she was furious at me every time she missed. She stomped
the ground and hid under the snowberry bushes. They're still
here, the bushes, with their perfectly succulent white and pink
berries. It's nine o'clock. I try to take stock of the situation. The
body in the sack, the wounded Russian. A possible war over
prostitution. And the hash traffic that might be much more
than just that. But nothing leads me to Lucille. Nothing. I con-
sider whether I should go to the police with my information. But
they weren't exactly helpful before. Besides, they have enough to
keep busy elsewhere in the city; there are gang wars and shoot-
ings in Nørrebro again. I don't know what to do. I fumble around
in my pocket for my phone and call Kirsten.

The white wine is rich and golden in the glasses. She nibbles
at her shrimp. Outside, people rush around—here inside we're
nestled in the restaurant's plush chairs. A waiter arrives with
the main courses; at my urging Kirsten has ordered lobster, I'm
having baked turbot. The music is agreeably muted, business
people and tourists are sitting all around us, dining. This is one
of the city's most expensive seafood restaurants, we have a view
of the canals and Folketinget, the Parliament.

Kirsten smiles at me, clinks her glass against mine. "To Lucille," she says. We drink. She tells me that she is studying literature at the University of Copenhagen. She is especially involved with poetry. We talk some about American poetry, I mention that I write poems myself. That seems to make an impression on her. "Tell me about them," she says, "tell me about your poems." I say that there isn't much to tell ("Life, death, love, you know"), but I love Walt Whitman—especially *Leaves of Grass*—and Eliot, of course (I recite from *The Waste Land*: "I will show you fear in a handful of dust"), but also the great Russians, Blok and Mayakovsky, not to mention Baudelaire. "Very predictable, all of them," she says with a smile, "and you don't even mention Anna Akhmatova?" She turns her glass in her hand. "What do you think about Sylvia Plath? You've read her, haven't you?" "I've mostly read her husband," I answer. "That's a shame," Kirsten says. She gives me a challenging look. "Listen to this: *Out of the ash/I rise with my red hair/and I eat men like air.*" She locks onto my eyes, then she smiles, sips her wine, and says: "You *must* be aware that she was much better than Hughes, wilder, much more talented and original, but she was the one who died and he had the last word. Have you read *Birthday Letters?*" I nod. "He abandoned her. It killed her," she says, loudly. I think she's being too simplistic, that if anything is predictable here—and stupid, and completely unfair—it's blaming him for her suicide; we discuss, her cheeks turn red, I promise to read Plath. She names a number of younger poets I should also read. She thinks I'm hopelessly behind the times. Which I'm sure she is right about. "Why don't you read Danish literature?" she asks. My hand is on the tablecloth, she covers it with hers. "Can't you send me some of your writing? I want to read you." I take this as a hidden invitation to something more than poems, my stomach tightens, I think I'm blushing. She goes to the ladies' room. I order another bottle of wine. It feels as if I'm floating. I feel my body clearly, I feel it not at all. And we sit there for another hour and a half, I have a hard time getting the turbot down, I get a little bit smashed, she does too. I enjoy watching her eat her lobster, sucking it all out, we talk and talk, especially her, I can't take my eyes off her, her sparklingly clear gaze, the smiles racing across her face, we toast again, this time to how she will come visit me in Brooklyn.

I'm giddy from a tickling, prickling anticipation. The imprint her lipstick has left on the glass. The delicate curve of her nose. I forget that dead girl, Lucille, everything. Kirsten's presence and the intimacy she offers me makes me light and carefree, almost ridiculously light and carefree (and I take note of that, but everything is radiant). Then we have coffee. I feel her pressing her leg against mine under the table. And I ask her if she would like to take a walk before picking up her daughter. She would like that.

We walk slowly around Kongens Have, the King's Garden, looking at the small castle, Rosenborg, that Kirsten (and Lucille) dreamed of moving into when they were grown up, because they would be princesses. The sky is soaring and blue. Kirsten links her arm into mine and shakes her hair into place. The cold air clears my head. I haven't told Kirsten any of the horrible details of the "case," instead I say that the college hasn't heard from her for a long time, that she hasn't been reported to the police as missing, and then I ask her to tell me more about Lucille. "She visited me at the hospital when I had Mia. That was three years ago. We hadn't seen each other in a long time. Her mother had just died, and she was very thin and desperate. I'd sent her a letter when I read in the paper that Isabel was dead. But Lucille was just like herself too. She is so much fun."

"Is she?" "Yes! She has the sickest sense of humor—black. Even right then, when she was holding Mia and talking about Isabel's funeral, she was funny. That's how she is. And I couldn't laugh because I'd had a cesarean. I bit the pillow. She said that she wanted to be a teacher and that she had traded Isabel's apartment for one on Turesensgade. She seemed strong and clearheaded somehow, even while grieving." "Did she know Dmitrij back then?" I ask. "She didn't talk about it. But I don't think so. The first several times I visited her she was living alone, anyway. And after he suddenly showed up, I stopped visiting her." "Because he scared you?" "Yes, honestly, he scared me to death. The way he stared at me. I think Lucille was smoking a lot of dope then. She seemed distant and listless. Totally different from that day at the hospital. And I was alone with Mia and just didn't have the energy to help her." I feel a rush of joy when she says she was alone. "Because she must have needed help. She was way out there, I think, really messed up. Apparently I couldn't see it. Or I didn't want to." She sighs and looks up at me. "If only I'd helped her. So all . . . this, maybe wouldn't have happened. I mean, that—that she would be here. Now." "But then we wouldn't have met each other," I say. "Do you have a boyfriend?" I ask, out of the blue. "A boyfriend?" She looks at me, confused. My ears are burning under my cap. Quickly I light a cigarette. "Does Lucille have many friends?" Kirsten looks up at the sky. "I don't really know. I don't know very much about her. She's my childhood friend. Mostly we talked about those days. What happened at school, things like that. If we'd seen this person or that person. What he or she had made out of themselves. She never really asked much about me, either."

While we watch the ducks swimming around in the moat's algae-green water, she slips her arm under mine again, and she leans her head lovingly on my shoulder. I sense for sure that she's coming on to me. Something hugely electric between us. And I take hold of the back of her head, pull her toward me, and search for her mouth, try to kiss her. But she tears away from me, abruptly steps back and looks at me, angry and frightened. "What the hell are you doing?" And there's no way to explain. I say I'm sorry, again and again. I say: "But I thought . . . that you . . ." Her eyes flash. She says: "You! You're like a father! That's how I remember you, like a . . . an *adult*. And you think it's okay to kiss *me*? Is that really all you're after? To get at me? I thought this might be the start of some kind of friendship. I thought this was about Lucille!" Now she shouts: "You are just a stupid old man!" And she moves off. Rushing and raging across the faded lawns with her shiny auburn hair swinging behind her head in the sunlight. And I know I've ruined it, I will never see her again. I misunderstood everything. I couldn't control myself, she's right, I am a stupid old man. I flop down on a bench and toss what's left of the morning's croissants to the ducks. Exactly like old men do. Feed the ducks, sit and stare.

All I need is a cane. And a goddamn set of false teeth.

The rest of the day depressed in the hotel room. I'm on the brink of going back home to Brooklyn, the hell with all this. First I get boiling mad (at Kirsten and at myself), then I'm resigned, apathetic. Then I yell: "Why am I running around here like an idiot playing *goddamn DETECTIVE*?" I alternate between lying on my side in bed and pacing around the room, punching the wall. Later I'm just plain exhausted. I step out to get something to eat. After wandering around for a half hour, unable to decide, I end up with a slice from the Sicilian pizzeria on the corner of Nansensgade and Ahlefeldtsgade. My pizza is thin and crispy like it should be. I eat at a high table by the window and look out in the dark while listening absent-mindedly to background conversations in Italian. I leaf through the local paper. I stop, then read: *The man who was abandoned Thursday outside the emergency room at Bispebjerg Hospital died late yesterday. The deceased has not yet been identified. He was in his late thirties, white but dark-complected, with a distinctive scar twenty centimeters long on his upper chest. Family of the deceased are requested to contact the police.* The cooks laugh loudly at something in the kitchen. I look out at the street where a few boys practice wheelies on their bikes. I leave the rest of my pizza behind and stroll down toward Turesensgade. The second-floor windows are dark. But someone has hooked the front door wide open. I can't stop myself, I walk cautiously up the stairs.

No sound comes from the apartment. After a while I open the mail slot a crack, still no sound, nothing to see, no snoring men, no water running from a faucet; it's deadly quiet. I pull out my knife from my inside pocket. But the door is unlocked. I hold my breath. It creaks when I push it with my foot. Still nothing happens. I step into the hall. Pitch dark. First I check the living room and bedroom to make sure I'm alone. The light from the street makes it possible to scan the two rooms, both are barren, the furniture cleared out. The kitchen is the same way. All that's left are dirty dishes, they smell horrendous. The refrigerator door is open, it's empty too. A small pool of water on the floor from the thawed freezer. In the living room, the stench from the corpse still hangs in the air, even though they have left the window open. But the sack is gone. I can just make out a stain on the floor where it was lying. I think: *This was Lucille's home. She lived here. Here is where she got up and put her clothes on, here is where she went to bed at night.*

Back in the dark hall, I fumble around for the frame. It's there. I take the drawing down and leave the apartment with the door open.

* * *

It seems as if there is nothing more to do. A few days go by rambling around erratically: another night in Vesterbro, a glimpse of the young prostitutes huddled together again, talking eagerly on a corner, a beer or three at various bars, shawarma and bad fast food, I visit the Russian restaurant in a basement on Israels Plads just one time, in hopes of something happening. I eat a fine bowl of borscht that tastes of more than boiled beets, but otherwise it's just tables of families with young kids. Daytime I aimlessly follow the stream of light, blond people on the streets, homogenous in contrast to the motley street crowds I'm used to in New York. Suddenly I'm desperately homesick. I want to go home. And I discover I have already buried Lucille, I've passed the point of acknowledging that she is dead, that I will never find her. I don't think anyone will find her. I think the Russians have shut her up for good, because she discovered that they were trafficking girls from Gambia. I think they've stowed her away forever. Buried her in a forest or dumped her in the sea, far from the Danish coast. Maybe they even murdered her in another land far away. The earth has swallowed Lucille. She called out to me and I was incapable of answering her. I didn't grab her hand. *I said to my soul, be still, and wait without hope.* Eliot again, *Four Quartets.* Wish I could. Wait calmly without hope. Once, at a distance, I see Kirsten bicycling up Vendersgade with Mia in her child's seat. Another time I think I recognize Lucille in a packed bus at Nørreport Station. But it's just my imagination. Finally, I call the airline and ask them to reserve a flight on my open ticket. I pack the framed drawing in with the few clothes I brought and put it all in the suitcase. I pay the sleepy man at the hotel reception desk. He hands me a brown package with clean clothes. The vomit clothes. The 28th of December, around ten a.m., I walk down to the metro that runs out to the airport, and I sense how relieved I am to leave this city that, for one reason or another, always ends up huddling in on itself, shutting out the world right in front of my eyes. It snows lightly. There is ice on the roofs. Sleet and salt on the sidewalks. I walk past the flower booths on the square where the vegetable market once stood, red-cheeked women and young girls with stocking caps pulled down over their foreheads. Buy a cup of coffee at Café Dolores, set my suitcase down in the slush, and light a cigarette. Once again, this is how I take leave of Copenhagen. And again I swear to never come back. But it's not until after checking in, as I sit calmly at the gate, waiting to board, that Kirsten forwards a text message to me. *Hi K. Sorry I haven't called until now, have a new # ;) Living in Århus with Johan. D threatened me and beat me 2 times when he found out about J. Bastard. So I got out of there. Am totally in love. Do you know anybody who wants to buy a cheap apartment in Turesensgade? Hehe. Â bientôt, L.*

L. for Lucille. I swallow several times. The world swims in front of my eyes. And it's as if everything inside me plunges down, down, down, everything gets swept along, broken. I squeeze my eyes shut and all I see is a chasm, a wild gorge of darkness. I see precisely how I lose my grip, fall, and disappear. I ask out loud: "Why?" Open my eyes. Look out at the gray, snow-laden sky the planes lift off into, land from.

I should be happy. I should be *so* happy.

ONE OF THE ROUGH ONES

BY JONAS T. BENGTSSON

Northwest

I'd thought these images would be less chilling without the sound. Nothing much happens the first few minutes. The screen flickers. *Slack,* they call it. You should always forward a new tape a little bit before you begin recording. Count one, two, three, four . . .

Then a girl on a bed. Somebody lives here, the walls are a faded yellow. Daylight streams onto her from a window that must be to the left of the camera.

The metal tool in the girl's hand looks cold. Like something a gynecologist would use. Surgical steel. I fumble for the word. What is it, it's on the tip of my tongue. She's lying on her back on an unmade bed, slowly spreading her legs while she smiles at the camera.

I don't think I know her. It's not Maria, definitely not. Though I can't help thinking I've seen her before. Maybe on a bus or sometime in town. Maybe I've seen her in another film like this one. But she doesn't have the look of a pro. Her movements are clumsy. It could very well be her first time in front of a camera.

She parts her labia with her first and middle fingers. When the point of the surgical instrument enters, it's hard for her to keep smiling.

Then I remember. A speculum.

That's what it's called, the instrument in the girl's hands.

* * *

I know this because I've been in prison. While others inside were getting an education or learning a trade—if nothing else, they got better at stealing cars or breaking into summer houses—I acquired a vast knowledge of pornography.

I shared a cell with a long-term inmate who had kicked his wife down a stairway while they'd both been drunk. A long stairway. When he wasn't crying and looking at photos of her, he was going through his collection of pornography, a library in alphabetical order. The entire back wall of the cell was filled with VHS cassettes and DVDs. We sat on his cot. He educated me. From the first films in the '70s, when Linda Lovelace gagged on Harry Reems, who later married a deeply religious woman and became a realtor in Utah, to the first ass-to-mouth scene, which my cellmate was reasonably confident came from the early '90s. He paused the tapes and explained.

The metal instrument goes farther up inside the girl on the bed.

The technical term for her position is *spread eagle*.

This style of recording, the private setting, the shaky picture, would sell under the label *gonzo* or *amateur*.

She's still smiling.

A rehearsed smile, copied from similar films.

This is what horny looks like.

She's opened the speculum all the way now. Smile, smile. Horny.

Even with the shaky home recording and the old television we're watching on, a good gynecologist would be able to make a fairly complete diagnosis.

The word I'm thinking of now is the color salmon. She's not smiling anymore.

* * *

A few lines over the screen. A break in the sound. Then flickering. The first few minutes with the girl on the bed was just an old shot that had been recorded over. The tape has been used again and again. DV tapes are expensive. Another girl in the same bed, this one has strawberry-blond hair gathered in a ponytail, she reaches for something off screen. Then she's gone too. More flickering on the screen. The tape recorded over again. A new room, maybe the living room in the same apartment. The girl on the screen wears black net stockings. Hair is dark brown and hangs on her shoulders. She wears a short dress of a red, shiny material. She walks awkwardly, her heels must be unusually high. She wears more makeup than I've ever seen her wear. Painted like a whore or an ice-skating queen.

The voice behind the camera says: "Show me your ass." She turns around. Slowly hikes up her dress.

I look over at Christian, he's fumbling around in his pocket for his cigarettes. He looks strained and focused. On the screen in front of us, his sister shows her G-string.

There's no doubt about it, it's Maria.

We're in the back room of the TV and radio shop I work in. I've been here close to two years. Landed the job a few months after I got out.

I stand there praying that the only reason we're here—the only reason Christian called *me*, not somebody else—is that he needed to see a videotape. A DV tape. Digital video. Nothing else.

It's ten-thirty at night. It's November and black as coal outside. Nabil is the third person in the room. He's a constant talker. All the time. Now he's quiet.

But of course this isn't where it begins, either.

I've just stepped out of Erkan's Diner, Frederikssundsvej in Northwest, the outer edge of the city. You get any further out and it's the suburbs, human storage and residential districts. I'm holding a kebab wrapped in foil and I already regret buying it. They always give me a stomachache. Erkan only sells to schoolkids at noon, to drunks at night, and to idiots like me. They let the meat sit on the stick way too long, sweating fat and whirling around and around several thousand times before the last scraps are sliced off.

I think about renting a film on the way home, but I don't feel like going all the way to Blockbuster and I can't find a parking spot anyway. Or I could double-park, like the ex-Yugoslavians do in front of the place right beside it, Café Montenegro. The place called Palermo until a man got shot there. I debate myself, back and forth. Then the phone rings. I don't recognize the number and I don't answer. I sit in the car and I'm about to stick the key in the ignition when it rings again. It's Christian.

I drive one-handed, eat with the other. Feel dressing on my chin, down my hand, on the way to Bispebjerg Hospital.

My stomach doesn't complain yet, but it won't be long.

I open the door to room 18. Christian is standing at the foot of the bed, he looks up, nods.

Nabil can't have been here more than a few minutes. He's still wearing his overcoat and hasn't recovered from the shock yet. *Fuck, fuck, fuck.* He repeats it slowly, to himself. Only when I'm all the way in the room can I follow his eyes, down to the girl in bed. Maria. Christian's sister. Her eyes are closed, but her sleep seems more drug-induced than peaceful. Her head is held motionless by a big white collar. Her nostrils are filled with dried blood. One of her cheeks is swollen, almost twice as big as the other. The hospital gown gaps and I see red and purple marks on the small patch of skin visible.

At first I think, traffic accident. A bad one. But something isn't right. I haven't seen Christian for several years. Well, once after I got out. At a bar in town, we said hello and agreed to get together soon. Which of course didn't happen. But why would he call me after a traffic accident? He has new friends now. People who understand him better.

Christian breaks the silence.

"They found her down by Fuglebakken Station. She was just sitting there, bleeding from her nose and mouth. Didn't have . . . all her clothes on. Head hanging down on her chest. Then somebody called an ambulance."

"What happened to her?" Nabil asks. Christian doesn't answer at first, walks over to his sister and smoothes a lock of hair behind her ear.

"The police were here a few hours ago. I couldn't help them. I don't have any idea . . ." He turns toward me, pulls me in, hugs me. His eyes, dead and distant until now, turn moist. "It's so damn good to see you guys," he says. "She had this in her pocket." He opens his hand, holds out a small DV tape, a videotape from a camera. "The police can have it tomorrow. I want to see it first."

We take the car, my car, an old Peugeot. Down Hovmestervej, Tomsgårdsvej toward Borups Allé. A ride through our old neighborhood. I could slow down and say, There's where we smashed a few windows, there's where we broke into a car. There's where I beat somebody up, there's where I got beat up. There's where we wrote our names on the wall.

The rest of the kebab sits on the dashboard, the greasy wax paper flutters above the air vent. None of us speak. I roll down the window and throw it out, watch in the rearview mirror how it hits the street and explodes into small pieces of lettuce and meat. Someone honks behind us. There was a time when that would have been enough for us to stomp on the brakes.

The boys ride again. The boys from the Bird section of Northwest. From Stærevej, Swallow Street. The boys from the block. There was a time that would have made me happy. Us, back together.

Your first friends are your best, you'll never have better. That thought warmed me while I was in prison. The thought that someday we would meet again, Christian in a shirt and tie, Nabil who had finally figured out what he wanted to be, a driving instructor maybe, pointing at a blue Audi parked and shining in the sun. I would pull out my wallet, show photos of a girl in her late twenties, a pretty girl. Another photo of two kids. Maybe just a boy who looked like his father. We would sit in a café, toast with beer. Talk about old times, laugh, and feel just a little bit ashamed of all the shit we did. Boys' pranks.

It's still quiet in the car, no one says a word. No one laughs. This wasn't how I pictured our reunion.

Maria on the screen. She's dancing without music. She pulls the front of her dress down, gives a shot of her breasts. Dances some more, shows her ass, striptease. She's much better than the first girl on the tape, and though she almost falls a few times from her heels, she's always showing a naughty smile.

"Now you're going to suck my cock." The voice comes from the man behind the camera. Maria grabs a pillow from the sofa and lays it on the floor. I would never say it out loud, but she does it so naturally that this can't be her first film. The camera shakes and turns upside down a moment when it's taken off the tripod. Then the man films down on himself. Films Maria with her knees on the pillow, reaching out for the zipper of a pair of dark blue jeans, pulling a half-stiff cock out of the gap in a pair of boxers.

The phrase for this is POV. Point of view. A subcategory of gonzo. I'm not trying to remember this industry lingo. But the words pop into my head, and I'm ashamed to think about them while Christian's little sister gives head on the screen. If I hadn't seen her in the hospital bed this would be hot. I try to hold the image of her in my mind as the little girl going to confirmation class in Grøndal Church. Nabil and I took turns following her there when Christian couldn't. Because we thought it was too far and because we knew the ugly side of the neighborhood better than she did. Knew boys like us. She laughed and said that we were being silly, that she could walk there just fine herself. But she never refused us. I think she was proud to have an older boy escort her.

Now she's lifted the guy's member and is licking it underneath, also his balls. Christian still says nothing. His face dead, eyes unblinking. If you didn't know him you would think he doesn't feel a thing. It's impossible to look more indifferent than he does right now, to show less emotion. Christian was always the toughest one of us three, the one always willing to go the farthest.

Being tough was something he had to learn and learn fast, because he was an outsider. If he had continued his suburban ways he would have been beaten up. And beaten and beaten and beaten again. So he turned tough and he was good at it.

With his free hand the man grabs Maria's neck, jerks her throat around a few times. She makes a half-choked sound, as if she's about to throw up.

More fumbling with the camera, he sets it back on the tripod, zooms in so it's filming the sofa.

Then he steps into the picture. Still only his upper body and part of his legs.

The condom he puts on is pink. It's hard to hear what he's saying but it sounds like: *Doggy*.

Maria kneels on the edge of the sofa, sticks her ass in the air. He lowers himself onto her. First time we see his face. A half profile, turned away from the camera. He has light-colored, curly hair. He's thin, the way you're thin if you're badly fed as a child.

"I think . . ." Nabil says, but doesn't finish the sentence.

The guy's ass moves up and down. Dimples.

She says: Fuck me.

She says: Fuck me, it's so good when you fuck me.

She says: Give me your cock, give me your big cock. Oh God.

She moans. An artificial moan. One she's heard in other porno films and she's imitating.

That's how horny sounds.

"I've seen him before," Nabil says.

The man on the screen turns Maria around on the sofa. Bends her legs backward as if she were a folding chair. Her head is lying on the sofa's arm, feet next to her ears. He presses his hands into the hollows of her knees and starts banging away. She still moans, tries to sound horny, but it's getting harder and harder for her to make it sound natural. Now more scream than moan.

He holds his hand over her mouth. "Be quiet," he says. "I have neighbors."

"Almost sure I've seen him," Nabil says.

I think we're all shocked when the guy on the screen hits Maria the first time. A hard smack with the back of his hand that leaves a big red mark on her cheek. She looks up at him, surprised. Then she tries to smile again. As if it was kinky, something she liked. "You want punished?" he asks. "You want punished?"

"Yes," she says. "Yes, yes, yes."

The next few slaps aren't as hard as the first one. Each time she tries to moan and cry out, *Yes*.

Then he starts using his fists.

I turn off the sound. Had hoped that these images would be easier to watch without sound. That they would be less real. Like old film, silent film. But it makes no difference.

It's still Maria lying on the sofa. The man on top of her is punching her in the side, in the ribs. Several times in the stomach while he holds her by the throat so she can't straighten up. Meanwhile his cock is still driving in and out of her.

He looks over at the camera a few times. Like to make sure it's still taping. That it's picking up everything he's doing.

"I know I've seen him before." Nabil is mostly talking to himself. The man on the screen slams a fist into Maria's mouth. Her lip splits.

"I can't take this anymore." Christian is holding his hand over his mouth, the words slip out between his fingers. "You'll have to watch the rest of it. You *have* to watch the rest of it, watch everything he does to her. And turn the volume up. I want to hear what he said. Get all of it."

Christian walks out into the hallway. I turn the volume up when he's out of the room.

On the screen the guy is covering Maria's nose and mouth. She's fighting off his hands. He lets go, and when she gasps for air he punches her in the side. It should stop now. But it doesn't. He keeps going. It goes on and on. It gets rougher. Her eyes start to lose focus.

He slugs her a few more times, then he pulls out and gets up.

I hear a lighter somewhere off screen, a cigarette being lit. Then his naked feet on the hallway floor. He pisses long and hard, a small waterfall the camera's mike captures. Maria is lying just like he left her. The girl on the sofa, I say to myself, just a girl on the sofa. She could be dead. Then an arm moves. The girl's arm. Slowly she turns on her side. Stands up with great difficulty. Hobbles a half-step before she falls off screen, lying somewhere below the camera. The camera films an empty sofa and a framed poster on the wall above. Two dolphins jumping out of the water, the full moon is so big that their snouts almost seem to touch it. Then Maria comes back in the picture. Her head hangs down halfway to her chest, she's sobbing very weakly. Falters a few steps forward on shaky legs. The sound of a toilet flushing. His naked feet on the hallway floor. Maria stops. Lifts her head just a little, eyes staring at a spot behind the camera, the doorway. It feels like minutes, not seconds. Her staring, the feet approaching. Then the sound of a cell phone. And the feet walk away again. Out into the kitchen, I'm guessing. He says hi, hey, how you doing. His voice cuts through clearly. First they talk soccer. A Brøndby match that didn't go exactly the way it should have.

Maria tries to get into the red dress. One of her hands is useless.

"I'm working," the guy says from out in the kitchen, and laughs loudly. "No," he says. "It's going to be one of the rough ones. Nobody buys the soft stuff anymore."

Maria goes off screen. She's gone a few moments. The sound of the man from the kitchen, he's still laughing. Then we see the red dress close up, her arm rising, reaching toward the camera. The picture goes black. She's taken the tape.

How she got past him and down the stairs, I don't know. But after she reached the street he probably didn't try to catch up with her. She looked too beat up. It would look like a rape, still in progress. And he wouldn't have known she had the tape. So he'd let her go. All they'd been doing was making *one of the rough ones*.

* * *

Nabil covers his mouth. "I've seen him before," he says. He makes a face, to concentrate. An escape from the images on the screen. Then he snaps his fingers.

"I've seen him with Ali's little brother. Down at Nørrebro City Center." Nabil pulls out his cell phone, makes a few calls. Speaks half Arabic, half Danish. His voice switches between sounding chummy, they laugh together, and a little bit menacing. Our time is over. That time when we were the boys on Swallow Street. The boys. The big shots. But even now, nobody fucks with Nabil.

He puts the phone back in his pocket.

"I know where he lives."

Christian is back in the room again. His eyes scare me. "Let's do it," he says.

"Let's go over to one of my friends' first," Nabil says. "He's got some things lying around."

I know what he means.

I had actually thought I would just follow along. Do what had to be done. But no more than that. I'm the one, though, who bends over and pulls the toolbox out of the closet. Opens it on the workbench, finds a sports bag. The one thing I learned in prison was to make sure I'd never return. Three young men, stopped in the middle of the night, the trunk filled with baseball bats, they spend the night in jail. And with my record I would be back in prison.

But a hammer, a wrench, a large screwdriver, and a pair of hobby knives, they're all tools. Even if you've just finished doing time for a violent crime, the police can't do shit. They have to let you drive away. I lifted weights with a man who always kept a set of golf clubs in his car. No balls, just the clubs.

* * *

We're out riding again. The boys from the Bird. Even though we have the streets to ourselves, rainy November streets, I stay under the speed limit.

It was on a night like this that the police caught me. Almost four years ago. I tried to run, but when a big policeman from Jutland cuffed me, it was a relief. I knew it would happen. It had begun a year earlier and it had to end, one way or another.

While everyone else went into job training or the military or found girlfriends who wanted to go to Ikea and buy coffee tables you assemble yourself, and many of them began talking about home entertainment systems with large, flat screens and surround sound, so they could hold each others' hands and watch *I, Robot*, I became a dedicated amphetamine abuser. A few months that came back to me in flashes as the indictment was being read. Like emptying the minibar in a hotel room and waking up hung over, then looking at the price list on top of the television.

Nabil enrolled in several areas of training at vo-tech schools, but always stopped after a short while. He talked about becoming a driving instructor. Next time I saw him he wanted to start up a cleaning service.

As quickly as Christian became part of the neighborhood, became one of the natives, he pulled out just as fast. He moved away, went to school. The last I heard he was about to become an auditor or bookkeeper or economist. Something with numbers and lots of money. When I met him he was wearing a polo shirt with a Gucci bag over his shoulder.

Now we're in the car together. Our reunion.

Nabil guides us. Down this street, make a right ahead. Otherwise no one speaks.

We're still in Northwest, close to Emdrup. "Here it is," Nabil says, and points to a redbrick building. I drive by, park the car on the first side street. We get out. Everything happens so slowly, infinitely slowly. Like underwater. Three men, one with a sports bag in his hand. They walk down the street, come to a door. Slowly, slowly. There's no intercom, one of them opens the door, and they continue up the stairs. So slowly, three men. Though I'm one of them, I'm watching from the outside. Feet climbing the stairway.

Nabil presses the buzzer.

If I hadn't answered my phone I would be lying on the sofa right now. I would be asleep in front of the film I'd rented, a few empty beer bottles on the coffee table. Tomorrow I'd have woken up, watched the rest of the film while eating breakfast, fed my two birds, and went to work.

The door opens. I recognize him from the video, a sunken-chested young man in a T-shirt and jogging pants. When he sees us he tries to slam the door. He doesn't stand a chance, the door rams his head. He stumbles back a few steps.

Then I see the knife in his hand. It must have been there in the hall, on the little table under the mirror, ready in case. He smiles for a moment, raises the knife. Then it happens. I wake up. No longer underwater, I feel the blood in my veins again. The world is suddenly hard and sharp. I can feel my hands, feel my legs, feel the air flowing in my nostrils and filling my lungs. I toss the sports bag full of tools in his face. Before he hits the floor Nabil has started hitting him. I was never hooked on amphetamines. At least not only. This was what I needed. What I was trying to snort up, to no avail. Now, in this moment, I know it. When I hear Christian close the door behind us, and we drag the guy through the hall and into the living room.

We're the boys from the block again. The boys from the high-rise on Swallow Street. We're together again.

I don't know how long we keep at it. Not just an hour, a lot longer. With the stereo turned way up. We sweat, we laugh. I lose my sense of time. Remember only short flashes. Postcards of violence. One where I've raised the hammer above my head. One where I hold him and Christian sticks the handle of the screwdriver down his throat. One where Nabil jerks the guy's pants down and reaches for the monkey wrench.

We might have been easier on him, stopped earlier, if the room hadn't reminded us of the images from the video.

At some point he starts screaming. Screaming so loudly that he drowns out the stereo. This is after we've got his pants off. Which wasn't easy, because he kept twisting, kicking. Nabil goes into the bedroom. He's laughing when he comes back out. He's holding a gag, a pink rubber ball hanging by two leather strings. In it goes, into the guy's mouth. "One of the rough ones!" Christian yells, while he holds him by the throat. "This here is going to be one of the rough ones!"

There's not much left of him when we leave. He's barely alive. It's hard to determine which sex he is. We destroyed him. How do you destroy a man? Keep at it. Just keep at it.

Early morning. It's quiet in the car again. I drop the two of them off. Stop a few times on the way home and throw the tools in various trash containers. Then the sports bag.

I take a shower before going to bed. Stuff the clothes in a garbage bag that I'll throw out on the way to work.

I lie in bed and listen to the quiet. My eyes are already heavy. I know that as soon as I wake up the hangover will check in. Far stronger and different from any I've had before. The first few minutes I'll think it's something I dreamed. A nasty dream I can blink away, that will be out of my body when I'm done pissing. A dream I'll have forgotten when I smell the coffee flowing through the machine. But then I'll remember that it wasn't a dream. I'll grab the duvet or sheet and try to hold on. I'll sit there like it's a bad movie and make a face and keep holding on until the alarm clock rings again. Telling me that the day has begun.

First I'll drive out and buy some new tools. Then to work. Be on time. Old Nielsen will be waiting with a new record player or transistor radio that should have been thrown out but some old lady has insisted it be repaired. The next few weeks I'll jump up whenever the doorbell rings. Every time I'll think it's the police. Whenever I'm about to forget what happened, my sore muscles will remind me. But that's not the hard part. Not at all. Time will pass. A new day will begin. New days always begin. The hard part will be forgetting how good it felt. To be alive again. To be the boys from Swallow Street, the boys from the block. Us.

AUSTRALIA

by Christian Dorph & Simon Pasternak

Vesterbro

Thursday, 6:05 p.m. E65 to Swinouscie, Reza's Bistro

Marek opened the camper door. Reza stood on a stool with her back to him and both hands in a tub. She had rolled up her puffed sleeves, and her elbows were pumping. The camper smelled like fish. She turned, stood with a large cooked roach in her gloved hand.

"I'm too old for this, Marek. I had to send Zbigniew out for gelatin for the aspic. And now I need shallots and coriander."

The rubber glove slid off with a snap. She stepped down from the stool, left the fish on the kitchen counter, and walked over to the laminated table at the back of camper, took out a cigarette from a silver case, lit up, and inhaled the smoke deep into her lungs. Then she came back, stood with her face inches from his. She had been drinking slivovitz again and had eaten something spicy. She lifted her forearm and showed him the z and the small green numbers of the tattoo.

"They've tried to kill us off, Marek. They injected phenol in the hearts of my younger brothers. They shot color in Sonja's green, green eyes and they got infected, but they didn't let her die, not before she got gangrene. But we will *never* die, Marek."

Marek lowered his head, he always felt uneasy here. Glanced around at the screaming-red sashed curtains, the brown laminate, the green, red, yellow lamps, the picture of the brothers and sisters, the cousins, and the mother and father in a frame beside the television, the press photo for *Zigeuner-Zirkus 1939*, the entire tiny band with a Great Dane to establish proportions—the violinist to the right holding the toy violin reached the dog's shoulders: Reza at nine years of age.

"Irina says that you pull out. And you're doing it less and less." She pinched his arm with her small, hard claws. "Look at me, Marek."

He turned to her, stared down at her wrinkled cleavage, the ample makeup.

"You fucking Polacks. Big men, but what are you shooting? Blanks? I want *grandchildren*, Marek."

She looked him hatefully in the eyes, but then broke off and walked over to the dresser, put on her large glasses. She brought out a folder. Marek glimpsed a passport and a pile of other papers.

"We have a job for you in Copenhagen. One of our Polish girls has run away. Adina something or other. Olek will tell you everything. Zbigniew has arranged another car."

"Can't I take my own car?"

"No. You are escorting another girl. Here are her papers, straight from Moldavia."

Marek walked past the well-lit bistro. Another hooker job. *Do they think I'm worthless?* He looked in through the glass. His wife, Irina, stood inside, flushed, red blisters on her body. *Five years and nowhere.* She was giving orders to a girl who stood trying to keep a tub from spilling. He could feel Reza's fingernails all the way into his soul.

He walked over to his own car, grabbed the spare tire, 100,000 euros stowed under the rim.

He'd reached 100,000 yesterday. Enough for a new life.

The girl, pale and silent, was already in the car when he plopped down in the driver's seat.

"Marek," he said. "I'm Marek."
The girl began crying.

Thursday, 7:10 p.m. Abel Cathrines Gade 5, Fifth Floor,
1654 Copenhagen V

Henry og Connie Jensen was the name on the oval copper name-plate on the fifth floor. Adina had run and run and run like a deer in a cone of light, she was all in, and it wasn't until now that she felt how cold she'd been, how scared. She had stood on the bridge above Dybbølsbro Station, wanting to throw herself in front of the train. Better to die than go back to Olek, better to do it herself. But then suddenly she didn't *dare* do it, and she remembered Henry. *You can come anytime, and I mean it*, he had said. He always repeated it: *Anytime*. It was stupid to hide at a client's place, impossible, but now he opened the door, welcomed her, stood there with his big furrowed face, the worried eyes, and she fell into his apartment, was sucked into the warm hall-way. Henry helped her over the thick wool rug, over to the sofa.

"You need to take your clothes off, Adina," he said. "I don't mean *that* way," he added, without irony. "I think I still have some of Connie's clothes. Wait here."

A brown bureau filled the wall to the right; tiled table, wing-back chair, floor lamps, TV. Christmas plates lined the walls, all the way around. With stiff fingers she lit up a cigarette and searched her bag; a half Rohypnol in foil, two codies, and a Valium. She stuck the pills in her mouth, swallowed them, and slid back on the sofa. She felt nauseous. Henry returned with a pair of much-too-large beige pants and a wool cardigan. He helped her off with her clothes, rolled them off her, the panty-hose, the clammy panties. She sat smoking through it all, it was nice to let someone else take over. He sat at the other end of the sofa and hugged her ankles.

"What happened?"

She didn't want him sitting there touching her.

"Adina, you have to tell me, or I can't help."

"Lenja is dead." It popped out of her mouth, and she doubled up; she wasn't going to cry while he was touching her.

"We have to call the police, then."

"No, no, no, Olek will kill me!"

"Do you want some soup?" he asked suddenly. "I have some broth I can warm."

A few minutes went by as he rummaged around in the kitchen. Then a bowl of steaming soup was sitting in front of her, and he handed her a spoon. She was insanely hungry.

"Lenja's the one with the blond hair, right?"

Adina ate with her face in the bowl, three dumplings and four meatballs, she counted them.

"I'll get out, Henry. I'll leave in a minute. I just need to lie down a while."

Friday, 1:30 a.m. Hawaii Bio, Oehlenschlægersgade 1, 1620 Copenhagen V

Just call me Yvonne, said the middle-aged fake blonde at the till in the rear of Hawaii Bio, a twenty-four-hour dive filled with porno films and sex toys at a corner on Vesterbrogade. *I'm looking for Olek,* Marek replied in English, the language she had spoken. Yvonne turned her head and yelled, *Olek!* Then she offered him a cup of coffee. She sat knitting a stocking cap with a purple border. The coffee tasted bitter.

The girl was asleep in the car. She lay there hugging his coat. Ludmilla, fourteen years old, from Moldavia. She'd just sat there on the ferry, blue-eyed, cold, and frightened. Marek couldn't get a single bite down her, so he'd gone into the duty-free shop and bought a box of assorted candy, which she ate in the front seat. When they drove off the ferry she said, *I have money for school,* in English, and showed him a brown envelope. He looked out over the turnip fields and stuck a Marlboro in his mouth.

She'd fallen asleep while he was filling up in Tappernøje.

"Where is she?" Olek said, barging in through the back door. His eyes were bloodshot, he was every bit as blistered as his sister.

"Who?"

"You know, the new one."

"We'll get to her. She's asleep in the car. Your mother says there's something that needs taken care of quick."

They sized each other up. Olek gave him *the eye* and turned on his heel. Marek followed him out to the stairway, where Olek took three steps at a time. Second floor: cubicles, they heard someone moaning in one of the closest. Third floor: rooms to let, they entered one and Olek passed him a photo—*Adina Sobczak.* Thirty-five years old. Disappeared yesterday morning, emptied her closet and tricked a moronic Albanian at the till into handing over her passport. Last job: four Polish workmen on Mysundegade 3, the loft, lunch break, two hundred kroner per. Her roommate Lenja croaked yesterday morning, that might have made Adina crack. Olek pointed out Lenja's things in the small room. Clothes, mashed down in a large sports bag. The breath freshener was hers too. *Why don't these fucking Lats brush their teeth?*

Only the metal case belonged to Adina. Quickly they dumped it out, a barrette lay at the bottom. Marek picked it up. *Hello Kitty.* There was also a receipt. She'd bought a brush and something in product group 16 for 67.75 in Føtex on Vesterbrogade, the day before yesterday.

Not much to go on. Four Polish workmen who had gotten it on the cheap. He turned the barrette in his hand.

"Find her," Olek said. "Find her and do her."

Thursday 9:23 p.m. Abel Cathrines Gade 5, Fifth Floor,
1654 Copenhagen V

Adina brushed her long hair. The rain had made it ratty. Her back hurt, her lower back. Olek's sperm burned inside her. All the humiliations, the beatings, the cold. Lenja had lain on the bathroom floor behind the shower curtain, naked, bloody behind her ear. Olek's signature. He fucked them in the ass, then before he came he smacked them behind the ear so they would tense up and contract; they laid there waiting for that clout. She went over and opened the curtain a crack. One of Olek's boys, Kofi, was selling dope on the corner. She'd have to wait until he left. She sat down and Henry came in with coffee and a plate of cookies.

"It's strange having someone in the apartment," he said, speaking into the air while he set the cups down. "It's two years now since Connie died. We had two wonderful children," he continued, calmly. "Tina and Jørn. I don't see Jørn very much, but that's because of his new wife. Tina lives in Perth, Australia. Would you like to see some pictures?"

He edged past the coffee table and over to the bureau, opened the lowest drawer, and returned with a photo album.

"Here, this is their ranch. Greg breeds horses. And here, that's William, and this is Bill and Evan, and what's his name, the little one, Ross, yes, his name is Ross."

They went through the photo album, it was filled with photos, of horses and red-haired boys, two, three, four of them stood together, smiling at the camera. Adina followed along indifferently, the back of her eyes ached, and suddenly, without warning, she began crying. The tears streamed down, she couldn't take it anymore.

"There, there," Henry said, and grabbed her shoulders with both hands.

She shook her head and wiped under one of her eyes with her index finger.

"You know what?" he said, looking at her seriously.

"No."

"There hasn't been anyone but you after Connie died."

"What do you mean?"

"Just what I say. I haven't had other women except you since Connie died."

"You're saying that you've been true to me?"

"Yes."

She started to giggle. She laughed through her tears. Henry looked hurt, which only made it worse. Her laughter turned hysterical, she doubled over, unable to stop. Everything that happened had been so horrible, she'd been all alone in the world, and now here he was, talking like this. It wasn't funny—it was absurd. Henry, with his friendly eyes and sheeplike expression, his wrinkled forehead. She threw her arms around him and kissed him on the forehead.

"Thank you, Henry. Thanks. That was beautiful, what you said. Too bad I can't tell you the same thing."

"No, obviously you can't. Do you think Olek will kill you?"

"Yes."

Friday, 9:45 a.m. Mysundegade 3, Loft,
1620 Copenhagen V

Karol: We tossed for her. Ryszard went first. I was number three, but I couldn't. She just laid there. Over there on the mattress, on her stomach. Yeah, that's where we sleep. She didn't even turn over. And I just couldn't. I asked her if she wouldn't give me a handjob. She didn't answer me, so I just sat down beside her. I thought about my son. His name is Krzysztof. After Krzysztof Oliwa of the New Jersey Devils. The hockey player, you know. He's also from Tychy. It was Witold's turn after me. He already had a hard-on and he told me to get away.

Ryszard: She just took her clothes off and then I fucked her. Her name? I don't know. I didn't marry her.

Witold: She was on time. Asked where she was supposed to lay down. We asked her if she wanted some salami and vodka first, but she didn't. So then Ryszard went at it and we sat there and watched. He smacked her and yelled at her. Karol didn't like that so he pushed him off. I turned her over when it was my turn. I like missionary best.

Jan: She wouldn't say her name. I was sorry about that. There aren't many Polish women up here you can talk to, you know. I asked her if she was going somewhere, but she didn't answer. She had a big bag with her. Time? Little after two, I think. No, that picture doesn't tell me a thing. I don't remember her face.

> *Friday 2:47 a.m. Abel Cathrines Gade 5, Fifth Floor,*
> *1654 Copenhagen V*

The yellow light from the floor lamp softened Henry's face, and suddenly she remembered her grandmother, her babushka in the mountains. They visited her in the summer and at Christmas, and she always sat in her armchair and watched TV, her big pale face, the deep wrinkles, her knitting.

They had watched *High Noon,* Henry's favorite western. He said he'd seen it a thousand times and he hummed along with the title song, *Do not forsake me, oh my darling, on this our wedding day . . .* Adina had cried during the film. It was so beautiful and sad. Why didn't he leave with Grace Kelly, why did he have to be so proud? They drank beer afterward, and Henry made sandwiches, piled high with lettuce and tartar sauce on the roast beef, onion and jellied stock on the liver paté. She lay on the sofa, she'd had enough. Vesterbro was a thousand miles away. She walked over and peeked down at the street. Kofi was still standing there, dealing. He looked purple in the yellow light.

"Do you know what I dream about?"

"No," she mumbled.

"Moving to Australia. I've saved up twenty-seven thousand, and when I have forty I'm leaving. What about you?"

"I just want to get as far away as I can."

"Australia! That's as far away as you can get."

"It is?"

"You don't know where it's at?"

"No," she lied.

The globe stood on a low table in the bedroom. He flicked a switch on the wall, and the inside of the globe lit up. Henry got down on his knees. She knew where Australia was, why was she playing dumb?

"See, here *we* are." He put a finger on the small, blurry speck that was Denmark. "And *here*," he said, turning the globe without letting go of Denmark, "we have Australia. And *here* we have Perth." He put a finger on the city. "You simply can't get farther away. It's on the other side of the earth."

"And here," she said, and reached between his arms and put her finger on a spot between Warsaw and Vienna, "is where my family lives."

"What's the name of the city?"

"Krosno."

"Are your parents alive?"

"No."

They sat for a while without speaking, squatting in front of the glowing world.

Friday 12:32 p.m. Skelbækgade, Driveway into
Den Hvide Kødby, 1717 Copenhagen V

It was sprinkling, and Marek was sick and tired of it all. He had asked around at massage clinics, questioned Thai masseurs, tattooists, pushers, stood on street corners, in back rooms, gambling joints, checked with Pakistani taxi drivers, *no one has seen anything,* he had bounced around among the street whores, he had found a Polish girl with her head between her legs and a rubber hose tight around her arm in a basement stairway on Colbjørnsensgade, *it's not her,* he'd put his nose to the ground, bribed a med student who opened the drawers for him at the morgue under the National Hospital, *it isn't her either,* to hell with it all, he thought, *why shouldn't she be allowed to disappear, crawl in a hole, die someplace warm,* he was freezing and Ludmilla was hungry and hysterical, he gave her a shawarma and some candy, no, he didn't want her brown envelope. No, he didn't know what would happen to her. Shut up. He grabbed her by the chin, hard, *shut your goddamn mouth,* and then it didn't matter anymore, he had a bad taste in his mouth and he himself had caused it, he bought a pack of mints. Finally, the wind whipping his coat, a Nigerian whore on Skelbækgade reacted when he showed her Adina's picture, *seen this girl?* She wore a T-shirt, *Ivory Love* with sweeping gold letters, long nails with screaming pink polish. He had to dish out a hundred euros.

"I saw her yesterday. She was standing at this bridge by the station. What's its name . . . Dybbølsbro. Looked like she was going to jump. Didn't do it, but she looked desperate. Stood there with a big bag and no coat on. And it was raining!"

"What time?"

"In the afternoon. Around two-thirty. Maybe three. Then she was picked up by this guy. Don't know his name, but he is real wicked. A bastard. Uses his hand. Always takes his wedding ring and Rolex off. Don't wanna pay."

She scrounged around in her bag, found her cell phone, pecked on it, her nails clicking on the case. She held the display out to him and he saw the rear end of a car: XZ 98754. It looked like an Audi 4.

*Friday 12:51 p.m. Abel Cathrines Gade 5, Fifth Floor,
1654 Copenhagen V*

Henry stood in the kitchen holding a bag of fresh bread under his arm. His windbreaker was wet and smelled of rain. They had slept in bed with their clothes on, she had dreamed about *High Noon*, and in the dream she had been Grace Kelly wearing a bonnet and a laced-up, lace-trimmed dress and all the time that song, *Do not forsake me . . .* But then she woke up and felt his erection against her back. She lay still and fell asleep again, they had slept way too long. He stood up and smiled at her, and then something snapped inside her. She couldn't take it, the big friendly face, the same slightly baffled expression as when he came inside her every Friday afternoon, leaving a pathetic little blob of semen in the condom. The punctual little postman with the gray sideburns and the kind eyes—she had the urge to scratch them out and rip that cheap dream apart. She lunged at him, punching him, tugging and pulling at his big square body, she was furious, hammered at his arms and chest.

"What do you want from me? You want me to be your cheap little whore the rest of your life? Is that what you want?" she screamed. "You want me to be your little hole?"

"No. Adina—"

"And all that shit about Australia . . . and Gary Cooper . . . and . . . and . . . it's all just a bunch of lies and bullshit!"

She screamed and shouted. But then he grabbed her. Grabbed hard. His arms closed tight around her, clenched her. A brutal look came over his face, a coldness she hadn't seen before. She was surprised at how strong he was; she pulled and pushed and scratched and bit. He hummed, *Adina, Adina, Adina,* as if she was a child. He gripped her even tighter as he hummed. The floor fell away under her, and she was sucked down in it.

Friday 3:25 p.m. ColonWelfare, Vognmagergade 11,
1148 Copenhagen K

The owner of XZ 98754, Audi 4, Gregers Ege, walked alongside the impressive instrument with its hoses and buttons, talking about it. Marek had spelled his way through the English version of the questionnaire out in the reception area, and he believed he had checked "yes" to a *bloated sensation in stomach area* and *headache* and checked "no" to *bleeding ulcer* and taking Prednisol. Gregers Ege realized that colon hydrotherapy, colon irrigation with the new hygienic and 100 percent odorless technology, crossed a line of modesty for many patients, but ColonWelfare used the open system, LIBBE, approved by the U.S. Food and Drug Administration. Marek could insert the funnel-shaped plastic gizmo into his anus himself, Gregers Ege showed him. No one would at any time touch him or see him naked; he would be covered except for the area in question, and he would be lying comfortably on the form-fitting examination table and he could see what came out of the closed tube right there. Gregers turned the plastic gizmo in his hands, lost himself in its small molded end. He wasn't wearing a wedding ring. There was a pale outline of a watch and band on his suntanned wrist. Marek grabbed hold of it with his left hand and rammed his right elbow into Gregers Ege's throat. The man went into shock. Marek maneuvered him down onto the form-fitting table, strapped him in securely, grabbed several dispos-able wipes and stuffed them in his mouth, pulled his white coat up and his pants down, and shoved the plastic gizmo in his anal opening. Marek showed him the photo of Adina, stuck it under his nose. Gregers squirmed and jerked his head around when Marek connected the hose, turned it to the max, all the way up in the red. Gregers's eyes went wide, and when Marek ungagged him it shot out like a cannon: *It was the first time, I'll never do it again. You want money? Is it those fucking whores . . . ? They take people's license plates or what?* Marek had only one question, *Where did you let her off,* but first he asked Gre-gers about something else. *How much did you pay to fist-fuck her?* He got answers to both questions. Two hundred and fifty kroner in the parking lot at Sjælør Station. And, the end of Istedgade at Enghave Park and the community building. She staggered along Enghavevej, down by Prima. He saw that she had taken his watch when he looked to see what time it was. Three-fifteen p.m. on his car's display. It was pouring, and she didn't have a coat on.

Friday 12:55 p.m. Abel Cathrines Gade 5, Fifth Floor,
1654 Copenhagen V

"Adina, are you okay?"

"What happened?"

"I don't know what got into me, I . . ."

"Henry?"

"Yes."

"When I'm all alone at night, all my customers run to-gether . . . They turn into hundreds of mouths that moan, snort, scream, slobber, spit in my face. But with you, there was something . . . a tenderness, I don't know . . . And then it ends like this anyway."

"Adina. Come over here."

"No. It's best I leave. We can't change our lives."

"You don't think so?"

"No."

Pause. "We're doing it."

"What?"

"We're going to Australia. Perth. I'll empty my account. We'll leave tonight. Will you go?"

Friday 4:10 p.m. Hawaii Bio, Oehlenschlægersgade 1,
1620 Copenhagen V

Marek sat in the back room of the Hawaii Bio, wishing he was somewhere else, far away. Yvonne smiled with a cigarette between her lips; one of her eyelids drooped a bit. She held his hand in hers. The knuckles on his right hand were bruised and bloody, his fingers tingled. He couldn't remember what he had done to his hand. Had he beaten up Gregers Ege, or was it Ludmilla when she'd started screaming and wanted to go home? Why hadn't he delivered her? He didn't know why. She had taken some of his Rohypnols and was totally out of it when he'd left her. Just as well. Yvonne brushed the palm of his hand with iodine from a green bottle. Suddenly he felt a tenderness for her. Did she have a life outside of this, did she have a grand-kid who would get the ugly little stocking cap with the purple border?

Zdrow bądź, krolu anjelski.

Why was he thinking about that now? He always saw his mother's face when he thought about that psalm.

He pulled his hand away, raised his fist to the corner of his eye. There was a tiny wet streak on the back of his hand.

He reconstructed Adina's route. Mysundegade yesterday around noon, Dybbølsbro at two-thirty, Sjælør Station two-forty-five, Enghavevej three-fifteen. Then: gone. At the most she had a few thousand and a red-hot Rolex. She was still in town.

"Yvonne?"

"Yes, Marek."

"Did Adina have any regular customers?"

"What do you mean . . . regular?"

"I mean . . . did somebody treat her nice? Have you heard of anyone who was nice to her?"

"Nice, I don't know . . . Hey. There is this one guy, comes every Friday at four o'clock. Wait a minute . . . he didn't come today."

Friday 4:50 p.m. Abel Cathrines Gade 5, Fifth Floor,
1654 Copenhagen V

Henry had left again. Adina lit up her last cigarette with the next-to-last; she didn't know what to do with herself. She trudged back and forth between the sofa and the window and ran her fingers through her short hair. Henry had cut it. It felt all wrong.

Kofi was gone. Another African was dealing down on the street, someone she didn't know.

Henry! He had nagged and begged and pleaded and had been down on his knees. At last she had said she'd go with him. Why not? And then there was no stopping him. He helped with her hair and went out for henna and was down at the bank to withdraw his entire savings. She added her seven hundred to show her solidarity. That much for Australia. He had packed two suitcases and called his son, they talked a long time. They argued. She got a headache and lay down on his bed, rested there in regret, it was all way too far out. He went off to get the tickets, Melbourne via Frankfurt, departure at eight p.m., a taxi was reserved. But when he returned he came up with the idea that she should have a nice dress to travel in. She tried to talk him out of it. But he smiled and said, *I saw one with a big rose on it. It will look nice on you, you'll be wearing it when we get to Melbourne,* and out he went.

Where was he?

A girl came out of the laundromat and walked over to the African, one of the young kids from Skelbækgade, thin as a curtain rod. She stood freezing in a purple leather jacket with a fur collar, and he stuck a bag of brown h in her hand. The taxi arrived. Where the hell was he?

Then she heard him at the door.

Friday 4:57 p.m. Abel Cathrines Gade 5, Fifth Floor,
1654 Copenhagen V

Olek kicked the door in and rushed into the living room directly to Adina. She was standing there with the cigarette and Olek slapped her. He was half a head shorter than her, but he punched her in the stomach and she collapsed on the sofa, still holding the cigarette between her fingers. The glowing end fell off onto the cushions. Olek beat her systematically, first in the face, then the body, her breasts, arms, and stomach. She didn't scream, but every breath had its sound. She moaned and groaned after each punch, and he continued punishing her. He worked with both hands and covered her body with blows. Only when he grabbed her by her short red hair and pulled her down on the coffee table did she begin to scream, and he threw her to the rug.

"Get your clothes off!"

Marek had screwed the silencer onto his Zastava CZ-99, 9mm pistol; now he stepped over to Adina.

"Goddamn, Olek. Your mother will go crazy if she finds out you came along."

"I don't give a shit about that."

"You probably don't. But get out anyway, let me do my job."

Her one eye was closed and yellow, her ear and lips were bleeding. Olek spat in her face. She had stopped screaming and lay panting hysterically. Her lungs rattled, her wide-open eyes looked wild, green with bits of gray. Marek spread his legs, bent his knees a bit, took off the safety, and pressed the silencer between her lips. The metal clicked against her teeth. For some reason he changed his mind and aimed under her left breast. But then another click came from behind him. Another weapon, another safety off.

"Marek!"

"Yeah?"

"This is for my sister."

"What the hell are you talking about?"

"You think you can run from *us*? And take your little whore with you?"

Their eyes met. Marek stood awkwardly; he had to turn his knee and shoulder to swing around, then he threw himself backward at Olek and stretched his arm out straight. But he hung in the air when the shot boomed out in the emptiness. Marek felt a hard blow to his head, then everything turned red and faded out as the bullet snapped around inside his brain like a bear trap and blasted out through his neck and made a star-shaped crack in a Christmas plate, 1972.

Adina crab-crawled backward on her elbows, over to the door, and put her hands in front of her eyes. Olek walked over to her nice and easy and kneeled down. Sat there pointing the gun at her.

"Here. Here . . . take it. Take it, goddamnit, take the gun."

"What?"

"I'm giving you a ticket to your freedom. Take it."

Friday 5:15 p.m. Abel Cathrines Gade 5, Fifth Floor,
1654 Copenhagen V

By an act of pure will she raised herself up on her elbows and scooted across the floor. She wanted to see her executioner. He was stocky, balding, his head was shaved. He lay with his mouth open and pale eyes staring out; he looked like an idiot. Drool seeped out of the corner of his mouth and his right cheek was slush.

Olek was gone.

She searched the man's pockets and found a wallet with four twenty-euro bills, a Danish five-hundred kroner bill, and a set of car keys. She stuck everything in her clothes when she heard Henry letting himself in the apartment. Moments later he appeared at the door with a sack from Soul Made on Vester-brogade. He sat it down on the bureau, but then everything began to blur for her. He walked over to her but it all happened very slowly. Everything sounded loud, and there was a shrill tone in her one ear, the day's last rays of sunlight slashing through the apartment. He stood looking down at her. He had beautiful eyes, she thought, he was actually a very handsome man. There was a glow to him. She was no longer afraid.

"Adina."

"Yes."

His lips curled as he squatted down. Was he smiling? What was it about his eyes? He stroked her forehead and everything began flickering. He lifted her up, carried her over to the sofa.

"It was one of Olek's men, wasn't it?"

"Yes."

"It was him or you?"

"Yes."

"It's good that you got him. I'm happy about that. But it's best that you disappear now."

"What do you mean?"

"You need to get out of the country. I'll take care of all this. Give me the gun."

She had completely forgotten the pistol she was hugging to her breast, but he untangled it from her stiff fingers. He sat a moment looking at her, he hummed a little tune, the melody from the film, *Do not forsake me* . . .

Adina ran down to the taxi. But of course it was gone. A rusty Mazda 323 with Polish plates was parked in front of the gate. She tried the key. She would have said more to Henry, explained. But he just kept on. It was all going to be okay, he said. He also wanted to give her half the money. She would leave first, he would follow in a few weeks when everything had settled down. He would get through all this. Wouldn't be charged. He kept his wits about him surprisingly well, considering there was a dead Polack on his living room floor, shot in the face. She ended up taking seven thousand.

The key turned in the lock, and suddenly she was behind the wheel of her executioner's car. She started it and flipped on the blinker and drove off. But she didn't head for the airport. She drove out of the city. She just wanted to get away! She didn't know where, but it felt good tearing out into nowhere. She held the ticket, *Copenhagen—Frankfurt—Melbourne*, in her free hand, checked the rearview mirror, *no one*, she doubted she could get anything for it. She rolled the window down. *Do not forsake me, oh my darling . . .* Then she heard a pop, and the car began swerving. She threw the ticket on the passenger seat and steered off onto the shoulder. But when she turned to get out of the car she saw a girl in the backseat, asleep under an old gray windbreaker. She grabbed hold of the girl and shook her.

"Who are you?"

"Ludmilla . . . Where's Marek?"

"Marek is dead. What are you doing here?"

"I'm going to school in Sweden. I have money. See?" Ludmilla took a crumpled brown envelope out of her jacket pocket and waved it around.

"No, you were going to work as a prostitute for a bastard called Olek."

"I don't believe you. My mother said I was going to school in Sweden."

"All right, fine."

"You're lying," Ludmilla persisted. "Who the hell are you anyway? Where is Marek?"

The spare tire was in the trunk. Adina dropped it, and it rolled onto the sidewalk; something rattled when she took hold of it again. She grabbed it with both hands and shook. There was something inside. She removed her pocketknife from her bag, made a slit in the tire, and stuck her hand in, and there she stood with a roll of hundred-euro notes! She sat back inside the car and cut the tire all the way around—it was filled with rolls. Ludmilla still sulked in the backseat. She began slitting the brown envelope open with her finger, turned it upside down. A birth certificate, a physician's statement, a stack of tourist brochures about Copenhagen in Polish. The girl looked unhappy and started hammering her knuckles into the front seat. Then she let her head fall between her knees. Adina laid an arm around her neck, squeezed her, and then stuffed the money into the bag; she could count it later. Ludmilla sat crying with her head in her hands.

"Come on," Adina said, and she got out of the car and started looking for a taxi.

"Where are we going?" Ludmilla asked, following her outside. She was skinny as a reed.

Adina didn't answer immediately. She felt strangely weightless, and the pale, thin girl made her feel sentimental. She wasn't dead, Henry had saved her. The girl could sink to the bottom as quickly as a stone. She put her hand on Ludmilla's cheek, wiped the tears away.

"Where are we going?" the girl asked again.

"I'm going to Australia, and you can come along."

"What will we do there?"

"Wait for a man. A good man."

ALL I WANT IS MY BABY, WOAH WOAH, WOAH WOAH WOAH WOAH

BY SUSANNE STAUN

City Center

So let us go then, you and I, down the dark streets we know so well we no longer see them, let us eat the last sidewalks of Knabrostræde and turn down Læderstræde, stomp off in the light from the last breathing windows of the night, you, my towering steaming rage, and I, who must recognize that things probably can't be a whole lot different right now.

Unless you decide to bug off?

Before I do something stupid?

To be preferred.

But noooh, you won't do it, you've dug in, you insist on reaming my ass like a dog, and I'm not talking poodles and puppies, I'm talking a big filthy doberman with long brown teeth, a rotten mouth, and a snout with no honor. Well good luck, and excuse me if I'm not wild about this. But I'm not, amigo, just like I'm not wild about how I wasn't any good this evening. I was somewhere else, funny, sure, they laughed, got their money's worth, but I was somewhere else, and I hate it when someone like you gets me way out there, which is also out where my rage grows so huge that my body can't contain it and I have to ship off the rest to Nowheresville, where it belongs, a grim place, far from me and me.

So take a hike! Can't you see what you're making me do, cawing and glowering on an empty street, as if talking to myself? *It's so very lonely, I'm a thousand light years from home.*

You've been following me for precisely a week, since last Saturday, when you said it, when it rolled right out of you like an old belch: *You fucking look like Keith Richards, you want a beer?*

It was just past three in the morning. I was standing there, minding my own business and a large draft, trying to ease stage-adrenaline out of my body. But: *your wit, your speech, your repartee, impressed me almost instantly.* I'd been present, really present, on that stage, had them in the palm of my hand, never better. And then it slipped in, ruined my night, day, week, month:

You fucking look like Keith Richards, you want a beer?

And me? Didn't say a word, stood there gawking, didn't mention your gut, your watery eyes, and your fat cheeks. Not a word. Not that I'm polite, I'm not, but words just wouldn't cut it, no matter how ugly. And I lacked the courage for the kind of brutality it would take. Plus I didn't have the time. I was way too busy watching my life fall apart.

You fucking look like Keith Richards, you want a beer? But if you'd just smile a little . . .

I'm not smiling, not at you, at any rate. *If the show must go on, let it go on without you.* Bereaved of my illusions, I pondered whether it was the young Keith Richards, the one with the teen acne and all the scars, that you had in mind. The one who recorded people's toilet visits on his tape player? Or the old sod with his Grand Canyon–junkie face, the silver skull ring and bandana and girlie crap in his hair? Is my face really already a map of the twentieth century?

And then I walked home. Not enraged, not enraged, not yet. Just speechless. *It's not easy facin' up when your whole world is black:* only seconds ago I thought I was young and beautiful.

When we pass by Kongens Have, in just a few moments, why don't you go on in and run around in the dark a bit? To unwind, maybe? You never know, that fenced-in tar pit may hold people more bizarre than me, and honestly, I'd really rather not be Kill Bill tonight. Look! So gorgeously black and dark behind the grating. So seductively blue-black against the moon, so murky, too murky, just right for you. The ideal place to go up in smoke.

Right?

All right. But if I'm Keith, it seems so right to murder you tonight—not you, your ethereal remains, but you with the fat gut and the runny eyes who ruined my life with a sentence. Short and sweet. For we are both full of violence, separately and together. You may not know that I kicked a Glasgow bully in the head with the pointed toe of my boot. That I nearly strangled Ronnie Wood with my bare hands. Hammered my fist repeatedly into Stigwood. And why? Because he kept getting up. And for you I have a real buffet: blue and yellow and dead. In that order.

(But I'm still nice, given the chance. "I am a lover.")

Ah, I see you stare at the park grating. Kongens Have beckons? Go! I'll retreat. Tiptoe away. Ever so quietly. Cut diagonally across the street to where the shadows are even blacker. Hide in the crowd, blend into the façades, disappear. But the crowds have gone to sleep, the city is nearly empty. One couple walks by, like tears. Wrapped around each other, and her coat grazes me as they and their conversation slowly pass by, *Pretty, pretty, pretty, pretty girl, you're a pretty, pretty, pretty, pretty, pretty, pretty girl, pretty, pretty, such a pretty, pretty, pretty girl, come on, baby, please, please, please, I love you, are you cold?*—yes, please! I'll have some of that, thank you. *For here or to go?* No matter, just need to file off the rough edges.

Now you cut across the street, dear towering steaming rage,

and catch up with me on the corner where I thought I'd faded into the bricks so you couldn't see me. You glower at me, I can't miss it: *Go on, go on.*

All right then, let's. Side by side we walk down Gothersgade, I paint you black so I can't see you, step up the pace so to avoid your presence, and keep a steady rhythm without looking back. My feet move beneath me furiously, but I make no progress on this deserted street, and I sense you behind me, a thousand arms, a thousand legs twitching pointlessly, hear you grunt like a frenzied pig, grind your long, loose teeth and lose them, *plink-plonk,* on the sidewalk. Maybe this *is* a dream. No drunks in sight, it isn't right. No drunks, no scum, and no slime. So wrong for this time of night. And no intense poetic airheads who write ART, who write *sitting in the leftovers. World's silence. All are drunk on ether hope. Also that will pass away. Violently. Suddenly. And now;* no lame *come on, baby, please please please;* no T&A with metal heels; no old gals with teased, sprayed hair; not even the odd lost specimens who only want to find a head they can hop up and down on until all that's left is cauliflower. *Don't you know the crime rate is going up, up, up, up, up, to live in this town you must be tough, tough, tough, tough, tough!* Naw, we have the street all to ourselves, you and I, and I'm getting nowhere. And it's as if you're growing. And the more you grow, the more nowhere I get, the more I want to headbutt you, both of you. *You fucking look like Keith Richards, you want a beer?*

Have you ever heard a mouse roar? If you don't get lost, your face ends up like mine: Fuckface with Beckett-like furrows. So take a long walk on a short pier, and if you don't drown right away I'll be at your service in no time flat. I have something in my pocket, it's sharp, it can scratch and prick, deeply if need be, or just sever and slice, and I want to do so, badly, besides which I have leather gloves in my pocket that I'll put on so I don't hurt myself. My face has to go to work tomorrow, you see, and I hate to get blood on my clothes.

I cross the street toward the hot dog stand and order a grilled one while staring straight at Andy's Bar opposite. They're all in there. I don't care how crowded it is. I can cut you up, rip your black heart out in full public view, and stomp on your head until it's cauliflower, as is the custom nowadays. Surrounded by people, I can carry out my hideous but necessary project without unwelcome interruptions. No one will react. Not in McDonald's, not in Nab-a-kebab, not in Andy's—especially not in there.

The grilled dog arrives, but my towering rage runs around and around the hot dog stand, faster and faster, unnerves me. I fix my stare on Andy's cheery colors, the cozy lights, silhouettes of rollicking, sloshy binges. If you're not over there, in there, it's death by rage for the World's Most Elegantly Wasted Human Being, me:

So, my friend, where have you hidden tonight? Couldn't find you yesterday, either. I've been looking for you for over a week, in the city streets, after streetlights came on, in front of dour houses with windows so black they ate the white curtains, the white sills, and what else, the occasional cactus? I've looked for you in the courtyards, on deserted stretches, out by the warehouses on Amager where they bet on dogs and girlz wrestling in mud, along the canals, the slopes, in noise and darkness, and in the still of artificial lights. I always think it's your back I see framed in cold neon, always your boots tromping up the stairs, opening the door with a bang, your hands passing me things from inside.

Fuck, it was just the bitch who sold the tickets.

Andy's is open. That means I'm drunk. If I wasn't, Andy's would be closed. So it is. Keith Richards with acne and/or wrinkles and heroin-assisted constipation in wonderland, where he eats a grilled dog with everything on it in front of the bewitched tavern that must have you aboard by now, you and your like-minded and their mass of wrong words, though the right ones exist, like *Beautiful Delilah, sweet as apple pie, always gets a second look from fellas passin' by . . . The better don't allow me fool around with you, you are so tantalizing you just can't be true*, sounds so much better than *You fucking look like Keith Richards, you want a beer? If you'd just smile a little . . .*

I won't! I smile only for money. Your heartless sentiment has been eating away at me for eight days, and I don't even play the guitar.

I chew the last bite, swallow it with a dry throat while you run around and around, and I want to cry because you've ruined my dream about *Come, let us go then, you and I*. Come, let us go out and watch the evening stretch out under the sky like an ethereal figure longing for the light, let us go then, through half-empty streets, still cringing from the ringing sounds and echoes of the days, the smell of cheap restaurants, the agony of long menus; one street after another goes by like boring arguments that distract you from overwhelming questions: What does your skin taste like? Where can my tongue go, everywhere or nowhere—where precisely? And don't ask who I am, and what I do, no more questions like, *What is it?* There isn't anything, so let us do everything I have dreamed about.

For all this time. That I have dreamed about, for *all* this time. But come along before the yellow fog arrives to turn your thoughts to things that aren't going to work, to what you can't do, what you may not do, like eyes in drafty windowsills, scanning the street with disgust and fear. *Love is strong and you're so sweet, and some day, babe, we got to meet, just anywhere out in the park, out on the street and in the dark.*

Where shall we eat, you and I? Alone. Together. At Pastis? They already took the trash out.

I lick your lips and mine at the thought.

First thing in the morning, last thing before I go to sleep.

Leaves go, leaves come.

Wind rises. Summer's over.

So follow me now, share a bottle of wine. With me and make my heart boil.

Look at me.

Across the rickety table.

Warm for a September evening, don't you think?

But why not simply smash your face in? Trailer trash for an evening, no problem. Red necks, white trash, black & blue girls, I'm all that.

I toss the paper in the trash can, wipe my mouth, *good dog!*, and tremble when you jump in through my stomach and we become one flesh, one concentrated killing machine, bad company in every possible way. We cross the road blindly, walk up the steps, and I open the door with these luminous black eyes I always get when someone crosses me, and there it is: laughter, loneliness, and sex and sex and sex, *fucked all night and sucked all night and taste that pussy till it taste just right,* look at me, I'm finished, I'm totalled, *Look at me! I'm in tatters,* and well suited for the absolute armpit of the city, the final cockroach left alive in the debris, and I notice that I sway while I search the place for you, and fumble in my pocket for my scrap of metal.

Almost no women, almost only men, but then again: there's pussy at the bottom of every single beer glass, it's just a matter of getting down in there. The poets sit over in the corner, shitting words without wiping their mouths afterward. I know them, some of them step on stage once in a while to speak words, as they call it, and they don't know it's just *chitter-*

chatter, chitter-chatter 'bout shmat, shmat, shmat. The rest are old and dying, dried-up organisms, rustling folds of skin and too-full beards, and there you are, walking past the kidney-shaped table, *here it comes, here it comes, here it comes, here it comes, here comes my nineteenth nervous breakdown,* my body stiffens, and only my hand has the good grace to close around the sharp edge of the ragged metal in my pocket.

You see me, you smile, my mouth falls open: confusion. You approach me. Smiling, sparkling eyes. What? Is it the sight of my elegantly wasted face that makes you so happy? And then you say it: *Beautiful Delilah, sweet as apple pie, always gets a second look from fellas passin' by . . . The better don't allow me fool around with you, you are so tantalizing you just can't be true,* and you put your arm around me and kiss me, and you have no gut, no runny eyes, why? Was my memory that hazy? It really was very dark, black as night, black as coal, very dark in my head, and maybe I had visions or hallucinations, heard ghosts, I really imagined that you said I looked like Keith Richards, and I know I do, but honestly, I'm just a girl, and you shouldn't say things like that. But all right then, come on, come, let us go out and watch the evening stretch out under the sky like an ethereal creature longing for light; let us go then, through half-empty streets, still cringing from ringing sounds and echoes of the day. *Raise your glass to the good and the evil, let's drink to the salt of the earth.*

A FINE BOY

BY HELLE HELLE

Vanløse

Every evening after work I wanted that French hot dog so damn badly. I took the last metro train home; the grill was wedged in under the viaduct. Until then I had controlled myself. I wore a green uniform with padded shoulders and a belt at the waist. I was the thinnest I'd been since Jørgen left. He was a vegetarian, we were into butterbeans. Then he found someone else, a red-haired singer; I threw his duvet out the window. Afterward I lay on the floor for over a day, this had been toward the end of March. When that one and only you want inside you is no longer there.

It was raining. I cut across the square. The sliding door stuck, I stood there tugging at it. The girl inside came over and picked up a clump of wet napkins in front of the door. Then she opened it for me, walked back to the counter.

"A French hot dog, regular dressing," I said.

"On the way."

She put the hot dog bun in the machine. Picked a cigarette up out of the ashtray and sucked on it. I had the exact amount ready. Her hand was pale and delicate, hair in a thin ponytail pinned up on her head. She might have been nineteen or twenty, her smile revealed a slightly crooked set of teeth: "Can you believe it, it's the first French hot dog all evening."

"Is that right?"

She nodded: "Mmm. Strange, with this weather. Usually people come in and stand around."

We both gazed outside, she sucked on the cigarette again.

I wanted a cigarette too; I fished around in my net bag. The floor was covered with napkins. I found the pack and shook one out, she shoved her lighter across the counter.

"Those are really pretty earrings," she said.

"Thanks. I like them too."

"I have nickel allergy, I can't handle anything at all," she said. She blew smoke in the air, I did the same. By coincidence we had both held back a mouthful for a smoke ring; we blew one at each other simultaneously, the rings met over the counter. We broke out laughing, her laughter was what you would call sparkling, it trilled out of her. Smoke caught in her throat and she began to cough. The bun fell out of the machine, she kept coughing while she filled it with dressing. She smiled while she coughed and shook her head at herself. She held the back of her hand over her mouth, the hand holding the hot dog bun.

The ponytail wobbled on top of her head.

Then the telephone rang. She pounded her chest with the flat of her hand and lifted the receiver. The hot dog bun lay on the counter, some dressing ran out of it.

"This is Christina," she said, her voice unsteady after the fit of coughing. "Sorry, but I can't, I didn't bring them with me. They're over at Vibse's. No." Someone spoke to her. She cleared her throat, she pounded her chest again. "We don't close until one-thirty. And Mathias is with me, I can't go anywhere," she said, and a moment later: "Can't I bring them over tomorrow morning? Hello?"

She stood a bit longer with the phone in her hand, then she hung up. Turned around for the tongs, hovered over the hot dogs without picking one up.

"Toasted or plain?"

"Toasted, please."

The hot dog entered the bun. She handed it to me, walked to the sink, bent over, took a sip of water. I had opened the sliding door halfway, about to leave, when she called after me: "Could I get you to do me a big favor? It'll only take a minute."

"What is it?"

"I'll give you something for doing it. Just stay here for five minutes. My boy is out back asleep, I can't leave him here alone."

"How old is he?"

"Five months. But he'll just sleep. I'm only asking because it's an emergency. I have to go get something."

"Okay, I'll do it," I said, and joined her behind the counter. She was really small, not much over five feet. She pulled a white raincoat off the hook and put it on, felt around in the pockets.

"I'm back in five minutes," she said. "If anyone comes in, give them a free Cocio. But nobody will."

After she closed the back door behind her, I threw my hot dog in the trash. I reconsidered and pulled it out, packed it in a napkin, and stuck it back in the trash. Covered it with several napkins. Then I opened the back door. The baby carriage was just outside under a porch roof, protected by a dark rain cover. I peeked down through the hood's opening and could hear breathing. I opened the door all the way to get some light down there.

He lay on his side with a pacifier in his mouth that shifted back and forth. His head was large and round, covered with thick, light-colored hair. He was a fine boy. I leaned over and touched his cheek; his eye twitched but he didn't wake up. I tucked the duvet around him, rocked the carriage a few times, and went back inside.

A man stood at the counter. He was lanky and wore a windbreaker. He looked at me without any particular expression. I nodded at him. He nodded back.

"Where's the whore?" he said.

I thought I must have misheard. I smiled at him. "Would you like a free Cocio? Since you'll have to wait a little while."

"Is she gone?"

"She'll be here in a minute." He hadn't closed the sliding door, the wind whistled through the room.

I stepped back, leaned against the sink. The cash register was open under the counter, it was nearly empty. Broken buns and a bunch of fried onions lay in a pile on the floor. I grabbed the broom by the back door and began sweeping. I swept neatly and thoroughly. I looked around for a dustpan but couldn't see one so I left the pile there.

"You're good at that," he said from across the counter.

"At?"

"She's lucky to have you, else it would never get swept."

"Oh, surely it would," I said, and smiled a bit too boldly.

He didn't answer. I pulled my sleeve up, as if to examine a watch I wasn't wearing. Then the broom fell down by the back door, and I took the opportunity to duck under the counter. Something was still on the floor down there. I leaned forward—it was half a hot dog. When I stood up he was gone.

I perched on the stool with my net bag in my lap. The ponytail was soaked and shriveled when she came rushing through the sliding door a little while later, the rain jumping off her coat. "Thanks so awfully much," she panted, and stood with her hands on her hips. "It was really nice of you. Did anyone come in?"

"Just one man. He left."

"Did you give him a Cocio?"

"He didn't want one."

"Didn't you tell him it was free?"

"I did, yes."

"What did he look like?"

"Normal. Lanky. Had on a windbreaker."

She gathered herself and walked behind the counter. We almost collided, my net bag banged into her. I wanted to go home now, but before I reached the sliding door she cried out, then moaned from the back door: "He took Mathias, he took him along to the bar."

"He took him?" I shook my head, kept shaking it. "He definitely wasn't up behind here."

"Maybe not, but he took him. He went around back, must have. He took him along with him."

She stood with the carriage's rain cover hanging from one hand, the little duvet from the other. "Please, can you go over there with me?"

"But why did he take him?"

"I had a key of his brother's. That's who called, his brother."

"Was that what you went home for?"

"Yeah, now he's sitting over in Jydepotten with him."

"With his brother?"

"No, with Mathias. I have to close early. Hold this," she said, and handed me the little duvet. "Could you fold it up into a package so it's not so obvious?"

I didn't understand what she meant. I rolled the duvet up and tucked it underneath my arm; apparently that was good enough, she didn't say anything about it. She locked the door from the inside, I followed her behind the counter, she shut off the lights.

"Wait a sec," she said, and poked around in the cash register, then: "No, I'll count up tomorrow."

We left the grill and walked quickly through the rain down Jernbane Alle.

"He's never come by while I was working before. His name is Leif, he's sick," she said.

"But why did he take Mathias?"

She was about to cry, her voice shook: "To have something on me. How do I look?" She ruffled her hair, stepped under the awning at Jernbane Bakery, tried to catch her reflection in the darkened glass. "Don't ever buy anything in here, I found a snail in a roll once. Shell and everything."

"The duvet's getting wet," I said.

"We'll hang it over something, come on." She herded me along in front of her on the sidewalk. "Didn't you even hear him? What were you doing while I was gone?"

"I just sat. And I swept underneath the counter. What's the key to?"

"To a place out on Damhus Lake. I haven't even been there, it was just because of this guy who called Vibse's little brother."

We turned the corner at Jydeholmen. We could hear music from inside the bar, something with funk bass. The door was open a crack, the smell of smoke and old carpets met us.

The man, Leif, sat up at the bar, his back to us. There was no baby in sight. She nodded at a round table off to the side, we sat down. I laid the duvet on my lap under the table. The duvet felt clammy, my uniform did too. Fortunately the radiator by the window gave off strong heat. The bartender came over to us: "What'll it be?"

"Two beers and aquavit," she said, and then to me: "I'm just about to faint. He spotted us."

"Are you sure he's the one who took Mathias?" I said, when the bartender had left.

"Yeah, it's him."

"Then why don't you go up there and give him the key?"

"I need to sit for a minute. I've got to be calm."

"Where do you think Mathias is?"

She shook her head, she had tears in her eyes. "He's here somewhere. It's so cruel." I couldn't help reaching over and putting a hand on her shoulder. Which caused the tears to run over. Meanwhile she smiled crookedly: "I used to run around with some real sickos, I was a big idiot."

"What about your boy's father?"

"He came from Køge. Originally," she said, and wiped her nose with her arm.

The bartender brought the beer and two small glasses of North Sea Oil, the aquavit. We drank. It burned my throat. We both lit a cigarette, no smoke rings this time. I felt how tired my entire body was. My legs ached, I had been on my feet all day.

"I don't even know your name," she said.

"I'm Helle."

"Helle," she said. "That's my sister's name too. I'm Christina."

"Yes, I heard. That's my sister's name too."

"Really, it is? So we have the same name, that's really strange. With a C?"

"Yes."

"Really, that's strange. My sister works on the Oslo ferry, she'll be forty next month."

"She must be a lot older than you."

"Yeah, we have different mothers," she said, and tears welled in her eyes again. She covered her mouth with her small fist.

"My sister is a reflexologist," I said.

"I tried that once, it really hurt," she said, from behind her hand.

We sat, nodded shortly. Took a few swigs of our beer.

"And I work out in Bakken," I said then.

"I figured that out from your clothes, I've seen you walk by a few times. What do you do out there?"

"I sell tickets for the rides and stuff."

"That must be fun."

I shrugged my shoulders: "It's only for the time being."

"Me too," she said. "I'm going to be a midwife. I'm starting high school equivalency classes next year."

"That's a really good plan," I said.

He climbed down from the barstool, the windbreaker short on his lower back. He disappeared through the door to an adjoining room, maybe the bathroom was out there. She straightened up, took a deep breath. "I'm following him and I'll give him the key, but he has to give Mathias back right away," she said, and stood up. "Mathias is out there for sure, they have this little sofa, I'm sure he's laying on it."

"You're a little bit black under this one eye here. There."

"Thanks. That's sweet of you. I'll be right back," she said, and left.

I drank my North Sea Oil. I lit another cigarette, avoided glancing around the place. I looked at the leaded window of lurid colors, blue, red, yellow, and green, I counted the panes, five times seven, thirty-five in all, minus the three black squares in the middle, thirty-two. I reached into my net bag for a piece of gum. Yanked my sleeve up.

I needed to pee but I wasn't going *out there*, I wanted to head home, I wanted everything cleared up now. I stood and walked up to the bar to pay, the bartender wasn't around, dishes rattled somewhere in the back. I leaned over the bar to take a look.

The boy lay sleeping on an overcoat on the floor behind

the bar. Now I could see how big he was. Chubby arms and legs, round cheeks, pacifier moving back and forth. It seemed strange a boy that large had come out of such a small person. The rattling from the kitchen grew wild now, I leaned all the way over, I couldn't see the bartender. Quickly I fetched the duvet and my net bag, went behind the bar, and picked up the boy. He didn't wake, his head fell into place on my shoulder. It was a battle with him in my arms, the duvet hanging from my wrist.

We made it out of Jydepotten, and I walked across the street into the narrow alleyway beside the butcher shop. I leaned against the wall, I was completely out of breath. I wrapped the duvet around him. The boy had some real bulk to him— I figured out a way to hold him with both arms, the net bag wrapped around one of them. We stood like that for a while. The rain had stopped. The water puddles on Jydeholmen were like mirrors. I waited, my eye on the bar's front door.

Much later I heard loud noises from the courtyard behind the bar, grunts and groans beneath that unmistakable pearly laughter, the moaning now from pleasure. I stood holding the boy until it was all over. At that point I had almost no strength left in my arms.

I left the alleyway and returned to the grill. I walked around the back and laid the sleeping boy in the carriage, tucked him in. I returned to the street, paced up and down the sidewalk for quite a while, and at last I walked home. I took a long shower, using all the hot water. The next morning I was late getting up and had to rush out the door. I waited for the C train to Klampenborg. My pocketbook wasn't in my net bag; it had been fat, Karen and I had secretly exchanged all the Swedish bills. Almost four thousand kroner. I might have left it on the bar, I kept on imagining that.

But I never looked into it. Two days later I quit at Bakken

and returned the uniform, the only one I'd ever had. The week after that I enrolled in a writing program.

PART II

MAMMON

WHEN THE TIME CAME

BY LENE KAABERBØL & AGNETE FRIIS

Ørestad

S hit."

Taghi felt the tires on the junker Opel Flexivan sliding and losing traction in the icy mud. If he drove any closer to the entrance they might get completely stuck on their way out. The marble sinks were heavy as hell, and right now a wet, heavy snow was barreling out of the black evening sky, forming small streams in the newly dug earth in front of the building. The walkway around the building lacked flagstones. Nothing at all, in fact, had been finished. The whole place had been abandoned, left as a gigantic mud puddle, slushy and sloppy, and they were forced to park out on the street.

Taghi backed up, swearing in both Danish and Farsi. It would be backbreaking work lugging all the stuff that far, but there was nothing he could do about it now. He wasn't going to risk getting bogged down with all that shit out here in the middle of nowhere. No goddamn way.

They hopped out on the street and stood for a moment, hugging themselves in the icy wind. The building looked like every other place out here. Glass and steel. He'd never understood who would want to live in such a place. True, there was a view of some sort of water if you were up high enough, but otherwise . . . Taghi sneezed and looked around. The other brand-new glass palaces were lit up as if an energy crisis had never existed, but there was no life behind the windows. Maybe nobody wanted to live this way after all, when it came right down to it, and it would for sure be a long time before anyone moved into this particular building. The workers had been sent home several weeks ago. Something to do with a bankruptcy. Taghi didn't know much about it, but he had been by a few times in the past week to check it out. They could pick up some good stuff here.

At the corner of the enormous glass façade, pipes and cables stuck up out of the ground like strange, lifeless disfigurements. A stack of sheetrock lay to the side, the top sheets presumably ruined by now; the middle ones might be okay but they were a waste of time. They were after the marble sinks in the ten apartments. Three men, three hours work, and a short drive out to Beni's construction site in Valby. It was exactly what he needed, Beni had said.

The front door stood open a crack.

When they had been by earlier that day it was locked, and Taghi sensed Farshad and Djo Djo exchanging glances when he carefully shouldered the door open and stepped into the bitter cold hallway.

"Let's go, ladies."

Taghi's voice rattled off the unfinished cement walls, and he regretted wearing hard-heeled boots. Every single step rang upward through the stairway, fading into weak echoes that vibrated under the large, clear skylights, the steel beams, and the tiles dusty from all the construction. He fished his flashlight out of his pocket and let it play over the steps.

Had he heard something?

Djo Djo stumbled over a few half-empty paint cans, and Farshad laughed at him, a loud, ringing sound. Djo Djo grumbled and hopped around on one leg, the paint cans clattering around on the dark tiles. Those two babies. Annoyed, Taghi bit his lip and decided the ground-floor apartment to the right was a good place to start. For some reason he had gone totally paranoid. Wanted out of here, quick. He felt a prickling under his skin.

"Shut up, you two. It's not that goddamn funny anyway."

Farshad held back another giggle, but at least they didn't speak until they reached the half-open apartment door, and now there was that sound again. A muffled, drawn-out moaning that rose and fell in the empty pitch-dark surrounding them.

Taghi stiffened. "What the hell is that?"

Djo Djo's whisper broke, his voice on the edge of failing him. "It's some kind of totally weird ghost or something."

The muffled moaning was weaker again. They stood listening until it died out, and now the only sound was Djo Djo's nervous feet on the dusty tiles.

"We're out of here, right, Taghi?" Farshad had already stepped back, he was gripping Djo Djo's arm. "We can always come back tomorrow."

Taghi didn't answer, he was gazing at the darkness in the doorway while he considered the situation. The truth was that he felt exactly the same way as Farshad. He wanted to get out. He felt sticky underneath the down jacket Laleh had found for him in Føtex-løsning, the discount grocery. He heard a faint scraping sound and possibly a sigh from inside the apartment. He felt unsure, but he was the oldest, after all, and he had to decide what they should do.

"It's not a ghost," he said, in a voice as strong and steady as he could make it.

The others hesitated behind him when he pushed the door open and entered the apartment, the beam from the flashlight bouncing in front of him like a disco ball out of whack. There was an open living room and kitchen, bathed in a pale orange light from the plate-glass window facing the canal. Taghi knew instinctively that this wasn't where to look. It was too open, no place to hide. An empty space at the opposite end of the living room led into what must be the guest bathroom. If there had been any doors in the apartment they were gone now. Maybe someone else had gotten here before them, Taghi thought. Something dark was moving in there. Rocking back and forth on the floor still covered by clear plastic from the painters. He heard Farshad gasping behind him. He had followed, while Djo Djo hung back at the newly plastered island in the kitchen.

Taghi pointed the beam of light directly at the black shadow, and before the figure even turned its head toward him, he knew he'd been right.

It was a woman.

She sat stooped over the toilet seat. Her skirt hung sloppily around her hips and thin legs. Her arms arched like taut bows over the toilet bowl. Like someone throwing up, Taghi thought. But he knew what the woman was doing. First it was as if she didn't know they were there, not really, anyway. But when he stepped closer she turned her head, and her eyes, completely naked and black, met his.

They had been so close. So close that she could see the bridge, see the long rows of lights leading to Sweden. After the nightmarish days on the open deck of the ship, after months of overcrowded rooms that smelled of fear, with nervous men who always wanted more money than agreed upon, with uncertainty and despair about her belly that kept growing and growing . . . after all that, only one thing was left: get over the bridge. When she got there she was supposed to call Jacob, and he would come and take care of everything, the rest of her life, he had promised, with her and the baby . . . She felt an overwhelming yearning in her gut, almost as fierce as the contractions, and her lips formed the words he had taught her to say, the magic words that would open the gate so she could be with Jacob forever: *Jag söker asyl*—I seek asylum. But don't say it before she got to Sweden, he had said. And for God's sake, she must not be discovered before she was inside Sweden, otherwise the gate to her life with Jacob would close. If she wasn't sent back—a terrible, horrifying thought—she would end up in some sort of refugee camp, someplace he couldn't get to her, couldn't be with her. It would be like prison, he said, and it could be for several years.

That was why Chaltu hadn't said anything about the jolts of pain shooting through her body. She had tried, *tried*, but eventually she couldn't hold it back. The sounds were coming out no matter what, just like the baby. And then it happened, the one terrible thing she couldn't let happen. Her water broke, came rushing from between her legs and out over the seat beneath her.

The driver stopped the car. This is no good, he said. He cursed about the seat that was wet now, but even worse was how she couldn't sit upright and keep quiet when the contractions came. They would be stopped, and he wasn't going to prison because of her, he said.

She screamed and wailed and begged, and they had to drag her out of the car by force. She even tried to run after them, but of course that was hopeless. The driver floored it and a shower of slushy gray snow sprayed up in her face, and then the car was gone.

I will die, Chaltu thought. The baby will kill me and neither of us will ever see Jacob. She slugged her stomach with both hands, punches of helpless rage, and she had to bite her cheek not to say out loud the curse that was on her lips. I must not curse my own child, she thought. God will punish me for that. Holy Virgin, what have I done? But she knew well enough. Her sin was love. Love for Jacob, a love that had no future in Adis Ababa, but maybe in Blekinge, where he had lived since he was seven and was now studying, in Blekinge College and Yrkeshögskolan, to become an agronomist.

She kept walking without knowing where she was going. First she thought she might be able to find the bridge again and cross it on foot, but she quickly lost all sense of direction. What kind of a city was this? There were no people, none at all. It was almost as if the buildings owned the city and the streets, as if they had decided that they didn't want any dirty living creatures crawling around.

A strange singing tone stopped her. For a moment she wondered if she were hearing angel voices, because she was so close to death. But then a light popped out, an entire snake of light, and she saw that it was a train, even though it zipped through the air above her, on a track supported by concrete pillars. There was water underneath the track, long shiny-black sheets of water reflecting the train light. Why couldn't it run on the ground? Chaltu wondered. It was as if someone had erected a bridge just to remind her of the one she couldn't get across.

There were people up there, she noticed. They were being carried through the dead city and they looked warm and cozy and cheerful in the belly of the snake train.

The wet snow was denser now, and the wind drove it against her head so she could no longer feel her face. When she noticed the building still under construction, with the fence knocked down and the empty, dark windows, she realized it might be a place she could stay without being discovered. No one could be living there.

And it was dark and quiet in there too, but there were so many windows. She thought the whole world must be able to see her. And it was almost as bitter cold as outside. There were no blankets, no furniture, nothing soft whatsoever. Some of the inside doors were missing. The wind whistled through the main hallway, and the wet snow slid quietly down the enormous panes of glass.

A violent contraction came—it felt as if God Himself had grabbed her with His giant hand and squeezed until she was close to breaking apart.

"Stop," she whispered desperately. "Stop." If only it would hold off again. If the contractions would stop; if the baby would just stay in there and leave her alone—then maybe she could cross the right bridge to the right country instead of dying in the wrong one.

She crouched down on the tile floor beside a toilet bowl because she felt least visible there. But the sounds from inside kept coming, and what good did it do to hide?

Here there is no one, she told herself. The building is empty, it is unfinished. No one can hear you now. But suddenly there *was* someone. She hadn't even heard him come in. She just opened her eyes and there he was. Her heart took a long, hovering leap and ended up stuck in her throat.

He was just a silhouette in the dark, a darker outline, and the glare from the flashlight blinded her even more. A moment earlier she had thought she would die either from the cold or from her baby. Now another possibility had shown up.

"Leave me alone," she said, but of course he didn't understand her.

The man said something, and she realized he wasn't the only one there.

"Don't kill me," she said.

And he didn't. To her amazement he took off his coat and put it around her shoulders.

His name was Taghi. She understood that much from his words and gestures, even though they shared almost no common language. And he was trying to help her. This was so strange that she could barely comprehend it. His hands were friendly, his tone of voice reassuring. And he said one word she understood.

"Doctor," he said in English. "We will get you to a doctor."

"No," she answered, the word scaring her. "No doctor."

"It is okay," he said, slowly and clearly. "It is a secret doctor. Okay? You understand? Secret doctor okay."

She couldn't answer. The next contraction hit her, and she was only vaguely aware that he brought out a cell phone and called the okay secret doctor.

Nina was staring at the vending machine when the telephone rang. For a measly five kroner you could choose between coffee with cream, coffee with sugar, coffee with cream and sugar, bouillon, pungently sweet lemon tea, and cocoa. Unsweetened and uncreamed coffee had once been options, but they had been eliminated sometime in the mid '90s, if those who had been here even longer than her were to be believed.

It's Morten, she thought, without taking the phone from her white coat. And he'll be pissed with me again.

She was tired. She had been on duty since seven that morning, and the Danish Red Cross Center at Furesø, commonly known as the Coalhouse Camp, was every bit as ravaged by December flu as the rest of Copenhagen, with various traumas and symptoms of depression thrown in, plus an epidemic of false croup among the youngest children in Block A.

Despite all that, she could have been home by now. If she

had left at four, after the evening nurse delayed by the snow-storm had finally shown up, she could have been sitting right now in their apartment in Østerbro with a cup of real coffee and a few of the slightly deformed Christmas cookies Anton had baked in the SFO, his youth center. Why hadn't she? Instead of hanging out on a tattered, tobacco-stained sofa in the Block A lounge, listening through the walls to Liljana's thin cough, her professional ear focused. How obstructed was the child's respiratory tract? How much strength was there behind each cough? Should she be suctioned again, and when *was* the last time her temperature had been taken?

The sick-staff excuse was about as worn out as the sofa—Morten wasn't buying it any longer.

"Damnit, Nina. She's *your* mother!" he had hissed the last time she had called home to say she'd be late. He was supposed to be going to some sort of show with the others from his work, and if she wasn't there it would be the second night in a row that Nina's mother would be alone with the kids.

The phone began to repeat its cheery little electronic theme. Reluctantly, Nina grabbed it out of her coat's pocket.

It wasn't Morten. It was an extremely frantic voice she didn't recognize until he said his name.

"It's Taghi. You have to help. There's a woman, and she's . . . she's about to have a baby."

Even then it took her some time, for Taghi had been out of the Coalhouse Camp for three years, and there had been so many others since then.

"Take her to the hospital," she said, even though she knew that wasn't an option. Not when he was calling her.

"No," he replied. "She's from Africa. She won't go to the hospital. You have to help."

I'm not a doctor or a midwife. The words were in her mind,

but she didn't speak them. Her exhaustion was already gone. Adrenaline shot into her blood, she was clear-headed and energetic. Morten will have a fit, she thought. But this would be so much easier than trying to explain to him why she couldn't handle spending another night alone with her own mother after the kids went to sleep.

She set the plastic cup of lukewarm coffee with cream down on the scratched table. "What's the address?" she asked.

Taghi glanced at his watch. Wasn't it about time she got here? He was out of his league here, he wanted so badly to hand over this woman and baby and the contractions and birth to someone trained for it. He was a man, damnit. He shouldn't even be here.

He heard a sharp metallic click, and suddenly the whole apartment was bathed in a piercing white light from the spots set into the ceiling.

The woman crouching on the floor grabbed desperately for his arm. Taghi heard Djo Djo and Farshad swearing softly out in the kitchen area. A second later they stood beside Taghi in the small bathroom, where they both squeezed their way in behind the wall, the only thing shielding them from being in full view from the street outside.

Someone had walked into the hallway, and Taghi immediately assumed it was the police, and thought that the residency permit he'd worked so hard for was about to go up in smoke right now, right here, in front of the entire fucking district of Ørestad. Someone had turned on the building's electricity and the harshly lit apartment made him feel like a fish in a very small aquarium. The bathroom was the only place to hide. He caught Djo Djo's eye and held his index finger to his lips, warning him.

The footsteps outside rapped sharply against the tiles. Whoever they were, they weren't afraid of being heard. They walked past the door and stopped farther down the hallway. There were at least two of them, maybe more.

The dark-skinned foreigner on the floor fidgeted and held both hands over her eyes, as if to protect herself from the whole world. Another contraction was on its way. Her backbone formed a round, taut bow underneath her summer jacket, Taghi noticed; soon she would be moaning again. Soon they would be discovered.

If they nailed him for theft they would send him back to Iran, or at the very least back to the refugee center. To the knotted-up feeling of not knowing where he would be the next day or the rest of his life. The letters from his lawyer, from the state. The stiff white sheets of paper folded perfectly with knife-sharp edges. How would he take care of Laleh and Noushin then?

Taghi caught the woman's eye when the next contraction overtook her and she moved to get back on her knees. As if she was trying to flee from the source of the pain. He stopped her halfway and pulled her head against his chest while shushing her, the way you would shush a young child.

Now the men outside were arguing. It was impossible for him to hear what it was all about, but one of them yelled that the other was an asshole. Then their voices were muffled by the creak of an elevator door, which slid shut and swallowed the rest of the argument.

Quiet.

"Shit."

Djo Djo was the first to stand up; he slapped the light off in the kitchen area. The snow outside swirled in the cloudy yellow spotlights illuminating the building's façade. Taghi rose and moved to the window facing the street. Farshad came to stand beside him.

"Why don't we just get out of here?"

Farshad looked warily over his shoulder at the bathroom door. He was more afraid of the woman than the men, Taghi thought.

Farshad was nineteen and Djo Djo eighteen. Childbirth was obviously not their strong suit.

Taghi's pulse was pounding in his temples.

"Okay, you called that woman," said Farshad. "Time to split. Me and him, we're out of here for sure." He gave a jerk of his head in the direction of Djo Djo.

"And leave her here alone? *Na baba*. You've got to be kidding." Taghi nodded fiercely and pointed out to the van.

A metro train whistled past on the tracks above the black canal. No conductor—it was some kind of new technology they had installed when the metro was built. It was all automated. The light from the windows of the empty cars reflected in the water.

He supposed the shadow came first, hurtling past the window, but it was the sound that Taghi reacted to. A hollow, wet thud, like the sound of a very large steak being slapped down on a cutting board.

The man had landed on the stack of wet sheetrock less than a yard from the window and was definitely dead. Taghi didn't need to go outside to check. He was lying on his belly, with his neck twisted back and to one side, so that they could see his forehead and his eyes. Or rather, eye. The part of his face that was resting against the sheetrock had been crushed so completely that it was just a pulped mess. His one identifiable eye was staring at Taghi, Farshad, and Djo Djo with a strangely irritated expression.

"Fuck! Fuck, fuck. What the fuck do they think they're doing?" Farshad's voice stumbled, shrill and pitched too high in the dark behind them, and Taghi knew right then that Farshad was a bigger problem than the woman in the bathroom.

Her eyes were wide, but she had stopped talking. He couldn't even hear her breathe. He felt the shock himself, like a strap tightening around his chest. Despite this he managed to reach out and clap his hand over Farshad's mouth.

"*Khar.* Shut up, you big idiot," he hissed.

Farshad thrashed around like a drowning man under Taghi's right arm. Now they heard quick steps on the stairs. The front door opened and slid shut with a quiet click. A moment later a pair of headlights swept over the glass façade. The car took off and the sound died behind the thick thermal windows.

Taghi slowly removed his hand from Farshad's mouth. He wasn't sure that Farshad was completely calm yet, but at least he wasn't shrieking like some old woman. In the bathroom the woman had begun to groan again. It sounded like she was calling out for someone. She no longer had the strength to crouch, she was rolling on the floor, trying to curl up as the contractions grew stronger. Her lips formed a fluid and nearly silent stream of words, and her long, slim hands clutched at thin air and then grabbed a corner of his sweat-soaked T-shirt.

"Jacob?"

Taghi rubbed a hand across his eyes. He needed to think.

Djo Djo had stepped right up to the window to get a better look at the corpse.

"What the hell we do now, Taghi? He's dead. The police will come. They'll be looking for us and they . . ." Djo Djo spoke slowly, searching for his words, as if the reality of the situation first struck him as he talked about it. "Maybe they'll think we did it. Then we're fucked. They'll throw us out, they'll kill us."

Taghi had been thinking the same thing.

Their fingerprints were all over. Farshad's gloves dangled from his pants pockets. One in each pocket. Djo Djo hadn't even brought any. All they had planned on doing was liberating a couple of fucking sinks. That's not something they nail you for—not seriously, anyway.

The woman had another contraction. They came every few minutes now. She was pulling him down, as if all she really wanted was someone she could drown with. She was crying.

"You have to find something to cover him up with."

Djo Djo glared silently at Taghi. Then he grabbed Farshad's shoulder and dragged him toward the door. Farshad stumbled, found his feet again, and trudged off behind Djo Djo, who was as agile as a cat in the dark.

A second later, Taghi saw the two brothers standing outside the window, struggling with the green tarp from the van. The wind grabbed the tarp, making it look like a dark, flapping sail against the multitude of brightly lit windows on the other side of the canal.

The woman on the floor loosened her grip on Taghi a bit, and as he straightened up he noticed a thin figure walking their way, leaning into the wind, hands over her face to shield herself from the big wet flakes.

She had arrived.

Nina zipped her down jacket all the way to her nose before getting out of the car.

Brave new world. The streetlights' reflections shimmered in the black water of the canals, and the elevated railway looked like something from a sci-fi film. Trees and bushes didn't belong in this vision of the future, the general impression was that organic life forms were unwelcome here. How in the world did an African woman about to give birth end up here?

Brahge Living, a big sign said, illuminated by a powerful floodlight. *24 exclusive condominiums—for sale NOW!* The colorful, optimistic drawing of the finished development formed a sharp contrast to the muddied mess of construction and the toppled wire fence.

Brahge, she thought to herself, hitching up her shoulder bag. He was the man who went broke. One of the most publicized bankruptcies in recent times, because Torsten Brahge had been regarded as one of the best and brightest, having just been awarded some business prize a few weeks earlier. Investor megabucks were in danger of evaporating. She had seen the man's slightly chubby, Armani-clad figure on the front page and in several self-pitying television interviews, though she couldn't remember what he had said. Usually she quickly grew tired of hearing wealthy people moan about the financial crisis and the real estate collapse.

A battered-looking van was parked beside the fence, and she caught sight of two young men grappling with a green tarp just outside the building. Life in the desert, she thought, and lifted her arm in a stiff, frozen wave

"Is Taghi here?" she yelled.

Both of them stared at her as if she were some monster that had crawled out of the canal. But one of them nodded.

"Yes," he said. "Are you the doctor lady?"

"Nurse," she corrected.

He shrugged his shoulder, *whatever*. "He's inside. Ground floor to the right. You'd better hurry."

She found them in the apartment's tiny guest bathroom, the woman on her knees in front of Taghi, clinging to him with both hands. The quiet hope Nina had been nourishing that it might be false labor and a touch of hysterics immediately disappeared. The woman's coat and skirt were soaked with amniotic fluid. If there were any complications, Nina decided, she's off to a hospital whether she likes it or not.

At that moment the woman's eyes flew open, and she looked straight at Nina.

"Hi," Nina said in English, in her most reassuringly professional voice. "My name is Nina, and I'm here to help you. I'm a nurse."

"Doctor," the woman gasped. "Secret okay doctor."

"Just say yes," Taghi said. "I don't think she understands much English. Her name is Chaltu." Taghi didn't look so hot himself, Nina observed. Anxious, nervous, but that wasn't so surprising, either. She had a good idea what he was doing here. Or anyway, what he would have been doing had a woman giving birth not gotten in the way.

He tried to stand up, but Chaltu kept clinging to him.

"No go," she said. "Jacob no go."

"Sometimes she calls me Jacob," Taghi said. "Don't ask me why."

Nina touched Chaltu's arm. Her fingers were bloodless and gray, her skin icy cold. She let go of Taghi with one hand and swatted at Nina, who was trying to see how far she had dilated.

"Chaltu," Nina ventured. "I must look. Look to see if baby is coming."

"No baby," Chaltu groaned. "No baby here. In Sweden. *Jag söker asyl.*" And she pressed her legs together so hard that her thigh muscles quivered.

Jesus, Nina said to herself, and took measure of the woman's desperation. If it was possible to delay a childbirth by will alone, this would turn into a very long night!

"We have to get her someplace where we can keep warm," Nina said. "Is that your van?"

Taghi looked toward the window facing the parking lot, and Nina followed his eyes. She saw the two young men outside, pulling a blue nylon rope through the green tarp's grommets. A violent gust of wind rammed them. One of them slipped in the mud and lost his grip on the tarp. It flew up, flapping like a bird trying to fly away. Underneath lay a dead man.

It took her only a few seconds to recognize him. The Armani suit had had a terrible day, and the man inside a worse one. There was no doubt, however, that it was the head of Brahge Living lying there, very much dead.

The two young men got the tarp under control and tied it down, and the well-dressed corpse disappeared from sight. But it was too late. Nina had seen him. And Taghi knew it.

They stared at each other over Chaltu's head.

"We didn't do it," Taghi said. "The guy just went flying past us and—wham!"

Nina nodded. She also stuck her hand in her pocket and began pressing numbers on her cell phone blindly, not bringing it out. But he noticed. He tore away from Chaltu, who screamed in a burst of fright, and suddenly he had a knife in his hand. The blade was barely two inches long. A pocketknife, Nina thought, no murder weapon, and he didn't hold it as she imagined a murderer would. It looked more as if he were about to sharpen a stick to roast something over a fire.

All the same. He had a knife.

"Give me your phone," he said. "Now!"

She thought about what was at stake for him if the police came. Everything he stood to lose. She gave him the phone.

Chaltu looked back and forth between them with eyes that could hold no further terror. Taghi plopped Nina's Nokia into the toilet. Then he brought out his own cell phone and punched a few numbers. Through the window she watched one of the young men let go of the tarp and put his hand to his ear.

Taghi began to speak, fast and in Farsi. Nina didn't understand a word. Yet for the first time she felt a jolt of fear.

Fucking morons.

Taghi could barely control his anger. He felt it, warm and throbbing just under his skin. No one had better touch him. No one. Especially not those two idiots standing there fidgeting by the door. Just covering up a body with a green tarp—you would have thought it was a pretty simple job. It wasn't like he was asking them to perform brain surgery.

They stood there staring at Taghi and the doctor lady and the woman on the floor. Farshad squirmed around like a three-year-old in need of a pee. His eyes moved back and forth uneasily between the doctor lady and him, as if he was trying to figure out what Taghi was thinking. Taghi knew he ought to say something, but he didn't know what. Plus, he didn't want to talk to that idiot. Not right now. They had a problem. The African wouldn't go to the police, of course. The doctor lady, on the other hand . . .

Would a Danish woman be able to drive away from here and forget everything about the squashed corpse on the sheet-rock outside? Could he let her go?

His thoughts were broken by Farshad, who again spoke way too fast and way too loudly. "Shouldn't we . . ." He hesitated and flashed another look at the women in the tiny bathroom. "Shouldn't we kill her, Taghi? Isn't that what we should do?"

Taghi caught Farshad with a whipping blow across the back of the neck. He didn't want to talk to him, mostly he wanted to hit him again, harder. Farshad's astonished expression stopped him, and instead he spoke slowly and clearly.

"No, we are not going to kill her. *Ajab olaqi hasti to.* You are as stupid as a fucking donkey." Taghi's low, tense voice quiv-ered. "Keep your mouth shut while I think."

Farshad, clearly hurt, stared at him, then he bowed his head.

"Taghi." The doctor lady's voice sounded like a gunshot in the tense silence. "You're all going to have to help me hold her. She won't do anything."

Taghi gaped at her. She couldn't be serious. Did she think they looked like a bunch of nurses? He was about to say some-thing, but he stopped. One glance at the sinewy little figure beside the African woman convinced him that there was no room for discussion at the moment.

The doctor lady had made a pallet for the woman consist-ing of Taghi's down coat and Djo Djo's fleece. On top of that she had laid clean white towels from the shoulder bag she'd brought along.

"Sit so you can support her head, and then shut up. Appar-ently you're Jacob at the moment, and it works a lot better if you're not yelling at your cousin."

Taghi trudged back into the bathroom, and slid to the floor without another word. He raised the woman's head and shoul-ders so she could rest against his thigh. He dared a quick glance at Djo Djo, who was still standing in the kitchen area, his ex-pression an absurd mixture of terror and amusement. A brief, nervous laugh escaped him.

The eyes of the doctor lady gleamed fierily in the dark. "You two can make yourselves useful and see if there's any hot water in the pipes."

Djo Djo and Farshad got going too. Taghi heard them swearing beneath their breath at the kitchen sink. There was water, but it was cold. The African woman hunched over and pushed so hard he could see the small veins in her temples standing out in the weak light from the streetlamp. He put a hand on her forehead and sent a quick prayer off to heaven. For her, for the baby, and for the three of them—Djo Djo, Farshad, and himself.

He turned again and looked at the doctor woman. Nina. Her face blazed with a pale, persistent concentration.

"It's coming," she said, glancing up at him with something resembling a weak smile.

"I know."

The African woman opened her eyes and looked directly at him as the next contraction hit. And he thought about what it must be like—to give birth here, among strangers, among men.

Down between the woman's legs, the doctor lady reached out with both hands and made a quick turning motion, and Taghi heard the wet sound from the baby slipping out onto the white towels.

It was a boy, and he was already screaming.

"Blessed Virgin, Mary full of grace, free me from this pain, Gaeta, Gaeta, Lord have mercy upon me, may all your saints protect me, and I will honor you . . . *honor* you . . ." Chaltu had to pause for a moment because God's fist squeezed the air out of her, but she continued the litany in her head and time disappeared for her; it was the priests' mass she heard, she thought she could smell the incense and feel the pressure, not from labor but from the crowd, all trying to catch a glimpse of the procession, the long parade of holy men clad in white costumes trimmed in red and gold. "*Hoye, hoye,*" the children sang, swaying and clapping their hands, and farther forward she could see the Demera, the holy bonfire waiting to be lit. The Meskel festival had arrived in Addis Ababa, and she was a part of it, swaying in rhythm to it, and she felt uplifted, she felt like she could float above the crowds and see over them instead of standing there among backs and thighs and shoulders and legs.

"Chaltu, push. Go on now, push!"

Hoye, hoye . . . be joyful, for today the true cross is found, praise God Almighty for today all sins are forgiven . . . and Jacob's eyes gleamed at her, his hands supported her so she didn't stumble despite all the people around her pushing and shoving. In that moment it made no difference that she hardly knew him, that he was only home for a visit, that he wasn't the one she was supposed to marry. She loved him, loved the open look in his eye, his rounded upper lip, the way his earlobe attached to his neck. Loved him, and wanted to make love to him. It was as if the holy Eleni herself smiled upon them and promised them that their love would be clean and unsinful. *Hoye, hoye.* Today life will conquer death.

But why did it hurt so badly? She no longer understood this pain, no longer remembered the baby, instead she called for Jacob, again and again, but he faded away from her, as did the priests, the singing and clapping children, and the bonfire, the flames of which were supposed to show her the way to salvation.

God's hand crushed her, she could neither think nor scream. She could just barely sense that she was surrounded by strangers, and that the arm she was clinging to wasn't Jacob's.

"Look, Chaltu. It's a boy. You have a son."

They laid a tiny, wet creature, a baby bird, on her stomach. Could it really be hers? She knew she should hold it, but her arms felt cold and heavy as stone.

It took several minutes before she realized that the baby had been born, and that she was still alive. A miracle, it was, and she only slowly began to believe it. For the first time in many days she felt something other than pain and fear. She raised her heavy arm and curled it around the baby-bird child. Breathed in its odor. Began to understand. *Hoye, hoye,* little one. We are here, both of us. We are alive.

Nina regarded Taghi's tensed-up face. She sensed that the truce was over. The umbilical cord had been cut and tied off. The placenta lay intact and secure in the plastic basin she'd brought along from the clinic. The little boy whimpered in Chaltu's arms, pale against her dark skin. And Nina's reign had ended with the birth. Now they were back to the corpse and everything death brought with it.

Farshad said something or other, his voice catching nervously. Taghi answered him, negatively Nina thought, but she wasn't sure. How terrifying it was that they could discuss what to do with her without her understanding a word. Taghi had said that they didn't kill Brahge, and she couldn't really believe he was a cold-blooded murderer. They aren't evil, she told herself, and tried not to think how absolutely normal, unevil people could do horrible things if they were pushed far enough.

"Why don't you just leave?" she said. "You can take Chaltu and the baby with you, and I'll wait until you're long gone before I call the police."

"Yeah, right," Djo Djo said, and scratched himself quickly and a bit too roughly on the cheek.

Taghi said something sharply, obviously an order. Djo Djo protested, and Farshad started to titter nervously, maybe at what Djo Djo had said. But finally the brothers left the apartment. Nina saw them through the window, lifting the tarp-wrapped body and carrying it over to the van.

All of a sudden they were rushing frantically. They pitched the body in the van, threw themselves into the front seats, and roared off. Seconds later Nina could see why. On the other side of the canal, on Ørestads Boulevard, a police car was approaching slowly, its blue lights flashing.

Eggers stopped the patrol car.

"There's a building with balconies," he said. "And that van didn't waste any time driving off."

Janus shrugged his shoulders. "We'd better check it out," he said. He had his regular black shoes on, not his winter boots. The radio hadn't mentioned anything about snow when he left Allerød that morning at a quarter past seven.

Eggers called in the address. "We're going in," he told the shift supervisor. "But it looks peaceful enough."

Janus sighed, opened the car door, and lowered his nice, black, totally inadequate shoes into the muddy slush. "Does anyone even live here?" he asked. The place was all mud, with construction-site trash everywhere, *for sale* signs in most of the windows.

"At least there's light," Eggers growled. "Come on. Let's get it over with."

The street door was open, a bit unusual nowadays. Eggers knocked on the door of one of the ground-floor apartments. After quite a while, a thin dark-haired woman opened the door. She stared at them with an intensity that made Janus uneasy.

"Yes?"

Eggers told her who they were and showed his ID. "We had a report from a passenger on the metro who saw someone fall from a balcony in this area. Have you noticed anything unusual?"

A whimpering came from within the apartment. It sounded like a baby.

"Just a moment," she said, and closed the door in their faces. Eggers and Janus glanced at each other.

"She looks a little tense," Eggers muttered.

Then the door opened again, and this time she held a very small baby in her arms. "Sorry," she said. "We just got home from the hospital and it's all a bit new to him."

The baby made a low murmuring sound, and Janus instinctively smiled. Lord. Such a tiny little human. No wonder his mother wasn't too pleased about the disturbance. She was looking at the baby, not at them, and even Eggers was thawing out a bit, Janus noticed. There was something to this mother-and-child thing.

"Like I said, we just want to know, have you noticed anything?"

"Nothing," she said. "It couldn't have been here."

"There was a van over here a little bit ago," Eggers said.

"Yes," she replied. "It was the plumber. There's something wrong with the heat, and now we have the baby . . . we have to get it fixed."

"Sure, of course. Well. Have a nice evening."

The woman nodded and closed the door.

"I bet that plumber was after a little undeclared income," Eggers said.

"Yeah. But it's not our business right now."

They walked back to the car. The snow felt even wetter and heavier now. Janus wished he'd at least brought along an extra pair of socks.

Taghi was elated when the police left. It was as if he'd forgotten all about threatening her with a knife a minute ago.

"*It was the plumber* . . ." he said, in a strange falsetto mimicing her voice. "Fuck, you were good! They totally swallowed it."

It took a moment for Nina to answer. "Get out, Taghi," she said. "Don't think for one second that I did it for you."

He came down like a punctured balloon. "I'm sorry," he said. "I got a little crazy, I think."

"Just leave. And don't call me again." She remembered her cell phone and got him to fish it out of the toilet bowl.

"It doesn't work anymore," he said.

"No. But I'm not leaving it for anyone to find."

All the way across the bridge Chaltu sat with her eyes closed, praying, as if she didn't dare hope she could make it without divine intervention. Nina let her off at the University Medical Center in Malmö and tried to make it clear to her that she should wait until Nina had left before saying the only three Swedish words she knew. Chaltu nodded.

"Okay, secret doctor," she said.

Nina looked at her watch. *11:03.* With a little luck her mother would already be in bed when she got home.

The snow turned slowly into rain. The gray slush around the building in Ørestaden was melting into the mud. The blood of Torsten Brahge mixed with the rain seeping into the sheetrock, which eventually grew so pulpy that not even Beni in Valby would be able to find a use for it.

SLEIPNER'S ASSIGNMENT

BY GEORG URSIN

Frederiksberg

W e are in Frederiksberg, which is a district of Copenhagen.

It is a colorful district, with old streets, quiet residential areas, large parks, a castle, a zoo with wild animals that the cautious fear, and theaters offering dramatic productions. As well as nooks and crannies where the law is trod upon and crushed.

One of these nooks is a lunchroom. It is large, low-ceilinged, and grubby, and patronized by a lively but not always amiable clientele. Sleipner sits at one of its many tables. He sits alone. That's nothing new. For long periods of time, in fact, he sits there every day, mostly by himself. He is thirty-eight years old, stronger than most but not brutal, and has a heavy face with innocuous features. The articles of clothing he is wearing are wrinkled. The shoes are comfortable to put on and take off, but otherwise they are nothing worth mentioning. His hair is of no specific color and can look a bit greasy. He has almost always been a bachelor.

Over the years he has had a number of occupations and has left them, either because they were not independent enough or because he was asked to get out. Now he is a private detective. Because he cannot afford to rent a place of business, he uses his regular table as an office. Those in his crowd know they can find him there. Because there aren't many in his crowd who have need of a detective, he also provides other similar services.

Most of the time his facial expression remains unchanged. A sleepy mask, seemingly unable to convey either alertness or boredom. Therefore, and perhaps for other reasons, practically no one seeks him out for the pleasure of his company. When someone approaches him and begins a conversation, it is professional in nature. Once in a while a client sits down across from him and begins to present him with a problem, but his only reaction is an acknowledgment of the greeting, should there be one, with a "Hi" and a serious glance. When the problem has been described, he might ask a few questions, then he keeps his mouth shut while thinking. When he has finished thinking, he offers his assistance and sets a price, which includes an advance. For the most part the amounts of money are small. His crowd seldom can afford more. When they have the means, a rare occurrence, usually they don't have the desire.

Today he has no clients. He has been served the cheapest item the lunchroom offers. It consists of smoked fried pork with boiled potatoes and parsley gravy. In addition to numerous thin slices of dark, heavy Danish rye bread. Not only is it the cheapest meal on the menu, it also is the only one served *ad libitum*, all you can eat. Sleipner often takes advantage of this by ordering it in the morning and devouring it for hours, such that it fills him up for the entire day. It has been a few hours since he ordered, and he is about finished. He concludes with a glass of draft beer, very cheap and, as his crowd puts it: fortified with water.

Just as he finishes, a client comes along. It is a man he knows, but not well enough to know his real name. Sleipner knows only that he goes by the nickname of Bruiser.

Bruiser claims to have a problem. Sleipner doesn't ask what

it is about. In the initial stage of the meeting he limits himself to gazing around the room. This maneuver is based on bitter experience. He knows that when someone sits at his table, the many people who have noticed his guest and recognize him can say to themselves and others: "I saw with my own two eyes that he hired Sleipner." Sleipner also knows that those who have such knowledge can contrive to hold the guest responsible for intentions the guest may not have, and to make Sleipner an accomplice.

But no one seems to take an interest in Bruiser's visit to Sleipner's table today. At nearly all of the other tables, men and women are sitting and having a good time together. Many of them are either stocky, corpulent, or obese. They are loud and resolute, and each wears clothes exhibiting very little harmony, especially regarding the choice of colors. Their attention seems to be concentrated more on their own distinctiveness than anything else.

Sleipner relaxes and lets Bruiser continue his confidential account. Bruiser speaks without passion, which after a while Sleipner begins to wonder about, since people with problems usually express their worry. Suddenly he realizes that Bruiser isn't seeking counsel, he is threatening Sleipner. Someone has stolen something from Bruiser, who now is twisting Sleipner's arm to retrieve whatever has been stolen.

Sleipner shows no sign of how he doesn't care for this type of stunt. He keeps his cool and tells himself that it would be stupid to resist because Bruiser would likely be quite dissatisfied, which in Bruiser's case means vengeful and crude. For the time being, Sleipner nods sympathetically at Bruiser, who explains that the stolen goods are securities that he wants back immediately.

Bruiser doesn't say that Sleipner has no choice but to help.

He doesn't say that Sleipner must do it for free, either. In fact, he says only that he assumes that Sleipner will take care of this matter for him, and that he will be paid to do so. Sleipner is certain both that the payment will be no more than a trifle and that it would cost dearly to refuse the difficult man across the table from him.

Therefore Sleipner says he will do it, and that all he needs to know is the type of securities and who stole them. Bruiser answers that the thief is Pistol, a nickname by which the crowd knows him because he occasionally carries a pistol, and that the securities are mortgage papers of considerable value. Sleipner is handed a list of the mortgages.

Sleipner sees no reason to continue the conversation. Bruiser concurs and walks off. Sleipner sits for a while afterward and takes stock of the situation. Then he stands and walks over to a neighboring table where a broad is drinking cheap champagne mixed with English porter, which is, according to many, a very agreeable mix when grown accustomed to. He has no intention of sweet-talking the broad. He merely asks her if she knows where Pistol is staying nowadays. The broad says that Pistol is moving in with Rattlesnake. She also tells him where Pistol has been living. Sleipner takes the opportunity to milk her for Bruiser's real name and where he lives. Finally, Sleipner unleashes a small, grateful smile, something he rarely does because he seldom has reason to, and he leaves.

Sleipner walks to the address where the broad claims that Rattlesnake lives. The building is in a rear courtyard. It is four stories high. Rattlesnake's name is on the intercom's resident list, fourth floor. Sleipner refrains from pressing the button, because he will get nothing out of announcing his arrival. He lays a heavy hand on the front door's handle, and it opens practically by itself. Then he takes the stairs up to the fourth floor, he stops and listens. He hears nothing from inside the apartment and considers walking in without talking to anyone. But he doesn't like that idea, and more than anything he feels relieved when he suddenly hears there is someone at home after all. He recognizes the voices of both Pistol and Rattlesnake. And goes quietly back down the stairs.

He takes a close look at the building's façade. It is a strange façade, because it is every bit as impressive as those of many of the buildings out on the district's streets, and it is hard to see why this type of luxury exists in a rear courtyard. But such is Frederiksberg. The façade has cement angels and gargoyles. In addition, a large area is covered with Virginia creeper.

It is little trouble for Sleipner to clamber up such a façade. Since childhood he has climbed all kinds of places, and here it goes very quickly. He reaches the fourth floor unwinded, plants a foot on a gargoyle, puts his arm around an angel, and takes good hold of the creeper. Then he looks in through a window and sees nothing inside except for a packing box and some papers lying on top. It is obvious that Rattlesnake and Pistol are pulling up stakes and moving to a better place.

Sleipner lets go of the angel, pulls a small pair of binoculars out of his pocket, focuses them on the papers, and tells himself that if he's not mistaken, and he is sure he is not, these papers are the very mortgages that Bruiser talked about.

Then Rattlesnake appears in the doorway to a neighboring room. Sleipner recognizes her immediately. Her nickname doesn't originate from any resemblance to a snake, but rather because she is every bit as terrifying as one, which makes her easy to pick out. She grabs the papers and disappears with them.

Shortly after, Rattlesnake steps out in the courtyard. Pistol, carrying the documents, trails her. They walk through the courtyard toward the street and disappear without noticing

Sleipner hanging on the façade. He is very pleased that they didn't see him.

When they are out of sight he makes his way down to the ground. He follows them.

The couple pick up their pace out on the street, chatting gaily as they walk to a bus stop and stand facing traffic, therefore not noticing Sleipner's arrival. He stands at a distance from them, making sure that he is concealed behind a man as big and broad as a heavyweight boxing champion.

Then the bus comes, and Sleipner hurries to get on before the other two. He walks quickly toward the back of the bus, sits down, and holds a hand in front of his face to avoid being recognized. Rattlesnake and Pistol sit in front of him and begin discussing their next move. He overhears that they plan to sell the mortgages to an economic consultant with whom they have an appointment at three o'clock. Rattlesnake says that she needs to shop for something, and that she will be done before three.

The two get off the bus and walk into a department store. Sleipner rides further, then he gets off and, knowing the address, heads straight for the consultant's office, where he asks the young lady behind the reception desk if the boss is busy. He is not in and will not be back until a little before three, the lady says. Sleipner asks if he may wait; permission is granted. He sits in the reception area and gazes wearily into the air. The lady walks into a kitchenette. She closes the door and bangs some utensils around. Sleipner gets up, treads heavily to the outer door, opens it, and slams it shut. Then he walks as quietly as possible into the boss's office, shuts the door softly behind him, and inspects it. There are several articles of furniture and quite a bit of printed material. An enormous velvet curtain hangs in front of a window.

Sleipner sits down in a chair and remains quiet. Twenty minutes later he hears voices in the reception area and therefore assumes that the consultant is back. Sleipner stands, hides behind the curtain, and sits on the windowsill.

The consultant comes in. Soon, Rattlesnake and Pistol join him. They say hello to the consultant and ask how he is doing, and the consultant answers that he is doing fine, and he asks them the same question and they give him the same answer. They all look as if they expect to quickly wrap up a profitable transaction.

The consultant reviews the mortgages and says that it's good work and he would like to buy them, that it can't be detected that the mortgages are forgeries. The couple says that it's because Bruiser did the work.

"He's really good at that sort of thing," Pistol says.

The three of them agree on a price for the mortgages. Pistol writes on the documents that they are hereby assigned to the consultant.

The consultant wants to give the sellers a check, but they smile coolly and ask for cash, which they receive. The sellers leave. The consultant walks out, leaving the mortgages behind on the desk. The receptionist closes the outer door as she leaves.

Sleipner gets up off the windowsill, sits on the edge of the desk, and counts the mortgages. There are thirty-two. He slips them under his arm and leaves the office.

That same evening Sleipner sits at his regular table. He is very relaxed, as if he isn't afraid of anything. He passes the time with some Danish beer. Then Bruiser shows up, sits down across from him, and demands to know how it went, even though Sleipner has had only a short time to complete the assignment. Bruiser enjoys doing this—making people toe the mark, giving them an order and asking them the next day if they're done yet.

Sleipner says that it went well, that he has the mortgages.

"Hand them over," Bruiser says.

"First I want my money," Sleipner says.

"Not a chance," Bruiser says. "First the mortgages, then the money."

"You get nothing before I have my money," Sleipner says.

Bruiser pauses a moment and thinks. His counterpart's resolute attitude has given him a sense that something is abnormal about the situation. That Sleipner has some particular basis for being so stubborn, or he has gone insane, which does not make matters easier. Bruiser, therefore, changes his tactics.

"Okay," he says. "Here's your money. Go get the mortgages. Right now." Bruiser removes a thousand-kroner note from his wallet and waves it around a bit, as if it is fish bait.

"Fine, now all I need is forty-nine thousand more." Sleipner is completely cool.

"What do you mean, another forty-nine thousand kroner?"

Bruiser looks at his table companion with sorrow and amazement, an expression that he uses occasionally as a warning that abuse and harm may follow. Sleipner recognizes this warning and swiftly deflects the danger.

"I'll explain it all to you," he says. "I got the mortgages. I found out they were forgeries, and that you're the one who made them. If I notify the police about it, you'll do time. But I won't say anything to the police if you buy them from me. It'll cost you fifty thousand kroner. You pay now, I deliver later."

"Wrong," Bruiser says. "If you tell the police I did the mortgages, I'll tell them you stole them. Theft is a crime."

"You're the one who's got it wrong," Sleipner answers. "Theft, according to the penal code, is a crime involving something of value. If the stolen goods have no value, there's no crime. Since the mortgages are forgeries they're invalid, and therefore worthless."

"It's like this," Bruiser says. "The police won't believe you if you tell them I did the forgeries."

"They'll figure it out soon enough. They have fingerprint and handwriting experts."

The decisive words have now been spoken by Sleipner. Bruiser is silent. He resembles a masculine version of the goddess of revenge as he pulls out forty-nine thousand kroner. He slides them and the previously shown thousand-kroner note over to Sleipner, who slips them into his inside pocket and stands up.

"You'll bring them to me now," Bruiser says. His tone is menacing.

"If I'm not delayed or find something better to do," Sleipner says, and leaves.

Outside, Sleipner makes sure he is not being followed, then walks to a supermarket and goes to customer service to request the return of a full grocery sack that earlier in the day he dropped off for safekeeping. He is given the sack, which contains groceries and mortgages.

Sitting on a park bench, he pulls out the mortgages. Later he walks into a post office and mails a thin envelope with fifty thousand kroner to an address in Jutland.

He walks back to his table, where Bruiser sits with four empty and one half-full whiskey glasses and waits for him.

"There," Sleipner says, and lays thirty-one mortgages on the table.

Bruiser counts them. "There's one mortgage missing," he says. He speaks slowly, almost lifelessly, yet with a threatening undertone, as if he is the quiet before the storm.

"Of course. Naturally, I've kept one," Sleipner says. "Otherwise I'd be walking around scared that you'll take revenge on me. That won't happen, now that you understand—I'm telling you now, anyway—that should anything bad happen to me, one of my friends you don't know and never will know will send the final mortgage to the police, with the message that you forged it. I can send it to the police myself, if I think you're beginning to act naughty."

Bruiser can't believe his ears. Then he thinks it's too crazy to really be true. Not until later does he realize the battle is lost.

Sleipner and Bruiser never again sit at the same table. It seems as if they both prefer the company of others, should they desire company.

But when Sleipner and Bruiser run into each other— something that cannot always be avoided, being part of the same crowd—Bruiser is always quite friendly, in fact very polite.

And that is worth taking note of. Politeness, you don't see much of that in their crowd.

DEBT OF HONOR

BY KLAUS RIFBJERG

Amager

The wind drove the rain in over the market's flat roof in gusts, and the sidewalk from Elbagade to Parmagade floated. The streetlights still retained some of their half-blind poverty from during the war, though by now it had been several years since the last Prussian had dragged his boots and himself southward. But maybe it was just his imagination, maybe it was just his inner light, turned down so low that it resembled a pilot light. Maybe that was it, that he, Aage Baldersen, was on pilot light.

He pulled up his coat collar and felt its clammy chill against his neck hair. Despite the blackouts and everything else, there had been more action during what some called the evil years, but what he thought of as the good years. There had been lots to do, and while most felt something was left missing when the police were nabbed on September 19, 1944, and sent to Germany, others—he included—felt a certain relief. Not because he was a German sympathizer, but no one would deny that it had taken a certain amount of pressure off the underworld when the law had been removed in one fell swoop and later replaced by the so-called Vagtværn, the private guard whose effectiveness in relation to the police was on the scale of a teaspoon to an excavation crane.

Someone had thrown a few snipped-up Christmas trees on the bare ground by the depot. Their limbs shook hysterically in the wind gusts and were mirrored in the large puddles formed by the rain. Disgruntled, Aage Baldersen blew out through his nose. Right now there was only mud and slush, but occasionally during the summer a circus slapped its tents up on the lot, and once, having nothing to do that day, he'd been stupid enough to buy a ticket for a show that should have had to pay its audience, that's how bad it was. One of the clowns was an obese former half of a comedy duo who'd had some success in film. Now he looked like a worn-out punching bag and was just as funny as one.

Parmagade stretched out before him into the horizon. The blocks towered up on both sides of the street, and the vanishing point was anybody's guess in the drizzly mist. But Baldersen knew very well what was hidden out east; back when the five-room apartment had a porcelain washbasin (women painted on it) and real booze and wasn't a dump like now, he had bicycled the route many times, past the hospital and along Italiensvej and down to the beach and public baths that had proven to be a convenient meeting place when the bosses decided how the work should be divided. Nobody was going to frisk someone in their birthday suit!

Those days had been great in a lot of ways, and he didn't even have to close his eyes to picture them. There had been a shortage of everything, but if you could get hold of a product in short supply it could be sold at a high price. Actually, he was very proud that he'd been part of what had to be called a major economy. True, it had developed underground, even though the retailing was done out in the open. But in front of the Lido by the Liberty Memorial and on Suhmsgade, it had naturally been only small stuff: single cigarettes, butter and sugar ration coupons, some 60 percent soap, and bike tubes with no holes. Baldersen's level was more wholesale, but it made him happy anyway to see all the activity when he occasionally—and mostly for pleasure—inspected the troops.

He blew rainwater out between his lips and stepped into the hallway, where a weak, sour odor met him. The place needed painting, and there wasn't much varnish left on the steps. While hauling himself slowly upstairs he felt the moisture that had seeped through the soles of his shoes.

Naturally, Aage Baldersen had understood that things wouldn't be the same after the Liberation, but the first few years went very well. People still lacked everything that made life a bit more fun; the promised boatloads of bananas arrived a lot later than most had expected. But now he'd hit bottom, and while others saw light ahead, he stared into a growing darkness. And that's really what surprised him the most: he'd lost his zing. It was as if all the fun had gone out of life. Once he'd been cheerful and energetic, now he was mostly surly, if not depressed.

Deep inside he knew what it was about: a lack of excitement. If he wanted he could get work—honest work—but he didn't seem to have it in him, his slide had been too severe, and when it was all said and done, he had been the one left holding the bag. They bought him out with cash, and he'd been dumb enough to take it (who says no to a truckload of C-notes?), but when the paper money exchange came after the war, he was sunk—there was no way he could explain where all that money came from. He was so depressed that he couldn't even enjoy the flames when all the bundles ended up in the furnace.

And this is where *he'd* ended up. Aage Baldersen opened the door to his apartment—room—that you walked directly into because it had no entryway, with the bathroom out in the hall. His shoes had dried enough from the climb up to the fifth floor that they left only small tracks on the floorboards when he walked in, yet he didn't know what to do with his coat. He stood undecided for a moment, then he unbuttoned it and let it fall to the floor in a wet heap. He was soaked from the knees down.

He sat on one of the two dining room chairs that were the sum total of the apartment's furniture and turned his eyes to the window facing the courtyard. One good thing the peace had brought: it wasn't necessary to lower the blinds, the blackouts were over, the view was open. No longer busy with anything else, Baldersen now permitted himself to enjoy the free entertainment from a distance. Being broke prevented him from enjoying the pleasures to which he'd had such ample access in the good old days, but he took a certain dogged pleasure in seeing how people made fools of themselves in the illuminated rooms above and below, arguing, fighting, or hunching listlessly over dining room tables, and the bitches, yes, there were bitches too, and when he discovered that he had a view of two dykes who weren't ashamed of performing most of the stunts their kind dreamed up, and in full public view, it both aroused and enraged him. A pair of cows like them should have been shipped south with the other perverts, but anyway he wouldn't want to have missed them.

He grabbed the half-bottle of schnapps he kept on the shelf beside the kitchen sink. Although he had only cold running water, it didn't really matter, since he still went to the public baths at Helgoland in the summer, and the water did a fine job of cooling off the liquor if it got too warm. He poured schnapps into a coffee cup and sat down at the table. Maybe it wasn't just the building that smelled sour, maybe it was him. He took a shot of schnapps and directed his sight to the entertainment on the other side of the street. But not much was going on, and should Aage Baldersen be completely honest he would have to admit that it was a poor show; like the circus, it wasn't worth shelling out money for.

The schnapps warmed him up, and a bit later he fell asleep. Naturally he was unaware of it, but in that crooked position, his elbow on the table and head in his hands and arm hanging, Aage Baldersen looked like a sculpture that could easily be entitled: "Tired Man." That was what he was, and when a while later someone knocked on the door and he opened his eyes and felt a shudder race through him, he thought: *Uhh, I never want to wake up again!* But of course he woke up—after all, he was still alive.

The man he let in was about his own age, wet only on the outside of his black, shiny oilskin coat. A military belt bound it in front. Without being invited, he sat down opposite Baldersen on the other dining room chair.

"Hey, Baldy," he said after a short pause, "how you doin'?"

Aage Baldersen said nothing, but he straightened up in his chair. The weariness that he had felt before was gone, replaced by a disgust as thick as pudding.

"I've got nothing," he said.

"Excuse me," the man replied, "I didn't quite hear what you said. What did you say?"

"Nothing."

The man laughed tersely. "So, that was what I heard."

The silence lengthened between them, and only the faint reflection from the windows across the street created any sort of movement in the room.

"You know what you owe." The man leaned forward. "You don't walk off with that much money without there being certain . . . debts. Debts of honor, if you want to put it that way."

"You want a schnapps?"

"No thanks, I don't drink on the job."

Aage Baldersen drained the coffee cup. "I don't know what you're talking about. Debts? Debts of honor? What the hell is that supposed to mean? You know goddamn well just like everybody else what happened to that money."

"Half a million? You're not going to goddamn sit there and tell me it's gone?"

Baldersen shrugged. He turned his head and stared out the window. "Fuck you," he said.

The man in the oilskin coat stood up, light reflected from the gloss. "Everybody trusted you, Baldy, it was a confidential deal. Everybody knew you had it under control."

"You bought me out."

"You've damn well never been worth half a million. You know that. Sure as hell you do, Baldy."

Aage Baldersen didn't even make an attempt at hunkering down. He just sat there.

"What you've done, how you've fixed it all up, I don't care. I've just been sent to collect."

"It was *my* money."

"Your money? It was *our* money. Fair and square. You hear?"

The man had stepped behind Baldersen's chair. A moment later he lifted his arm and hit Baldersen behind the ear with a small sandbag.

"Just a sample," he said, "there's more coming real soon. If you don't start talking."

Aage Baldersen rocked back and forth on the chair. That damn rain, the damn darkness. In fact, he was soaked.

"Leave me alone. I'm tired," he said, "tired, tired, tired . . ."

Soon the man started pounding him. It was almost like a machine. It was as if he didn't just want to beat Baldersen to the floor, he wanted to beat him into it. Slowly the figure melted and slid down off the chair.

"Night, Baldy, goodnight. And sleep tight," the man whispered.

After a while the man stuck the sandbag in his pocket, opened the door to the hallway, closed it behind him, and began the long walk down to Parmagade. Outside, the rain had stopped, but the wind still blew, and the figure's shadow moved uneasily over the walls of the buildings in the streetlights' glow. There was no traffic, but the steady *ding-ding* from a small bell announced that a late trolley car was backing into the depot.

WHEN IT'S TOUGH OUT THERE
BY GRETELISE HOLM

Istedgade

Despite a double gin-and-tonic and two of the small pink pills that she preferred to call "muscle relaxants," her hands shook when she punched the number. And she held her breath while listening to the amorous voice: "You've reached City Sex and Luxury Massage. For telephone sex, press 1. For information about net-sex, press 2. For appointments, press 3. For personal service, press 4—"

She hung up as if she'd been burned, mixed a dry martini, and curled up in the well-preserved, original Arne Jacobsen Egg chair.

She looked out over the sound through the coast road villa's picture window, waiting for the alcohol to relax and embolden her. Her Philippine au pair gave a friendly smile through the glass, which she was cleaning.

A half hour later Claire Winther felt she was ready. It was the only solution, the only way out of this situation, she told herself.

She punched the number again and pressed 4 for personal service.

"This is Bonnie. What can we do for you?"

"My name is Michelle Jensen, and I'm interested in hearing if there's a possibility of working for you."

"There's a decent possibility if you look really good and know what you're doing. How old are you, and how long have you been in the business? You specialize in anything?"

"I'm thirty-four but I can easily pass for twenty-six, definitely. I have to admit I don't have a lot of experience, in fact I'm a beginner. But you know how it is, it's tough out there right now, you need a little extra cash, so why not . . . if you have a natural talent?"

"We'll take a look at you and talk about it. Come in around six if you can, and if you have some porny pictures of yourself, bring them along on CD."

"I don't."

"No problem. We'll figure it out. In fact, we could use a Danish girl right now, so if you're okay . . ."

Claire felt calmer. Bonnie had sounded like a normal, everyday person. How hard could it be?

She chose a dark wig and large sunglasses. The oldest pair of jeans she owned, and a red lace top under the black leather jacket that hadn't been outside the closet for five years. Given her exclusive wardrobe, this was the cheapest she could look, she decided, and she topped it off with crimson-red gloss lipstick and a shot of a much-too-heavy and sweet perfume, a shopping mistake.

Obviously she couldn't arrive at the brothel in her Jaguar, so she called a cab and asked the driver to drop her off at the main station. It came to eight hundred kroner.

The November murk lay wet and heavy over the city, so she pushed her sunglasses up on her forehead as she walked down Istedgade, first past the row of hotels next to the station, then past all the porn and sex shops decorated for the Christmas season.

It was fascinating, she had to stop and stare through the shop windows. A Christmas manger scene with the tiny baby Jesus—surrounded by dildos. A blow-up sex doll with a silicone pussy wrapped in a chain of red heart-shaped Christmas lights. Handcuffs, leather whips, half-masks, and chastity belts hung on a plastic Christmas tree with a star on top and icicles covering it.

At the shelter, the Men's Home, the guests for the night had already begun to gather. Hoarse voices, the clinking of bottles, and tubercular coughs rose from the group of ragged, dirty, homeless figures. Claire decided to cross the street to the other sidewalk.

There was more dignity to the slick black kings of the street, who in two- and three-man groups marked off their territories, while the black females busied themselves braiding hair in salons, the walls covered with wigs and hairpieces of all colors.

The African hair salons were something new, thought Claire, who hadn't sat foot in Vesterbro since she left as an eight-year-old.

A drunk wearing only an open leather vest on his upper body tumbled out from one of the half-basement tattoo shops and knocked into her. His skin was totally and colorfully illustrated from his bald head to his waist.

More sex shops, more Asian grills, more stores with weird combinations of souvenirs, Christmas decorations, porn underwear and sex toys, more bars, more brothels.

At Skelbækgade, the street prostitutes—the lowest in the pecking order, the most desperate—were already busy. Addicts and Africans, as far as she could tell. Several men walked back and forth, openly sizing them up, while others crept past in their cars.

The nine-to-five shift, they called these early sex customers, when she was a kid.

At the spot on Istedgade where the place begins to look respectable again, she turned right, down a side street.

* * *

She stopped when a text message beeped in. It was John, from Rio: *All's well, dear. Brazil is the land of opportunity. Great deals. Looking forward to getting home December 9. Hug and kiss.*

She answered at once: *Thanks, hon. On the way to new fitness center. Trying to get in shape for Christmas. Take good care of yourself.*

The fitness center was to be her alibi. She had a membership card in her pocket.

"Wow! You've got class!" Bonnie said, looking almost lovingly at her as she pulled her in through the hallway to the reception area.

Ikea, Claire Winther noted. Cheap, but light and clean and less sleazy than she had expected. A beige corner sofa and a coffee table with porn magazines. A counter with a coffee maker and plastic cups. A flatscreen on the wall, fastened to a swinging arm.

"Here's where we receive customers, who come in only by appointment. They call or book on the net. As a rule, anyway. If it's totally dead we'll take them in off the street. I keep track of the shift schedule and the appointments and do the books, and most of the time I'm sitting right there."

Bonnie pointed at the chair and desk behind the counter.

A madam, Claire thought.

Bonnie was closer to sixty than fifty. She was overweight in the way alcoholics can be, a bulging stomach and thin arms and legs, her face ruddy and spongy with large pores that looked even larger because of her makeup, and she spoke with a hoarse, nasal voice.

She continued: "Five of us are full-time. Take that back, five of us *were* full-time. Alette, our Danish girl, died two weeks ago. Sad story. There's so much bad heroin around right now. Not that Alette was an addict, no no, she only fixed once in a while to feel good, she just got unlucky . . . You don't look like . . . ?"

Claire shook her head. "No, I stick with the supermarket drugs you can get in Brugsen," she answered.

"Good, because drugs—they'll just take you farther and farther down!" Bonnie put a protective arm around Claire's shoulder, looked her right in the eye, and almost whispered: "I can't count how many I've seen kick the bucket with their stilettos on . . ." Then she continued, more businesslike: "Right now we have two Thais and one Romanian, sweet girls, all of them, but the Thais don't understand Danish. They're here on tourist visas—three months at a shot. Theresa from Romania has a residency permit here and speaks pidgin Danish. Problem is, more and more of our customers only want Danish girls. It's all this talk about trafficking that's scaring them. God's sake, the foreign girls beg for a job, and now for example we're saying no to all the African girls, so they're on the street—painting the town red, as they say."

Bonnie smiled at her own wittiness and went on: "I take care of the phones and the cheap net sex, where they can jerk off to the sound and video files I send them, along with some live talk, moans and groans. Ten kroner a minute! Doesn't sound like much but it actually brings in quite a bit. Then we have a webcam so they can buy direct live shows. Most of them want girl sex, that's a lot more expensive of course, if it's direct and interactive, but all this about the money, you just let me take care—"

"How much?"

Claire received a warm smile in return: "You—you can hit the jackpot! You're exclusive, high-class—and you're Danish!"

Claire kept quiet, Bonnie became eager: "As a guesstimate, a good day, taking eight or ten customers, you'll go home with five thousand kroner. Times twenty . . ."

"But the clinic here takes their cut?"

"The clinic takes 60 percent of your overall earnings. That's the way it is. The money goes to rent, ads, equipment, supplies, transportation, security. Nothing under the table here. I guarantee you won't get cheated, and there'll be plenty of work. We're counting on a lot of Christmas business, and Copenhagen is the only place left in Scandinavia where it's still legal to buy sex. The Bangkok of the North, ha ha!"

Bonnie showed her the rooms. Three had double beds, a large bathroom with Jacuzzi and whirlpool bath—also for servicing customers—and a dressing room and wardrobe, complete with everything necessary to the trade.

Bonnie measured her by sight and concluded: "C-cup, 38. We have everything you need, but it's all right if you bring something along."

A back stairway led from a kitchenette down to a soundproof S&M room in the basement.

The room was dimly lit, and Claire shivered inside as her eyes adjusted to the gloom. Rack, gallows, iron-bar cage, tongs, whips, chains, masks, rubber and leather clothes, and various instruments to stick into body orifices.

"Down here you'll be a queen and dominatrix, I think. You should know that many of our masochists are very important men with exclusive tastes. Have you done it before?"

"No," Claire said. "But there's nothing wrong with my imagination."

"You'll get some recordings and film to take home with you. We have videos of most of our regular customers. They all have different desires. The most bizarre, right now anyway, is someone who wants needles stuck through his foreskin—can you handle something like that?"

Claire nodded. "If it's part of the job . . ."

"Also, you're an obvious choice for doing high-class escort. Lasse is our driver and bodyguard. When you're out with a new customer we have a security system. It's a special cell phone that stays on so Lasse can hear everything. He's also Teddy Bear's man."

"Teddy Bear's man?"

"Teddy Bear is our owner, he owns the whole building. We pay rent to him, Lasse takes care of that. Teddy Bear's okay. He comes around once in a while for a session down here in the torture chamber. You'll meet him. He's going to be wild about you."

"I don't want to be whipped or tortured myself," Claire said firmly.

"No, of course not. That's no problem. One of the Thai girls, Cindy, is pretty tough. She takes all the sadists . . . and Theresa is good with all the seniors, the gross-looking ones, and the handicapped . . ."

The problem came up back at reception.

"I'm going to get our photographer to take some gorgeous shots of you now, for the website. I'll show it to you," Bonnie said, and sat down at the computer.

"I won't appear on any website. If that's a condition we'll have to forget the whole thing," Claire said.

Bonnie looked serious, thought for a moment, and then said: "They need to, like, know what they're buying. Couldn't we show your body without your head?"

"No," Claire answered.

"Okay, we'll make an exception and put a different body

out. You're so beautiful, nobody will be disappointed if they even notice they've been tricked."

The website popped up.

Bonnie pointed: "Here's our Thais, Cindy and Lara. That's what we call all of them. We bring new ones in about every three months. They don't show their heads here, either. It's more because of the authorities. They're only here on a tourist visa . . . And here's Alette. We haven't taken her off the site yet. Isn't she sweet?" A tear ran down Bonnie's cheek and was slowly absorbed by her open pores.

Claire stared at the picture of a skinny young girl with empty eyes, a half-open mouth, and disproportionately large silicone breasts, "playing with herself," as the text claimed. She was in the process of inserting a black dildo.

"Apparently she didn't have any family. We were the only ones at her funeral, anyway," Bonnie sighed. "What would you like to be called?" she then asked.

"I'm Michelle," Claire answered.

"But do you want to use your real name?"

"Just call me Michelle," Claire said. "And I'll give you my cell number, but not my ID number or my address."

"That's fair enough," Bonnie answered, looking as if she was thinking like crazy about the story behind this elegant woman's decision to debut as a whore.

Bonnie started gathering up DVDs so Claire could study the servicing of customers, and she handed her a sheet of paper filled with writing.

"This is the list of our services and prices. We call it the menu," she explained.

Claire ran her eyes over the text. Danish, Swedish, French, Greek . . . female sex, bathtub sex, S&M, escort and out-calls, one girl and two girls. The typical price was thirteen hundred kroner an hour at the brothel, but it was noted that the fees were only guidelines, and that customers could have individual programs made up and prices calculated.

"Actually, we're in a situation right now where we need someone to replace Alette. When can you start?"

"Tomorrow," Claire answered. "I need to take a look at all this." She nodded at the DVDs.

Just as she was leaving, Cindy and Lara walked in with Lasse, a friendly, smiling, solarium-tanned bodybuilder with a ponytail. They had been at a customer's place on an out-call.

Lasse tossed four thousand kroner on Bonnie's desk.

"This is Michelle, she's starting with us tomorrow," Bonnie said as an introduction.

"Michelle, you're totally gorgeous!" Lasse said, and groped her breasts appreciatively, winking flirtatiously at her.

The two Thai girls held limp hands out to her and smiled shyly, their eyes on the floor, then they walked into the dressing room together to get ready for the evening customers.

Claire Winther stopped by the fitness center on the way home and spoke loudly and amiably with the receptionist and the man beside her on the treadmill, making sure that she was noticed.

At home, she poured a double gin-and-tonic, which she drank while taking a long and luxurious bubble bath. Just as she had settled in her adjustable bed with her laptop and Bonnie's DVDs, John's goodnight text came in: *Dear, what do you think about spending Christmas and New Years here in Brazil, I've found a wonderful beach hotel and the weather is great?*

She answered: *Wonderful. Just what I need--to get away from this wet and cold darkness.*

I'll reserve the luxury suite and arrange the trip. Okay with you if we leave around December 20?

That's great for me. Kiss hug and goodnight.

Then she put the first DVD in to study the whores and their customers in action.

By midnight she knew she could do this. She had a plan. Abandon her body mentally during the act, but leave her brain in charge. Most of it was banal and cliché-ish—as Bonnie had said it would be.

"They want to believe that they're fantastic, that they have an enormous cock and make you really horny. If you play that role you almost can't go wrong."

First and foremost in her mind was to take good care of herself. No sadism, no anal sex, no kissing, no sex without a condom, and no appointments without security. There were alarm buttons at the clinic, and Lasse was on duty with his phone on out-calls.

She could be firm with her demands because of her status as a luxury escort.

A week passed, and the others at the clinic were impressed with the stylish novice.

The customers were also thrilled.

A local politician, a police sergeant, and a real estate tycoon made new appointments with her as soon as they were finished. That was unusual. Most customers slink off, slightly embarrassed after the conclusion of a session, and aren't heard from again until the urge overcomes them.

She learned quickly how to answer the eternal question: "What makes a sweet, pretty girl like you . . ."

"Times are tough right now, and it's a job just like any other," she would answer.

On the third day, a straightlaced high school teacher already wanted to "save" her.

"You are far too good for this. I'm single and wouldn't mind having a girlfriend like you," he said.

When she told the story to the others in the kitchenette, they doubled over with laughter.

The catastrophe came on the seventh day.

A sadist went amok with Cindy down in the S&M room and ran off without paying. Cindy was shaken up from several violent blows to the head, in addition to suffering a hand wound from trying to avoid being knifed.

She sat in the kitchenette with a dish towel wrapped around her wounded hand, crying in anguish.

"She has to go to the emergency room," Claire said.

"That's a problem, because she's here illegally," replied Bonnie.

"Yeah, that's not gonna work, but I'll call Teddy Bear," Lasse said. He punched the brothel owner's number, explained the situation to him, and had a long talk, after which he updated the others: "Teddy Bear will under no circumstances have her go to the emergency room. But we can send her home and get a new . . . You want to go home?" he asked her in English.

Cindy looked at him blurrily, then her head fell on her chest.

"I think she has a concussion," Claire said. "I have a proposal: I know a doctor at a private hospital who will be discrete about this. Let me take care of it."

They all agreed, provided no one told Teddy Bear.

"But I have to drive Lara and Theresa out on three outcalls, so you'll have to take a taxi," Lasse said.

First Claire had the taxi take them back to her home on Kystvejen. She picked up her Philippine au pair's residency permit and passport, then they rode to the private hospital.

"My au pair has been hurt. She hit her head and cut her hand . . ." she explained to the doctor.

"She seems disoriented. We'll have to do a brain scan and hold her for observation. Her hand isn't serious, no tendons or vital parts have been cut, but it will have to be stitched," the doctor said, after a quick examination. Then he looked questioningly at Claire. "It looks like an assault."

"Yes, she had a fight with another Philippine, a boyfriend, but he was on his way out of the country, leaving today, presumably he's already flown the coop, and she won't go to the police . . . Would you like me to pay a deposit?"

"Yes, thank you."

Cindy was wheeled away on a trolley while the doctor did her case sheet on his computer, entering various details from the passport.

"Her name is long and it's hard for us to pronounce," Claire said. "So she calls herself Cindy. She doesn't speak Danish and understands only a little English, but we've found ways to communicate, so get in touch with me if there are any problems—and let me know when she can be picked up. I'll stay in touch."

First name: Cindy, the doctor wrote, and nodded politely at Claire.

She paid a deposit of twenty thousand kroner, putting it on her gold card.

That evening she told Bonnie: "I have some family coming next week. I'll have to work quite a bit from home, so don't put me on any shifts."

The truth was, John was coming home from Brazil the day after tomorrow. She had given a lot of thought to how she would conceal what she was doing. Her excuses would have to be the fitness center and visiting friends. Fortunately, he wasn't the controlling or suspicious type.

It was Sunday evening, and he would be home Tuesday morning. She debated whether she should surprise him by going out to the airport. No, that would seem peculiar. His car was parked out there, he always drove home alone. She should just stay home and greet him with a warm bath and a nice lunch. That's how he liked it.

"Monday is okay, but I'll have to take Tuesday off," she said to Bonnie.

Bonnie frowned, worried: "Then I'll have to start calling around to freelancers. It's tough right now. Christmas rush. But anyway, it's okay. You have to take care of things at home," she sighed.

Monday, Claire had three out-calls before Bonnie rang her at six o'clock:

"Okay, listen. Teddy Bear wants a session tonight. He's coming in at nine, and he's really looking forward to you after all the good things Lasse has told him. As you know, Teddy Bear is a little bit special. He wants it really hard, for a long time. Bound and gagged. The rack, cage, gallows."

Claire looked at her watch: "I have appointments until nine, and I have to get something to eat."

Bonnie: "Perfect. Lara and Theresa can tie him up and gag him, then he can stand there and wait until you appear as the dark mistress of the night, the slavedriver . . . Also, he likes the big black wigs and lots of black around the eyes. Oh, and by the way: when he blinks with one eye, stop with the pain. That's the game."

Claire visited the private hospital with flowers for Cindy and to hear the results of the scan. The news was bad. The scan revealed a hematoma in the brain, and Cindy needed a serious operation.

"We'll operate tonight and hope for the best, but there is a risk of permanent damage. The hematoma is in an unfortunate location . . ."

The doctor brought out the scan and pointed and explained. Claire was only halfway listening. Her other half boiled with anger.

Back at the brothel, she put on the entire circuslike garb: stilettos, net hose, leather costume, half-mask, whip, and black wig. Then she slipped on the long gloves.

The long gloves that she had never taken off in the S&M room.

"The deal is, he'll stay down there until tomorrow, but you can just leave him after he's had two or three ejaculations. That's the deal. Then he'll have another ejaculation early tomorrow before he goes home to his wife, but Lara and Theresa will take care of that . . ."

Just before ten she walked into the soundproof basement room.

John Winther, nicknamed Teddy Bear, stood buck naked on a small platform that his leg irons were fastened to. His hands were manacled behind him, and the handcuffs were chained to a heavy iron shackle. The lower part of his face was covered by a peculiar leather creation that served as a gag. And loosely around his neck hung the gallows noose.

He could communicate only with his eyes, and Claire read the eager anticipation in them. She let her gaze glide down the length of his body, to where his erection presented itself.

He hadn't recognized her, she was surprised at that.

She fought off a sudden impulse to flog him as an outlet for her rage, for his penis already stood greedily up on his stomach, and the mere thought of giving him a climax nauseated her.

Instead she first flung off her wig—and then her leather mask. His penis fell and shrunk into itself like a frightened snail, and she read genuine terror in his eyes.

In a moment of weakness she considered removing his gag so he could answer her question: WHY?

But no, she had made up her mind long ago. No explanations and excuses, no more lies. Instead she held a monologue: "You've surprised me in two ways, John. One: I'd been expecting you, but not tonight. And two: I didn't know that you were the pimp. Just thought you were a customer."

His cheeks moved, and a weak whistling sound escaped from the leather clump in his mouth, while his questioning eyes shone with horror.

"How did I find out? Oh, it was so banal: your secret cell phone with the prepaid card! It was lying in your desk drawer, vibrating, the day I was waiting in your office—when you were late for lunch at King Hans. I read all the text messages about Alette's death. It was a bit cryptic: *A is dead from an OD—that's how it looks.* I understood that. My own mother died of an overdose. Murder or suicide? That'll never be solved, right? I call it murder, whether the poor woman stuck the needle in herself or not!"

She drooped and went quiet. Tried to recall the image of her mother but could remember only her scream and her frightened eyes.

When her mother entertained customers, Claire had hidden in a cubbyhole behind the clothes hanging in the closet. That evening she'd fallen asleep in the cubbyhole, and when she crawled out the next morning her mother lay cold, dead on the sofa. The needle lay in the ashtray.

Claire was put in an orphanage and later placed with a number of foster homes. She did okay for herself, and had never set foot again in Vesterbro.

John Winther rattled his chains desperately.

She continued: "At first I only thought divorce, but then it hit me: why should I divorce myself from a few billion kroner? A text from 'the mistress' gave me the idea. I've been waiting for you, waiting for this hour in this room. Before you die, I want you to know that Cindy, the girl you wanted to ship out of the country with a brain hemorrhage, was operated on tonight. She'll be okay. I'm guessing that the only reason you bought this building was to have easy access to sexual services, and the income from the whores was just a little bonus that in your habitual greed you pocketed. But it's a lot of money to them, so I plan to pay them back when your estate is settled. Goodbye, John."

All she had to do was tighten the noose around his neck.

He climaxed as he died.

The next morning, wearing her warm mink, the tall, elegant Claire Winther stood in the airport and waited for her husband. When he didn't show up on the flight from Rio, she contacted the airline, then the police. She showed them the text message about his arrival and seemed to be on the verge of tears. A few hours later it was discovered that he had arrived the previous day.

At approximately the same time, the police were notified of a brothel customer found dead in Vesterbro. The two incidents weren't immediately seen as being connected. Claire Winther received a call on her secret cell phone with the prepaid card. The conversation was short, something about her making sure that the bill would be paid.

Then she tossed the cell phone down one sewer drain and the card down another.

Toward evening the police showed up at the coast road villa. There was reason to believe that Claire's husband was dead, and would she like to sit down.

Claire broke down when she identified the body, and she was offered emergency counseling, to which she said yes, please.

The tabloids all carried essentially the same story the next day: One of Denmark's unknown billionaires, the Danish-American John Winther, had died in a sex game gone awry at a brothel in Vesterbro. In connection with his death, the police are looking for a small Spanish-speaking woman answering to the name of Michelle. She is possibly from South America. According to the brothel's other prostitutes, the woman had recently been hired for a trial period and was servicing John Winther in the brothel's S&M room, where the accident occurred. John Winther, 46, earned his fortune as an international developer. Recently he had bought up and developed sites in Russia and Brazil, where his company was presently involved in new sub-divisions. The company owned many properties, both in and outside of Denmark.

The doctor had recommended to Claire that she check into a hotel to avoid the press storm, so she took a suite at D'Angleterre. The chairman of the board for John Winther Development, a prominent business lawyer, briefed her in the suite.

The company was in good shape, it could carry on as if nothing had happened, with one difference—she was now the majority stockholder.

"I'm going to spend the winter at our house in Florida, but

I want to be kept informed of anything significant happening with the company, and to participate in all the board meetings," she said.

The chairman nodded: "Naturally."

Again she stood in the airport. Had just checked in her luggage, when someone tapped her on the shoulder. She turned and looked into a puffy, yeasty face with pores like craters.

"Bonnie!"

"You won't forget us, right?"

"Of course not. You know me! But things need to settle down a bit. You understand that, don't you?"

"Of course."

They waved for as long as they could see each other.

PART III

CORPSES

SAVAGE CITY, CRUEL CITY

BY KRISTIAN LUNDBERG

Malmø

Translated from Swedish by Lone Thygesen Blecher

We must start at the very beginning.

Our story is simple. Just like life itself, it has no beginning and no end. We're in Malmø, one of the larger suburbs of Copenhagen. Our story is about death. Death is at the core of everything. All stories about life and love contain a kernel of death.

Those who must die are getting ready. Those who must die prepare themselves. They read and write, breathe and watch. Those who must die set out on a journey. One showers to be clean, cleaning especially well to smell fresh. Another writes his will and testament—he has already made up his mind, days and weeks ago. A third measures out precisely as much of the drug necessary to make him disappear. The vein responds, his eyes cloud over, and in a matter of seconds the world is dark, black. Everything hangs in the balance for a moment, the living and the dead. We who are still here, and those who have given up.

From Västra Hamnen, this community within a community, one can see Copenhagen glitter like a string of diamonds in the night. The neighborhoods Nils Forsberg loved were the ones close to the discontinued ferry port, Nyhavn, home of the shabby beer taverns where a Swedish policeman was allowed to be exactly as intoxicated as he wanted to be.

* * *

We are all in the same space. All the invisible people. Everything that creates a city, with sounds and echoes, time passed and time to come, dreams and hopes, the unborn and those who are vanishing. We are all here. This is a story of guilt and redemption, of hope and despair.

We are human beings. We live, breathe, love. We are the ones who are going to die. You are the ones who are going to die. We are each others' mirror images.

Those who are going to die look around the room, brush their hair, kiss their children, flush the toilet. They are the ones who know they are going to die, who long for death, for the great, soft darkness, the final hot flash, and then that final, last silence. And those who want to live, and who do all they can to stay here, who are frightened of the great darkness surrounding us. We are like each other, like day and night in the same city, alike as only human beings can be. Our story must start right there: in the city, with a description of death—the savage city, if you will. From a distance, and from far above, we might seem like insects, cockroaches, reptiles. We live off of each other. Out in the suburbs lights are coming on, slowly, one window at a time. It is morning, the first day for some, the last day for some, and in between we meet up. The commuter train shoots out between Malmø and Copenhagen, penetrating the morning like a flaming arrow.

Life.

All these breaths creating a chain of life, of time. We know we are being eaten by a hunger we can never escape, and yet we pretend we are not touched by it. That everything is as it should be. That time doesn't count us in, that we are not worried by time. For every breath, for every day that lights up, we move closer and closer, and one day, just like this one, we stand face-to-face with our own destruction. Then what is it all worth? Nothing.

Death is no stranger who suddenly appears in your room. Death does not pull the curtains aside, revealing an empty backyard. Death does not appear like a shadow that grows darker and then black, like a bruise that deepens in color. Death is just another kind of light.

It happens that Nils Forsberg thinks this way. That on the other side of this light there may be another kind of light, a darker light which your eyes need time to get used to. On other days, most days, he doesn't think at all, just wants to disappear, thinks that all that is left for him is to drink himself to death. At the center of the city the day deepens, the morning sings its city song. Everything we have will be taken from us, death can come like a thief in the night, he can come like an arrow shot from a distance.

Life.

Fragile as the delicate veins in fall leaves, strong as the stubborn pulse, strong as hope, stronger than love.

The water in the canal is still, translucent, and bottle-green. Every section of town seems to be linked by a bridge. Malmø is a town surrounded by water. The streetlights. Central Station. The taxi lines. The empty moments. Bicycle messengers steal a moment's rest, between hope and despair. Everything is in movement, the city is breathing and living.

And here we all are, spinning, hopeless.

She who has to die this early morning is getting ready, planning the next few hours, trying to remember names, people, and places. She knows the time has come, that it has been here a long time. She quickly brushes her hair, removes a speck of food from between her front teeth. She knows how much she owes, knows she must pay. She cannot free herself of it. Her debt grows with every breath she takes, and yet there's nothing new in this, she's used to being hunted, she is prey. She no longer knows what it feels like not to be hunted.

The withdrawal distorts her thoughts. She's not able to follow a straight line of thinking. There's no beaten path she can follow along, or leave behind.

Debt.

It's all about that.

The debt.

That she has to pay and cannot do so. She who has to die has tried in vain to settle her debt by offering herself as mule. She said: "I can fix it, I can take it. You know I can handle the pressure."

It would be so simple, just a transport through Copenhagen to Hässleholm, but that prospect turned out to be futile as well. She had been hoping for it, it had been a straw to cling to, that she could put her debt aside by carrying a kilo of amphetamines from the head supplier.

She has offered to transport goods from Poland to Sweden—but that's just as futile. She has, to put it mildly, no credit left in her "trust account." Istvan is many things, but generous and forgiving he is not. She's still short four thousand kroner. A piddling amount, really. But every time she's managed to save up something, it disappears just as fast. There are always new needs. The big problem is that the money runs right through her fingers, that she needs the drugs to be able to work and save up more money, and to do that she needs to use more and more.

It's an evil cycle. She's in the rat race, but unlike the rat, she knows she's doing it—which of course makes everything worse. She knows there's neither beginning nor end. She just runs.

She who must die gets dressed. Thinks of her mother who is still asleep, sees her in her mind's eye as she lies in her bed, breathing. She who must die cannot this morning help thinking about how much she loves her mother, how she wishes she could give her what she dreams of. A daughter. That she would come back, return from this shadow world. Become alive again. Be a human being, at least for a little while. That's by now the only wish the aging mother has—to get her daughter back.

Traffic is still almost nonexistent, but the city keeps changing. Roadwork is going to detour traffic from Exercisgatan during the early-morning hours. According to a report from the traffic department it has something to do with a minor gas repair job. These things happen all the time, everything changes.

She who must die thinks about yesterday when what she has feared for so long finally happened—a friend from her school years picked her up in the street. She didn't notice until it was too late.

Rickard is his name. She remembers him. He always sat at the front of the class raising his hand and sucking up to the teacher. Even then he was an ass, a pig. Rickard. He didn't recognize her, paid up front for a blowjob without a rubber. She's almost the only one on Exercisgatan who does it.

Everyone knows about it. She doesn't need to advertise her special products. For her it doesn't mean anything anymore. It isn't true that there are levels in hell. Everything is equally black and hopeless. After she threw up Richard's sperm by the cemetery fence, she thought, for the umpteenth time, that it had to stop now. *No more!* she'd thought. Her eyes had teared and she still felt sick from the stale taste.

She who must die knows that it's inescapable, that it must

come to an end. Death from her own hand or an accident—it makes no difference, not any longer, she is tired, tired to the core. She looked into the mirror this morning and saw a ghost looking back at her: a skull with a thin film of skin stretched over the bones. She saw the badly healed scars all the way down from her upper arms. She saw the badly healed veins winding across her underarms. She is no longer a human being, she just doesn't know what she has become. A reptile.

A cockroach.

She assumed that's what she'd become.

He who this morning will do the work of death is calm and methodical. He doesn't hurry, his hand never hesitates. He strangles her completely, without effort. He's not a passionate man, he is calm and calculating. He knows what to do.

However, it takes longer than he'd expected. She resists— a kind of passive, hopeless resistance. It's unbearably exciting, and he can't help letting go of his grip a tiny bit, just so she can take a quick breath, just enough so she cannot scream, but enough oxygen to draw it out for a few more seconds. His pulse speeds up a touch, not much, but enough so that he's irritated by his own weakness. He finishes his job, his assignment. He's annoyed about his sudden weakness—that he couldn't resist the impulse. It all takes just a few minutes. He wishes he could have dragged it out longer.

The murderer covers up her body with a blanket, not from caring, not because the exposed body tells of the unspeakable— he throws the blanket over her from mere habit. The dead body is then rolled into the backseat of the car; the blanket has a small checkered pattern. He's reckless. It's a preposterous thought that he should ever have to succumb to letting his car undergo a criminal technical examination. Although the woman's body is covered with an abundance of DNA traces, he knows that there are neither trails nor suspicions anywhere, that he's a free man. He eats when he's hungry, drinks when he's thirsty. Now he's excited in this undefinable way that makes his body shake from inside out. To be like a god! Freedom is pleasurable. He sits still for a few seconds in the car, breathes deeply, thinks of the dead body in back, thinks that he must stay present now, that he can feel the whole world breathe against him, intensely and burning. He's beginning to change, growing harder, more like an animal. This is what he's been striving for, to become true to his instinct.

It takes time before one begins to see the pattern. The various parts do not make a whole, they're not noticeable, though it's so obvious—and perhaps it's for just this reason that the simple becomes the difficult. The solution is so obvious that it becomes banal. We search for more depth, a more complex solution. But it doesn't exist. Everything has to do with desires, with needs.

It's like emerging from a dark basement and being surprised by the bright summer light. You know what you're going to see, maybe you even feel it, but in the moment itself—just when the world is going to appear—you see nothing. You're blinded, thrown to the ground, covering your eyes with your hand to protect against the sharp light. This is what truth is like.

This is the merciless light biblical texts speak of, a truth so penetrating that it's almost impossible to survive. You must die in order to take part in eternal life. Therefore: better to squint than be blinded, better to be chosen, to be inside, than to be excluded.

Nils Forsberg wrote in one of his few letters to his former friend Father Pietro, as an answer to why he can no longer believe: *I think it has to do with a kind of stinginess, your faith, your feeling of presumptuousness—that there should be an answer, incomprehensible for those of us still living in this world. Yes, you are right, I am a coward. My way is the coward's way, but this way I only have myself to depend on.* He knew he would never send the letter, that it didn't really matter, and that the most important thing was to put his thoughts down on paper—that writing was a kind of mirror.

That's how it was. It was in the writing that he was able to see himself. *You think you have a mandate on truth, and through your very faith you make everyone else an exception. I spit on that!*

Father Pietro had for a short time been Nils Forsberg's father confessor. The aging priest, who'd been exiled to the edge of the world, had been Forsberg's path into the church, into what he imagined was the world. And then the real world came along and changed everything. The world where death attacked like a splash of ink on a white sheet of paper. Between the inner and the outer world, boundaries were no longer possible.

Body and spirit.

The city is Malmö.

The year is 2008.

The old year left only senseless tragedies behind, incidents that could just as well have been stopped in time before the wheel of death started rolling.

Now it's January. The month when everything stands in the balance. When everything is both too late and too early.

A series of deaths occur within a very limited time, and within a very limited geographical area.

Everyone is dumbfounded.

The general public. The police. The media.

The cruelty. The meaningless violence. The ominous sense

of aggression. It has become like an itch that can never be stilled.

The press is full of meaningless speculations, not the least of which are supported by Alexander Hofman's inflammatory editorials. There's a rising sense of anxiety that always sets in when weaker groups become even weaker. Everything rolls along, takes on a life of its own. There's a small part of the larger picture which at first you cannot see, a pattern not decodable at first. The light of truth is blinding, impossible to grasp.

A crime scene might very well be compared to an archeological excavation. You want to know what has happened and who is involved. There are clues, suggestions, a sense that something lies hidden.

The world is a riddle to be solved. We all become more or less suspect. Guilt is a disease, contagious, transmittable. He who turns his face away, he who starts walking faster, she who laughs off the facts, uncomfortably.

Nils Forsberg finished his letter to Father Pietro: *There is no longer any reason for me to not say exactly, and I mean exactly, what I think. And that way is, as everyone knows, a blind alley. We lie because we don't have the energy to tell the truth! Truth does not make us free, it makes us lonely.*

Of course, a social and ethical explanation can be found to interpret the reasons why a particular person commits a crime. There are also psychological models. For Nils Forsberg the answer to the "Why" has crystalized into a "Therefore": greediness, terror—because it was possible, because you could.

January is a month when everything hangs in the balance, when quick or well-thought-out decisions take on unknown consequences. To allow yourself to let go, or to deny yourself the right to act out your dark side. To kick someone lying down one more time, or to let it be. To jump out into it, or not to. Violence vibrates in the air: repressed hatred is like a dense fog rolling through all the alleys and squares of the city.

Life is unfair and cruel, and so is time. Cities grow, cities disappear, children grow older, stars fall and incinerate. Everything is in movement, the only constant is the actual feeling of meaninglessness. That we are on our way somewhere and that we don't know why.

Between us, the living, there is a transparent wall. Stay or leave. We never touch each other, we just turn our faces away, look down at the ground.

In the end, that's what it's all about. That some disappear, while others stay around. That we are weighted down to earth, as though we are carrying an invisible yoke. The dead can be whirled off into time, be recreated, placed into some context, delivered the justice they are thirsting for, and then even the memory of them will be gone.

The final problem is, of course, that any kind of fundamental justice is lacking. That we cannot see the whole picture, only parts of it. That we grope for each other in the dark. And the murderer remains alone, blood singing in his body, images haunting him. He is who he is, he owns this bottomless thirst and this voraciousness that fills him. He knows it should not be this way, he also knows he cannot stop himself. It's like an invisible wound that can never be healed, an itch you must not touch, and yet you cannot help yourself.

Is this how we become what we're supposed to be? Nils Forsberg is doubtful, he still believes there is a hope for mercy, for change, that life is not static.

Nils Forsberg had crossed several boundaries in the course of his life. It was not a conscious choice but the sum of a series of events taking place beyond himself. It was possible that he once had been free to choose, but no longer. He'd given up, been tossed here and there, taken paths he had previously not even known were there.

Nils Forsberg had chosen to remain in his job, long after he should have left. When he should have left the dead to bury their dead, and he should have stayed with the living—and lived. The very first time he'd had to deliver the news of a death, he should have refused to pass on the information. He should have said that he could not be the messenger of the underworld, that the living and the dead should take care of each other, and leave him out of it.

But then who the hell would do it?

That's how it always went. It was the responsibility. His feeling that he was more capable of dealing with the world than his colleagues. It was better that he did it than to have Nils Larsson come stomping into the home of the victims saying, "Your boy is dead, he fell onto the tracks . . ."

It's all still there, all the thoughts and actions are there, deep down in him, buried in sediment. And every time he takes action the dregs are stirred up, just like when you throw a stone into water and everything muddies.

Now he was in a gray zone, neither alive nor dead, and yet—a bit of both. He looked at himself in the mirror in the bathroom and could hardly recognize the face looking back at him. At times he despised what he saw. New Year's had passed, the nights were deep and dark, the days as short as a breath, gray and grainy. Nils Forsberg experienced a certain amount of pleasure in giving up, admitting defeat, with a tiny bit of self-pity mixed in. *Tasting the whip of degradation!* to quote his favorite author, Eric Hermelin, in one of his introductions to a book of Persian poetry. To summarize: in order to get back up you first must have fallen down. Forsberg had fallen down so many times by now, and he no longer had the strength to get back up. Nils Forsberg was a man who carried his story around with him, who was always telling and changing his life's story. He was also a man whom no one wanted to listen to anymore.

The morning news in Malmø reports of break-ins in three nursery schools; four people are arrested in a stolen car; a twelve-year-old girl is chased out of her home by her own father—she runs crying around in the yard in front of the apartment building; a middle-aged man is found dead in a parked car on Östra Förstadsgatan. He sits with his head leaning against the steering wheel. The autopsy shows that he's been dead for at least twelve hours before he was found, which means that he's been sitting dead in his car during daylight hours on a busy street in the middle of Malmø. Everything is changing. Though we are as alike as only human beings can be, we are still strangers. The girl gets to sleep late in the afternoon, her father will stay away overnight, and the three break-ins at the nursery schools are never solved.

Death is waiting.

Death bides its time.

Everything is about waiting, about doors thrown wide open.

The only thing we can really know is that time measures us carefully, it waits until we have finished all we are here to do, all that is written with invisible letters in the book of life.

Time.

Drops of time, trickles of time. Time scratching, carving its deep lines in your face. Time for the poison to leave your body the same second it's taken in. We're like black flares in a world of sudden light. The soon to be dead get on the bus, log onto their online bank, wait for a traffic light to change. Everything continues as though nothing is going to happen. The soon to die take their stuff out from the pawnbroker, try to ameliorate a bad cold.

The police station down by Slussplan, right by the canal, lies mostly in darkness. It's that time, right between night and morning, and slowly the city wakes up, revealing all the secrets of the night. Rain mixed with snow falls heavily. The water in the canal reflects the light, traffic lights blink yellow, again and again. Down by Midhem, at one of the many twenty-four-hour gas stations, a small fire ignites and spreads quickly along the back wall—a neglected area where trash has accumulated for many years. Three or four homeless people who've been using the area as a shelter from the wind run off, leaving the fire behind. They stumble along Lundavägen like evil-smelling ghosts, on their way toward the dense bushes right opposite Hedberg's car dealership. And then everything is recognizable yet again, from the acrid smell of burned plastic, damp leaves, scraps from a fast food place, a worthless windbreaker. The rancid smell of urine, alcohol, rotting food. Three of the four who run from the fire will not make it through February, the month of the death god. The youngest of them will be found dead in a gateway on Zenithgatan, right next to Rörsjöskolan. Life is in motion, it happens. We have so little to fight back with. We've created a world that turns its back on us.

Malmø is Sweden's third largest city.

The city is growing, in constant motion. The boundaries between Copenhagen and Malmø are growing more and more diffuse with every year that passes. Transportation is fast now—and everything can be transported. Huge sums of money change hands every day. The economy, lust, and desire itself move freely, like underwater currents. You see the ripples on the surface but never the big currents, the big fish.

Stars can just be made out in the grayness; far away a siren is heard from an emergency vehicle. Everything is within everything. Even chaos creates its own pattern, like looking through a kaleidoscope. Down in Rosengård a basement fire starts up. In the last few weeks there have been several, almost always basement fires, lit with rubbing alcohol and matches. The rental agency has emptied all the storage rooms, nothing of value has been left behind, nothing that could be ignited. Which means that they drag the trash in there themselves and light it. Why? The answer is simple: because they can.

A security company makes rounds, drives slowly through the badly designed alleys. They've been ordered never to stop, never to leave their car, always to call, "Patrol in danger," at the least sign of trouble. This of course contributes to aggravating the mood, to the feeling of being out on a dangerous assignment. The divisions become sharper and sharper. The difference between them and us more and more pronounced.

Windows in the stairwells are brightly lit. The city is besieged by its inhabitants, and a ghost walks through the city, a phantom.

Then the fire in the eastern parts of the city gets going. The night worker at Statoil strikes the alarm for the fire department and within a short time the gas station and the fast food restaurant have been shut down for customers. Someone also decides to block off the upper part of Lundavägen. Two big cranes block off the street. A lonely policeman is given the task of directing the scanty traffic. A rain storm is gathering, clouds quickly pile up above the city. This gray, miserable city of no mercy. On this day, in this city.

This morning finds Nils Forsberg sleeping at his kitchen table. A string of saliva has run down his chin. Forsberg doesn't dream. He's sunk into a deep black hole—the dreams are happening somewhere else. The alcohol rushes throughout his body, shakes and shivers in all his body's nooks and crannies, searching for cells, thirsty cells wanting to be saturated again. Time will burn off the alcohol. Time is our only friend. It moves on, rushing like an ocean. Everything tears and jerks inside of him and he can't see it or understand it. He's like the living dead, what's left over at the end. Finally, that's what it's all about: time. It changes us, it teaches us, if only we'll listen.

In the end, it all comes down to one question: who is it you belong to?

Who do you belong to? Your car? Your job? The alcohol? The drugs? You allow yourself to be defeated, vanquished, conquered, beaten. Eventually, that's the only thing Nils Forsberg can subscribe to: that he's owned. To live becomes like being on fire for one moment. To flare up like a star in a black room, imploding, then disappearing with a faint hissing sound, like when you drop a burning match into a glass of water. One quick fizzle, then all is quiet.

"Even time is political," Mats Granberg once said. Forsberg's answer had been blunt, not to say aggressive. "Ah ha? And what the hell do you want me to do about it?" How do you answer something like that? Which of course only meant that Forsberg tried to make sense of it because he missed his friend. He also knew that he couldn't admit it to himself. He couldn't allow himself to be human. All his mistakes, his failures, his problems lived their own life in Forsberg's consciousness, soaring and surging through his body like a separate ecosystem.

In the course of his career, Nils Forsberg had seen more dead people than he cared to think about. He had seen them in every condition, at all ages.

Children and adults, men and women. The dead all carried a common burden. Their spirits floated weightlessly, while the memory of them nailed them to this world. It was as though a special kind of energy had been released around the dead. A human being who disappears in a crime leaves a string of loose ends behind. Connections that are not cleared up, explained, will haunt the rest of us, force out an answer. Nils Forsberg lived in a dark maze, groping about and finding nothing, not even a flicker of light. Only the voices from the dead looking for answers, crying out to him when he tried to sleep, hesitantly reaching for him when he let his thoughts float. He knew he was not alone in this, that most police officers were haunted this way, yet it was rare that anyone said anything about it. As long as one didn't speak of it, it didn't exist, that particular problem.

A police report is at best a slow journey, two steps forward and one step back. At worst it's a march in place. Most often it's a balancing act between madness and discipline. This was a phrase Forsberg liked to repeat to anyone who cared to listen: "Madness and discipline! And all we have here is the discipline! Where's the creativity! Where's curiosity?"

The dead.

Some of these deaths he had shared with Gisela Eriksson. They had attempted to recreate times, places, and events to such an extent that the dead had become like distant friends, or relatives you haven't seen for a long time. The dead. He knew Gisela Eriksson also walked around surrounded by the shadows. She'd been his closest friend, the only one whom he could share his thoughts with. And then he'd gone and ruined it all, pushed everything to its ultimate conclusion so that finally there wasn't anything to be done but shut the door behind him. He'd always thought she'd be the one to take over after him. And that's what happened, but not the way he'd wanted it. He hadn't chosen to leave, he'd been kicked out. He had envisioned himself and Eriksson walking side by side through the city-jungle. Forsberg teaching what he knew, and Eriksson eagerly soaking it all up. Oh, what an idiot he was, what a naïve and narrow-minded view he'd had of himself, a complete idiot!

That's what he was.

The dead. The missing.

You could say they were one and the same, that they all spoke the same language. There was nothing conciliatory about them, they just didn't want to be forgotten, brushed aside. At night, and sometimes like a shadow in the middle of the day, Nils Forsberg could feel how they walked right next to him, whispering to him: *You are one of us*. On those days all he could do was drink, try to drown out the droning voices, just let them sink to the bottom, dragged down by alcohol, saturated. All those dead who sought to go back to their original context, who demanded justice, who wanted to be placed in a *true* context.

"And what about love?"

He'd never answered Granberg's question, mostly because there was nothing to say. When everything turned bleak and black, Granberg used to remind him: "And what about love? Love can make the impossible happen!" There was nothing to say to that. Love is a flame that suddenly appears in a dark room—and then it disappears. He would never say that love could save us, it certainly couldn't bring Mats Granberg back to life.

Death and time, love and the abyss.

Nils Forsberg had been a police officer his entire adult life.

He'd never married nor become a father. He'd become a police officer, and he knew only two kinds of people: those who committed crimes and those who searched for the people who committed crimes. Obviously that's a precarious situation—an unofficial health statistic published by the police authorities themselves states that more than 25 percent of police in active service find that they drink more than they should, while the average for the rest of the population is 4 percent. Also, suicides and divorces are overrepresented. To enter the abyss has its price, and it's paid for in life, in time. To be the Virgil of our times, to step down into the inner circles of hell with only a lantern, very quickly takes its toll. It very soon grows lonely and dark.

Time is the master of death. Time is a flash of light in a dark forest. Time is kaleidoscopic: it's what's keeping you painfully awake locked in a cell with a hangover—it's what's whiled away during a conversation along Strandpromenaden in Malmø. Whoever owns time conquers death. Nils Forsberg often thought that it was a kind of irony of fate that the center of the city, the very inner kernel of Malmø, was occupied by a cemetery, a place where time is suspended and at the same time fixed. He frequently ended up in the cemetery on his walks. He would buy a cup of coffee at the newsstand café on Gustaf Adolf's square and sit down among the other retirees, the ones who also lived in this no-man's-land. He always mixed the hot coffee with the liquid from his hip flask. But it had been a long time since he last took a walk. A great exhaustion had besieged him.

Forsberg used to spend days and evenings on the benches in the cemetery. It was an absurd feeling sitting there, absorbed in rest, while buses and taxis passed by. He'd heard voices. Shouts. All the sounds of the city.

Here they all were, the dead he'd learned from when they were still alive, the ones who could no longer answer when he talked to them. He'd come to the cemetery when Granberg's ashes were spread. Then he'd kept going back there for several days—probably not more than a week—until he could no longer do it, and the alcohol took over. He'd drowned himself from the inside out. The only people he was really able to talk to were the homeless whom he met on his random wanderings. They understood this particular condition, when you are suspended between life and death and lack any kind of anchor, when you are simultaneously hanging and falling, living at the outer edge of everything.

There are times when we want to escape, and times we want to hold on.

Greger's Antiquarian Bookstore is just a short walk from the cemetery. Forsberg no longer goes there, nor to the Catholic church situated in the same area as the store. It feels like swimming against the current. Every thought and feeling contains endless resistance. Nils Forsberg spends his time in his own rooms, drinking, sleeping, dreaming, screaming, beating the walls. He writes a couple of lines in a notebook, draws what looks like a map, sorts papers and books. Again and again he arrives at one and the same name.

Nils Forsberg imagines that he's following a trail, that he has an assignment. To anyone on the outside it's obvious that we're looking at a human being who's lost all ability to act like a human being. He's chasing the wind, a phantom. He sees a fundamental problem. It has to do with a pattern and intentions. It has to do with probabilities. The important question is:

is it possible to see what's going to happen? Yes, Nils Forsberg answers himself, if you can see what's already happened.

Forsberg had thought a lot about Greger lately. In between the alcohol attacks, and during moments of clarity, it occurred to him that he should have gone there, that he ought to have visited Greger in his bookshop in the basement, at least shown him that he too was struggling. But he'd just not had the energy. Nils Forsberg simply sank. Of course, he also should have settled all his small debts. He didn't do it. Sometimes he had the same dream, a recurring dream he'd had this past year: He was by a lake, the water was still, lake water, black water. The forest surrounded him, sighing, alive. In the middle of the lake floated a naked body, facedown. It was important, he had to get there, into the middle of the lake—but he couldn't move. He saw the body, how it tipped downward, more and more until it completely disappeared—and then he screamed out into the silent forest. The dream kept coming back to him. It wouldn't leave him alone. There was something that should have been said. He never got there in the dream. The naked body floated on in the black water.

The wind grew stronger, heavy rain-wet snowflakes spun through space and immediately melted away when they touched the ground. Nothing lasts forever.

Even when there were memorial services for people completely unknown to him, Forsberg still sat there. It was as though all the dead belonged to him, as though he carried so much grief that he was forced to unload it onto other people as well.

It's January, and the rain comes sliding in over town, then blows off again. The homeless people look for refuge, in gateways, public shelters, bicycle storage rooms, huddled together in small camps, seeking protection from the violence, the gangs who come at them with bicycle chains and sticks. House fa-çades are deteriorating, tree trunks are rotting. Forsberg has expanded his two earlier categories—those who commit crimes and those who have to prevent crimes—with those who long to get away and those who long to go home.

We want to be everywhere we're not. That's one of the rea-sons Malmø forces itself into a state of anonymity, of having no history. The new city has no room for the ugly, the limited, that which reminds us of the passing of time, of work and death. That which makes us what we are: live human beings.

We do not want to be broken, changed. It makes Nils Fors-berg think of a flickering flame in a dark room. Life is like that.

Violence. Cruelty.

Faceless, meaningless, cruel violence runs through the city like quicksilver, pulsating, forcing out opinions, points of view. All the places Nils Forsberg loved had in some way been left to themselves: churches, libraries, parks, antiquarian book-stores. They were places that were in some ways open, in other ways—finished. They were places where there was room for the abandoned, the leftovers. Of all these places, it was especially the antiquarian bookstore that attracted Nils Forsberg. That's where he felt at home, and often he thought about what this might mean. Why just antiquarian bookstores? Perhaps it had to do with the curious fact that time became a paradox within these rooms. It was both past and present, one layer on top of another, and unlike at a museum, it was possible to touch and smell everything. Every book carried an impression of its read-ers, but also carried a hope of being rediscovered.

Such light, happy days, and some darker, more profound days. Life could slide right along while he browsed his way through it, and love would suddenly be present, be real.

* * *

The city grows smaller and smaller, while at the same time it's bursting its own embankments and boundaries. Everything is in flux. Of course, it's all controlled by economic interests. Everything originates in greed. You eat sugar and fat and what you want is more sugar and fat. The changes in the city are also controlled by the economy, and eventually what will remain are only vapid cafés and anonymous shops.

Malmø's oldest porn shop, The Cave, will finally be crowded out of the Herman neighborhood, along with a small furniture store, a hat shop, a photo shop, and a knick-knack boutique.

Because Värnhemstorget, this complete social and architectural mistake, is about to be restructured. A new area, Gateway to Malmø, will be built up right along the approach to the city. The homeless people have been forced into Rörsjöparken, near the city center. They too want to be near where the money is, it's that simple, whether you're a bicycle messenger or a CEO. The easternmost parts of the city are moving further and further in toward the canals. The boundaries are being erased.

All the falafel stands have had their rental agreements canceled. The only constant in the area are the junkies who circle back and forth. The address Hermansgatan number 8 has been junkie central ever since the square was built. If you've lost your bicycle or your stereo, you can be certain that's where you can find it, number 8, third floor—the only apartment in the area with a glass-enclosed balcony.

Every evening and morning security guards patrol the area. Along the back of supermarket parking lots and construction sites found all over the area, the streets are filthy with construction dust and refuse. Everything with any kind of scrap value has already been stolen or carted away. The copper thieves come out at night, digging and drilling like moles for anything that can be melted down and transformed. Even here in the underground, everything is a constant hunt for money.

"It looks like a warzone . . ." the security guard Jan Brandberg thinks when he walks his nightly round, shining a beam behind the scaffolding with his powerful flashlight. The dog pulls at the leash, searching and straining—but no one's out there, all is empty, the world is on standby. As usual, Brandberg turns at the end of Hermansgatan and walks back toward the park again. He usually stops by the tent camp to make sure no one's about to freeze to death. He was taught to show this consideration by an older colleague: "It has to do with finding a balance . . ." He couldn't help asking: "Which balance?" "You must try to be careful with human life." And since then he's made sure to check in on the rag piles—made sure there was life, that they moved when he poked them with the tip of his foot. "Even they are human beings, in a way . . ."

During the last few days the water in the canals has risen. Cans, twigs, and plastic float about on the surface. The water slowly rises toward the edges of the canal. Everything's in movement. The public shelter has just opened its doors, and the first guests take off, always junkies first, the mentally ill last. It's all driven by hunger, by need. The mornings are always chaotic, and everything's again pushed to the extreme.

To live. To survive.

Rörsjöparken is empty. The pond in the middle of the park is filled with rainwater and garbage. The benches were moved inside the municipal storage buildings at the beginning of September. A siren cuts through the morning as the fog comes rolling in from Öresund. In the last few years the population has grown more and more quickly. At the same time, organized violent crime has become rampant in the city. We cluster together. Everything's about ownership. The alternative being: to be owned. Between these poles we are tossed about, like balls in a pinball game, more or less out of control, at the mercy of the times we live in, of our desires.

Morning arrives. Pale gray, it comes like a swollen wave, at first silently, then with all its violent power. So much happens when a town wakes up, so much it's not possible to catch, to describe, no matter how hard you try. Birds take off into the sky, light flickers on the water in the canal, traffic becomes heavier. All these sounds, all the sudden feelings. Life is suddenly in the balance: to jump or not, shoot up or not, sleep in or not. The big and the small, it's all caught in a whirl of hope and despair.

There's light and there's darkness, the dry and that which is still damp. On this day, Christian Westin sits in the basement storage room belonging to his mother's apartment at Allhemsgatan number 7. Westin has now been awake for seven days straight and the demons are getting closer and closer. They breathe and hiss in the dark basement. Westin's mother usually comes down to check on him at some point during the day. There's very little left of what was once the man Christian Westin. He's quickly transforming into a chemical monster. Today he's going to collapse in epileptic spasms and repeatedly beat his head against the cold basement floor. That's to be expected, nothing out of the ordinary. At the edge of one of the larger and more spectacular investigations in Sweden, his name is going to appear momentarily in public when one of his knives is found near a crime scene and it is thought, or rather hoped, that Westin might be involved. It would have been the easiest explanation. But this is not to be. Nothing is as simple as you hope. The morning is like an arrow, shot into space at random.

And death, too, might seem this way.

* * *

On this early morning, while the sky slowly deepens and brightens, the gray growing slightly grayer, a woman will be murdered. She will be thrown into the backseat of a large sedan and transported to a place she hasn't visited for quite a while—the outer edges of the housing ghetto Västra Hamnen. The last time here, she was in a professional capacity. And one might say that now she's also here acting that role. She plays her part, even in death. She died somewhere else and the murderer has brought her to a one-way street out here in Kirseberg where he parks next to Sven-Olle's car service. Alongside the construction sites, there are trailers where the company houses their employees: Poles, Latvians, Germans. The illegal workforce imported from surrounding countries is big business, worth millions. But as with everything else—it's within the pyramid where power figurings and transformation take place, where undeclared, almost invisible money is laundered.

It was all about time.

Fragments of time, dark oceans of time. Time by the drop, time like water-filled underground cavities. Time that curses and time that liberates, that heals and tears apart. All that must be changed, all that holds the eternal.

There's a time to love. A time to die.

Everything existed side by side, shoulder to shoulder.

The housing areas in and near the center of the city were being pushed further and further out toward the suburbs, while the inner core of the city was becoming populated by the wealthy and the homeless, all those who were free to move across boundaries. Everything was a question of time. He who owned his time, also owned his life—Gisela Eriksson often thought that what she really had to offer the anonymous police authorities in Malmø was her pound of flesh. She gave them her time, a part of her life, the only thing she could never get back. Within her, like rings in a tree, was all the time she'd experienced in her childhood, her youth, her early middle age. All time was in motion, sloshing back and forth. Whatever she'd experienced, whatever she'd thought or done, could all be used. There was a creative element to the job that she could not deny, and it was probably what made her stay. She was able to come up with solutions, not merely formulate problems.

Eriksson stood in the stairwell and watched as the aging mother slowly shut the door to her apartment, to "the crypt in which she would mummify herself." The civilian car she was driving was parked halfway on top of the sidewalk downstairs, and traffic was increasing as the day went on. Exercisgatan functioned as a kind of thoroughfare, connecting various streets of the city, and when Eriksson stood outside the apartment house gate, she could glimpse the square by the Jewish synagogue, surrounded by tall walls.

The morning had slipped through her fingers. Her thoughts came and went, rattling like train cars on a rusty track. She didn't know what to think, what she believed. Josman was still being processed. Her body, Eriksson had been informed, had been taken to the forensic department in Lund. There was always a rush, even with the dead. She reminded herself to call Hofman and Nordgren later today—always easier to pose the questions directly to them.

On the morning of the fourth of January rain was moving across Öresund, and you could see heavy clouds passing back and forth across the open expanse. Wind tore at the sea, throwing up water along the rock walls protecting walkways and lawns around the swimming area. Nature, yet again victorious. It was not possible to imagine nature's power. It conquered all obstacles. The sea will still be around when we're no more than a memory.

Time.

The time to leave, the time to come back.

Time to open one door, time to close another.

The wind increased in strength. There were places in Malmø that were in constant movement, where the wind always got in. The entire town was one big construction error from the beginning. There were no natural breaks, no given boundaries. Everything had been made by man. Time had changed the town, its inhabitants, its language. It was neither good nor bad, it was just the way it was.

Cruelty alongside consideration, life alongside death, love alongside hate. One thing depended on the other. In another part of town, on Fågelvägen, just a few hundred meters from Exercisgatan, was where Nils Forsberg stayed, more or less busy scrutinizing himself—always arriving at the same dreary conclusion.

That it was too late, that he had already lost, that now he had to listen completely to the inner voice telling him that the only thing he needed to do right now was to remain sufficiently drunk around the clock, then everything would take care of itself. If he'd counted right, then this was day sixteen. He had trouble in between rounds, telling where one day ended and the next began—so, for simplicity's sake, he'd drawn a thick line on the refrigerator door with a black marker. He counted sixteen lines now. And he knew that Mats Granberg had been dead longer than that. Those days, the ones without Granberg when he was still sober, were white, frozen, inhuman. *We're not created to lose, nor for defeat—we're made to win!* he thought, and at that moment it seemed obvious to him that he'd committed his whole life to failures, to losses. He was his own loss, had created his own degradation. He knew that he was beyond human help, that he was like a stone, sinking deeper and deeper down into the water. "Oh, damn it all!" he wailed his mantra, over and over again.

Nils Forsberg had lived very close to his own edges. In one moment everything could be changed. He shifted his inner positions as regularly as the tides. A more psychologically astute staff manager might have demanded an explanation about him from the social insurance office a long time ago. It was not difficult to discover that Nils Forsberg was a bipolar personality type with autistic traits, a diagnosis he could be proud of, by the way, not least because Robert Johnson gave Einstein the same diagnosis in a biography of him.

It was all a question of circumstances and chance. In truth he was really just odd. That's where his thoughts mostly went, deep down, to a feeling of embarrassment, about who he was—who he'd become. The difference between what played out in his mind and what took place in the real world was enormous. His main purpose, at least that's how he saw it himself, was to create as much trouble as he possibly could. He'd made a final decision when he first met the personnel consultant, a woman who it appeared didn't have all her marbles, but who made decisions about the world around her in the way she herself saw fit—if the shoe didn't fit, then the world around her would just have to change. He'd almost succeeded in driving Annelie Bertilsson out of police headquarters. But in the end he'd had to admit defeat. Bertilsson was the new order and Forsberg was the time that had passed. Like blowing out a candle—right now. And then everything goes quiet and dark.

THE ELEPHANT'S TUSKS

BY KRISTINA STOLTZ

Nørrebro

He wasn't the only one waiting for the author. Hannah, busy serving the other customers, had set the glasses and Sebastian Søholm's favorite whiskey, a Laphroaig, on the bar. The speakers spewed out Nick Cave's "There Is a Kingdom." People were already packed in around the small wooden tables. The room was buzzing, and all the cigarette smoke lay like a heavy blanket due to the bad ventilation. Andreas, sitting at the end of the bar, held a hand over his mouth and coughed. Though he tried to be as discrete as possible, it still caught Hannah's attention. She smiled and waved him over to three men sitting and talking together at the other end of the bar. Andreas knew very well who two of them were, a poet and a critically acclaimed novelist. He'd read them both but had never managed to get into a conversation with either of them. The third, a heavyset man in a checkered shirt, he'd never seen before. He walked hesitantly over to them. Hannah poured him a glass of whiskey. She said that it was Sebastian's birthday. They were going to celebrate when he arrived. Andreas said hello to the men, and immediately they returned to their conversation.

He looked up at the clock above the espresso machine. It hung amongst postcards and snapshots of bar employees and some of the regulars. His eyes nearly always lingered on the photo of Hannah and Sebastian. They held their heads close to each other. Hannah wore a cowboy hat. Her tongue was sticking out. Sebastian was just smiling that smile of his. The photo had been taken at the summer party. The employees had dressed as cowboys, and a country band played. If he remembered right, the band was lousy. It was the night he'd talked to Sebastian for the first time. Since then they had spoken often. Sebastian had told him about his mother, who was so ill that he'd had to move in with her. They played chess now and then, and one evening, at Sebastian's request, Andreas had brought along his writing. That had been over a month ago.

Hannah stuck a cigarette between her lips. Andreas reached down to feel in his pockets, but the poet was quick to strike a match. The smoke shrouded her face. Erased it for a few moments. Andreas stared at the small white particles that moved like some dancing organism in front of her. She waved the smoke away and poured a large draft for a man at the bar.

Normally you could set your watch to Sebastian. Hardly an evening went by without him stopping in, if not precisely at ten then never more than a few minutes past.

This evening the expected guest didn't show until twenty-five minutes past. Andreas spotted him at once. As always, he wore an Iceland sweater and a deep-blue windbreaker. His dark hair had fallen over his eyes, and he ran his hand through it as he stepped in out of the murk. Stooped shoulders and a dragging gait. The usual preoccupied expression on his face.

"He's here now," Andreas said, turning to the others. "He just walked in."

The poet raised up on his barstool and scanned the bar. "Well I don't see him. Where is he?"

Andreas pointed toward the door. Sebastian must have slipped into the crowd, because he couldn't see the author now.

"He was right here just a few seconds ago."

The poet snorted and sat back down. Andreas squinted and tried to make out the figures. Most of them melted into the haze. Until he showed up again. Sebastian. There was no mistaking him. It looked as if he had fallen into conversation with some people at one of the tables. Without so much as glancing at the bar he unzipped his jacket, ran his fingers through his hair several times, and seemed to let himself be drawn deeper and deeper into the conversation. Slowly the clouds of smoke enveloped him, blurring him out.

"He's here," Andreas said. "I see him."

"Then what in the world is keeping him?" the novelist said. "You'd think he's trying to avoid us."

"He *is* turning thirty-nine, poor guy," the man in the checkered shirt said, laughing.

"Yeah, that's just it," the poet said, and asked Hannah to turn down the music. "Come on, boys." He lifted his arms and prepared to conduct. "One, two, three: *Happy birthday to you, happy birthday to you, happy birthday dear Sebastian, happy birthday to you.*"

The three men sang the birthday song at the top of their lungs, and soon the rest of the bar joined in. Except Andreas. He didn't like it. Didn't like singing. Actually, he never had.

Sebastian came into sight through the haze. He gazed stiffly at them. Possibly he considered turning and walking off. That would be just like him, to get up and leave, but no, he nodded to the people at the table and shuffled up to the bar. The men kept howling. Louder and louder.

When Sebastian mounted the one available barstool without batting an eyelid, the men fell silent.

"Happy birthday, old boy," said the man in the checkered shirt, slapping Sebastian on the back.

"Happy birthday," the novelist said, and poured whiskey into a glass.

"Happy twenty-five." The poet burst out in loud laughter. The other two joined in, swept up in the moment.

Sebastian didn't show any response. He laid a hand on Andreas's shoulder. The hand was slender and cool. Bad circulation, perhaps, or else the raw cold outside had turned the thin pianist-like fingers quite red and stiff. The cold penetrated Andreas's shirt and raised the hair on his body. In the six months they had known each other, this was the first physical contact they'd had. Maybe the hand on the shoulder was a spontaneous act, to show that he liked Andreas's writing, or maybe he was just pleased that Andreas hadn't joined in on the song. Who could know. Sebastian was not often easy to read.

He removed his hand and turned, smiling at Hannah behind the bar. That classic, boyish smile that was always written about in interviews. The perfect rows of chalky white teeth. A *true Hollywood smile*. The front teeth were broad and a bit longer than average. It was a splendid unit, that set of teeth.

"Happy birthday, Sebastian," Hannah said with a gleam in her eye. She raised her glass. Andreas noticed that she had color in her cheeks. Sebastian nodded and held his smile. That's all it took. That's how easy it was for him.

The man in the checkered shirt pulled out a present and laid it in front of him.

"How touching," Sebastian said. "It *is* touching, isn't it?" Still smiling, he looked at Andreas. "On such close terms with the editor, indeed, indeed." He began loosening the ribbon. His fingers were still freezing, almost blue. Though it was warm inside. Very warm.

Several women had bare arms and shoulders, and Andreas

took his shirt off, which left him wearing only an old, dingy T-shirt with faded-out printing on the chest. *I Love New York*, it had once said, but now it was unreadable. As far as Andreas knew, Sebastian always kept his outer clothes on. He had never seen him wearing anything other than the Iceland sweater and the blue windbreaker that he always unzipped when he came in the bar and zipped up when he left.

"Would you look at this," he said, and lifted a small elephant made from dark mahogany out of the box.

"I was thinking it could sit on your desk," the editor said.

"On my desk, a cute little elephant on my desk, huh? That was what you thought?"

The editor cleared his throat. "Yes, that's what I was thinking."

Sebastian looked at Hannah.

"You get presents?" she asked, and leaned over the bar. Her low-cut blouse exposed the upper part of her breasts and made the pale skin appear even more radiant than usual. Sebastian gave her the elephant.

"Those tusks are really long," she said. She held it up in front of her.

"Do you know how many sets of teeth elephants go through in a lifetime?" he said. "Six. When the last set wears out they starve to death."

The editor grinned and nodded with satisfaction. "It's a brilliant novel. The best you've written."

"There *is* no novel," Sebastian said, thin-lipped.

"What are you talking about? I have the second set of page proofs lying on my desk."

"There will be no novel." He held his glass out to Hannah, who filled it. She set the elephant on the bar, but Sebastian grabbed her wrists and closed her hands around the small wooden figure.

"Put it on your nightstand and think of me," he said.

"I'd rather read your novel."

"Do you read novels, sweet girl?"

Hannah smiled mischievously and set the elephant aside. She leaned forward again and nearly blinded them with her luminous breasts.

"I read almost everything," she said. "But a novel about elephants is probably not something for me."

Her cleavage was like a dark and warm cave between two snowdrifts. Andreas reached over and picked up his glass. The smoky whiskey burned his throat.

"It's not about elephants," the editor said.

"Small cute elephants." Sebastian smiled and stepped down off the stool. "Small cute elephants to hide under your pillow, to rock yourself to sleep. Small cute elephants can go everywhere, they can be hidden between your legs, Hannah, they can rock you to sleep."

He left the elephant where it was, sent the bartender a kiss with his fingers, and, without uttering another word, turned to go.

"There's shooting down on Blågårds Square," a man at the door yelled.

Sebastian disappeared into the crowd.

It was the second time that week. Andreas had seen it on television. Gangs at war, they said. It had happened just outside his apartment building's door, but he hadn't heard a thing.

People grew uneasy. Several stood up from their tables and gathered around the bar. Hannah blew smoke down over the elephant and turned the music off. It was for the best, given all the confusion. People were quick to turn panicky, even though nothing had happened. Several chairs were overturned and candles blown out. Perhaps it was like being on a boat about to capsize, knowing that you'll be one of the few to survive. Andreas couldn't help smiling. He looked toward the door, but the dim lighting and all the jittery customers made it impossible to see if Sebastian was still inside.

Like Andreas, the three other "birthday guests" were still seated at the bar. They were silent. Dejected, perhaps. But not scared. Andreas considered saying something about Sebastian—or the shooting. Hannah poured them more whiskey. He smiled at her. She smiled back. Wasn't it times like these that you should go for it? He drank up and stepped down off the barstool. Put on his coat and turned to go. That was how it should be. So simple.

He had to push his way through the crowd. The sweat from all the bodies. A woman's hair brushed his face. The smell of paraffin and smoke. There were sirens outside. The blue flashes lit up the dim bar.

He waited until the sound of the sirens had disappeared before leaving. It was drizzling, but it didn't feel as cold as it had earlier. The water puddle at his feet reflected a blurry moon. He looked up, but he couldn't spot it anywhere. Empty racks stood at the vegetable shop across the street. A few cardboard boxes lying in front of the shop were getting wet. Everything seemed normal, except there were no people. He turned and peered down the street at Blågårds Square. He was alone out here unless someone was hiding in a doorway. There were no police cars, either—maybe they'd already left the area. It had been a false alarm, no doubt about it. He considered going back inside the bar to assure everyone that the danger was past, but he decided not to. It seemed as if the panic had created a certain mood, a common bond among them. He wouldn't be the one to break the illusion. Instead he headed toward the square.

Something must have happened, for even though midnight was more than half an hour away, all the cafés and restaurants were closed. The shop windows weren't lit up as usual, either. Several streetlights had gone out. On a Saturday evening. Even the World Cup never left Blågårds Street deserted.

The square seemed lifeless too. The naked, dark trees surrounding it stood stock-still. Andreas walked over to Apoteket, where the intellectual alcoholics sat in the summer and listened to jazz under the linden trees. There was not a person in sight.

He eyed the ball court, which was lined by a low granite wall. Dark statues sat silent along the edge—he knew each one, but now they were indistinguishable from one another. He'd forgotten that the court was iced over in winter so the kids could skate. Now it seemed almost radiant in the dark. Andreas wanted to feel the ice under his feet. He walked down the stone steps and caught sight of someone out in the middle.

He saw at once who it was.

The rain had made the ice extremely slick, and he almost slipped. He jerked his hands out of his pockets and regained his balance. Idiotic. He headed toward the middle. The court couldn't have been more than twelve meters wide, but it felt much bigger.

When Andreas reached him, Sebastian smiled his smile. "The story about the sick mother," he said. "You've got something there."

"The sick mother?"

"Yes, that's the best one."

"I haven't written any story about a sick mother."

"'The Elephant's Tusks.'"

"I thought that was the title of your novel."

"Why did you think that?"

"I don't know."

Andreas looked over at the redbrick buildings at the end of the square. It could be called a ghetto of sorts, and almost all the people living there were immigrants.

"Who got shot?" he asked, and looked again at Sebastian. His teeth were the same color as the ice under their feet. Gleaming white.

"It was deserted when I got here," Sebastian said. "There's nobody here at all."

Andreas looked down at his sneakers. His toes had begun to freeze.

"'The Elephant's Tusks' is a good title, but there are a few things I'd like to discuss with you."

Andreas nodded. He crossed his arms and slapped his body for warmth. "What about the other stories? I don't remember the one about the mother."

"The one about the mother is the best one. No doubt about it, the best."

Andreas felt his lips stretching into a smile. This was what he'd been waiting for. Why couldn't he remember the story about the mother, then, and that title? Sebastian took his arm and led him across the ice. Apparently his leather boots were better suited than sneakers for slippery surfaces.

They walked together back toward the bar. The drizzle was letting up. Blågårds Street still looked dark and deserted.

"Did you hear all those sirens too, just awhile ago?" Andreas said.

"No," Sebastian replied. "It's been quiet the entire time I've been outside."

At the corner of Baggesens Street, right beside the bicycle shop, at number 10, Sebastian took a key from his pocket and opened the door.

"Are you living here? I live right across the street, number 13."

"Yes, I know." Sebastian turned the hallway light on and stepped inside. "Come on."

"Won't we wake your mother?"

"No, she's a heavy sleeper." He pulled down the zipper of his jacket. Andreas could feel his socks, wet now.

The apartment was on the top floor. The dark hallway smelled old and dusty. It was easier to get their bearings after Sebastian opened the door to the living room, but the smell persisted. It was a strange odor. Andreas took off his shoes. "You don't have to do that in here," Sebastian said.

In the living room, a door to another room stood open. The door couldn't be closed because the end of a bed extended over the doorstep. A pair of feet. A pair of feet stuck out from under the blanket at the end of the bed.

"It's my mother," Sebastian said, his voice low. "She loves to have the bottom of her feet massaged. If you'll do that, then I'll go out and warm the soup."

"The soup?"

"Yes, I've made soup for us."

Andreas walked over to the feet. The nails were long and thick. A few of the toes were crossed, and the bunion on one foot stuck out like a sharp weapon. How could he have made soup for both of them when he hadn't invited Andreas over? Sebastian had yet to budge from the doorway. He still wore his sweater and windbreaker.

"They're horrible," Andreas said.

"No, they're just deformed," Sebastian answered, and went into the kitchen.

They weren't merely deformed. There was something threatening about them. He craned his neck to see inside the room. The bed took up the entire space. He could barely glimpse the bedstead in the dark. The mother's face lay hidden somewhere in there. He looked again at her feet. He was alone with them now, and he realized he had begun shaking. His hands and knees. He could simply not do it. But he felt as if he didn't have a choice. He reached out for the feet, brushed against the thick nails, then quickly pulled his hands away. Took a deep breath. Thought he smelled basil and thyme. That must be the soup.

Outside the window, a cloud slid off the moon and lit up the room. The pale feet seemed almost transparent. Blue-violet veins stood out, thick as earthworms, under her skin. He leaned over the foot of the bed, but still he could see only the white blanket that covered her entire body, hiding all of her limbs except her feet.

He looked out at the moon and noticed the building across the street. For the first time he realized how close the two buildings were. Light shone from the upper-floor windows. He recognized the bookshelf in the living room. He could almost read the titles on the books' spines. They stood in alphabetical order. Usually he cleaned them off with a feather duster—one of those old-fashioned ones, in cheery colors. Someone was walking around over there. He'd forgotten to turn off the lights. Andreas recognized every movement. The T-shirt with the faded printing. The temperature was different over there. The smell. But the body. The body was the same one. It surprised him that that was how it was.

He took a deep breath and turned back to the feet. The skin was thick and waxy. The heels rough and hard. They were cold, the feet. Ice cold. It didn't help to massage them. He understood that immediately. Yet he put everything he had into it.

THE BOOSTER STATION

BY SEYIT ÖZTÜRK

Valby

K ris stops, and I barge right into him. The winter cold makes my nose hurt. "What the hell are you doing?" I yell, and I think I can taste blood in my mouth, but what do I know? After all, most of my face is numb from the cold.

Kris doesn't answer. He reaches around, trying to grab something. His big hand rams the middle of my chest, and I'm about to topple backward, but he has a good grip on my coat. With his other hand he points at something down in the ditch ahead.

"What? What are you doing?" I ask, when I've regained my balance. "You trying to kill me?" It feels as if his hand has left a crater in my chest.

Kris stands completely still. His arm is still stretched out. I follow his index finger.

At first I can't see what he's pointing at. I can see the railroad, the rails that disappear around the curve, the noise barrier, the gray sky . . . what is it he sees? What is he pointing at?

Then I spot it. Right there. In the ditch, all the way down by the barrier, a naked pale foot is sticking out of some sort of bundle; at the opposite end, right at the barrier, a head is visible. Wet hair blocks off the face, but it's a head. No doubt about it.

We stand, frozen. He still has hold of my coat, and I'm

clutching his arms with both hands. The bundle lies motionless. A strange silence. A wrong silence.

"Is it a dead body?" Kris whispers, and he looks at me.

I shrug, I don't know. He gives me a shove, wants me to go down and look. I shove him back, but Kris is bigger, that means I've got to do it.

Dickhead!

"If it's a body, what are you afraid of?" I ask, and hop down in the ditch. I pull the hammer from my belt just in case it isn't a body, but some psychopath luring teenage boys down there so he can eat their eyes out.

The brown bundle must be easy to overlook if you ride by on a train. How did Kris even spot it? It's the same color as the brown stones it lies on. Almost the same color. It *must* be a body. You can't lie there like that in this cold without being dead.

I look back at Kris, still on the tracks. He nods toward the bundle, moves his lips, like he's egging me on to investigate, but not a sound comes out of him. It looks a little bit ridiculous. A boy Kris's size. Afraid of a corpse.

I take a deep breath. In. And out. Have to remind myself to do even that. To remember to breathe. Slowly I approach, my hand grips the hammer, my teeth are cemented together. If it's not a corpse, it would be nice if the person stood up now. A homeless person who fell asleep out here. Someone who went to a wild party, or a bachelor's party. Sit down, boys, listen to this. Something or other. Give me something. Just so he sits up.

I reach the bundle. It looks like a girl. The foot sticking out is way too small and delicate and white to be a man's. And the face . . . I still can't see it from the hair, but it must be a girl.

Kris clears his throat behind me, and I wait, but nothing more comes. He doesn't say anything. Just clears his throat.

She's lying totally still, no sign of life from her. I hear myself say, "Hello?"

No answer. Of course.

I lean down and lift a corner of the brown felt blanket and glance underneath. It *is* a girl. A naked young girl. Small white breasts, chalk-white stomach, light pubic hair below. Hard to tell how old she is. Or was. With one finger I pull the hair off her face as best I can.

Fuck!

"What's the matter?" Kris yells behind me. He hops down in the ditch and walks toward me.

"Nothing," I say. "It's just that her eyes are still open."

Not just her eyes, but her mouth too, frozen in an expression her murderer left her with. Because she must have been murdered. Why else would she have been abandoned here?

I try to warm my hands by blowing into the little cave they form in front of my mouth, but it's no good. Kris is still standing by the body. Leaning over it. It looks as if he's investigating it. What does he think he's doing? He must think he's a detective or something. It can't be someone he knows. We've grown up together here in Vigerslev, gone to the same schools, been around the same people. I'd know if he knew her.

The sound of a train rumbles in the distance. It will be here in a minute, for sure. Kris walks over to me. "It's a woman. I packed her in again," he says.

We jump back around the noise barrier. It's pure reflex. We always hide up here when the trains come by. If the engineer sees two boys on the tracks, the police show up shortly after.

We stand on the slope behind the barrier and look down at the community gardens, while the train roars past behind us. It's dead down there. Just like everything else in the winter. Like the girl behind us. I realize that I've lost my hammer somewhere back there. I have to remember to grab it before we leave.

"Do you think it was him?" Kris says all of a sudden.

"Who?"

"The guy down at the booster station?"

I stare at a cottage in the community gardens, a small green house with red shutters and wide flagstones set in herringbone, all the way through the garden to the door, which has a row of potted plants on each side, and hidden underneath one of them is a key, but I can't remember which one. I think that the owner must switch them around to confuse potential burglars, to confuse me, and yeah, fuck yeah, it makes sense. The guy we saw down at the booster station.

"Of course it was him!" I say. "If he was an electrician or a guard or had something he was supposed to be doing down there, he would have been in something his company owns. He'd be driving some lousy van and not that shitty little car."

"He had these big dark sunglasses on," Kris says. "I figured it was because of the sun in his eyes, but there wasn't any sun down there."

I don't think Kris is right. It was sunny, but I don't say anything.

"The license plate! Did you get his number?" I ask, even though it's a dumb question.

He shakes his head. I do the same. The idea was good enough: call the police and tell them about the body and hand them the murderer at the same time. Just like that! Heroes of the day. TV and newspapers. *Local boys find dead body*. How much pussy could a guy score from that at school? Or in town?

"Have you seen anything in the news? Anything about reports of missing girls?"

I shake my head. I don't watch much TV and don't read any papers, but I'm pretty sure there aren't any girls missing. Not right now, anyway.

We're back with the body. I lift the blanket up again. It's soaked, heavy. It hasn't rained for several days. Must be the night frost or something. She is so white, there's nothing on her that isn't white. She looks like a doll. Almost so much that it's hard to believe she's a corpse.

She doesn't look very old, maybe a few years older than us, but no more.

Kris reads my mind. "She's not a day over twenty."

"How do you think she died?"

There is no visible sign of violence. Her body, her arms and legs, are the way they should be, there aren't any broken bones, no bruises. She looks so perfect that it's strange she isn't.

"There," Kris says, and points. There are marks on her throat. I lift her chin up a little, exposing a hand-sized dark spot that stretches around her throat. Kris shakes his head. "Twenty minutes. If we'd just been here twenty minutes earlier." He has brought the screwdriver out again without me noticing it. "Just twenty minutes. It's typical, why do bastards like this always get away with it? It would have been cool to catch him up here when he threw her off. Caught in the act. Fuckhead!"

I'm about to pull the blanket around her again when Kris grabs my wrist. He points the screwdriver at her stomach. "What the hell is that?"

"What? Her stomach?"

"No, *on* her stomach."

I lean down a bit. Small white spots dot her stomach and breasts. It's hard to see them because her skin is almost the same color, but they're there. Sperm.

"Fucking sperm! So that fucker stood up here in broad daylight and came all over a girl he just killed?" Kris's grip on the screwdriver turns his fist white, and he starts talking through clenched teeth. "Twenty minutes, man. Just twenty minutes earlier."

I cover her with the blanket as best I can, and I try to throw up. But nothing comes.

It's getting darker. We lean against the noise barrier. Even though I'm wearing three layers of clothes, I can feel the cold metal on my back. Kris is cooling off, but he's still gripping the screwdriver. I can't see the hammer anywhere. It won't be easy to find now. But our little trip out into this residential area isn't going to happen.

I try to pack her in better. The blanket really isn't big enough, surely that's why her head and foot were sticking out. I try to fold it around her anyway. It's wet and heavy, and the tips of my fingers start to ache. It comes to me that she's been out here longer than we thought.

"What if he comes back?" I say.

Kris looks at me. "What? Who?"

"Him. The killer. What if he comes back tomorrow to get off again? Isn't that what they do, these sex killers?"

"What do you mean?"

"Think about it," I say. "That blanket is soaking wet, and it hasn't rained a fucking drop for several days at least. So it's the frost at night that made it wet."

"Wouldn't the blanket be frozen stiff?"

"Not for sure. It's warmer in the daytime. So she's been laying here since at least yesterday, and he came up here again today to get off."

We stand there for a second, looking at each other under

the railroad lights. Our breath forms small clouds of steam. Kris comes closer. You can almost see the wheels turning in his head.

"So you think he'll come back?"

"Don't they always? They have to admire their work, or whatever. That's how they get caught. Kris, we saw him down on the street. If we wait till tomorrow and catch him there, we'll be fucking heroes."

We look down at the girl. "So we just let her lay here till tomorrow?" he asks.

I shrug my shoulders. "She won't be any less dead from laying there. And nobody's coming up here, so she won't be found."

"So your plan is," says Kris, and looks around, "we pretend we haven't even been here today, and we just happen by tomorrow and catch a sex-crazed psycho?"

"Yeah, we won't even have to overpower him or anything, if he has a gun on him. We just get his license plate."

"But don't you think he saw us down on the street? I mean, since we saw him, he must have seen us."

I think that over a second. "We're just a couple of boys out drinking some beer to him. It doesn't mean we found the body. Especially since he hid her so far in from the rails."

On the way back we agree that he'll return to the body at the same time of day. He's been afraid of drawing attention to himself in the daylight, so he'll want to come late in the afternoon when it's nearly dark. Nighttime is no good because it's too dark for him to enjoy his work. He needs enough light to get off on it. He might also come at sunrise, but people are more alert at that time of day, before going to work. We don't dare take any chances, though, and we decide to meet here early tomorrow morning in case he shows up.

"He'll for sure be coming from the same direction," Kris says. "It's the only place he can park in private. He'll definitely be coming from the booster station."

Kris is already there when I return at eight the next morning. He's waiting at the end of the barrier, but I see him sticking his head out once in a while.

"You're early," he says, then bursts out: "What? What is it? What are you laughing at?"

"*I'm* early? How long have you been here?"

He doesn't answer, he just looks at me as if he needs a few seconds to think. "So okay, I've been here ten minutes, fifteen at the most. I couldn't sleep last night, how about you?"

I shake my head, even though it's not true. I have slept, not much, but long enough to dream something weird, where I was chasing someone who was constantly just out of reach. Just when I was about to grab him, he disappeared around the curve of the railroad tracks.

The bundle is exactly the way we left it yesterday. And yet something is different. Not with the blanket. With her. Her head. And her foot sticking out. Is it just me, or has she turned gray?

"Kris, is she starting to stink? Does she stink?"

Kris shakes his head. "My nose is stopped up, I can't smell for shit."

I take a deep breath in through my nose, and even though we're several meters from her I can smell it. A weak odor of rot. Apparently that's how death smells.

It's completely light now, and we hide behind the noise barrier. We settle in to wait. We stand on the slope, shivering from the cold, but we don't leave. We both thought the only times he might show up were morning and evening, but we stay anyway.

Neither one of us suggests we go home and come back later.
We stay.

The trains pass by. Those from Sydhavn roll toward Roskilde, the
ones from Roskilde toward Sydhavn. We stay hidden, counting
them. Two pass by toward Sydhavn. Then nothing happens. A
third toward Sydhavn, then one toward Roskilde. When it's totally quiet on the tracks we can hear traffic down on Vigerslev
Allé. The cars and buses driving by. We can hear people down
there. Kids yelling at each other.

"I've had enough of this," I say. "Let's get something to eat
somewhere."

"What the hell are you talking about? We can't leave now,
what if he shows up?"

"Kris. I'm freezing my ass off. He's not coming now, it's too
light. Come on, let's go down and get something to eat. We can
be back in an hour."

He shakes his head. "I'm staying right here."

I turn and walk down the slope. "I'll pick something up for
you."

"Let's call the police."

Kris stuffs the last of the burger in his mouth and washes it
down with soda. "Why?"

He's pissed at me because it took longer to bring the burg-
ers back than he'd expected. Incredible, how paranoid you can
get when you're on surveillance. All the way to the pizzeria and
back I tried to find a route where I wouldn't be seen. In case
the killer was on his way. I crawled along the slope by the community gardens, looking for the hole in the fence, and when I
couldn't find it I had to climb over. It was harder on the way
back because I had a big bag of food with me.

It's already getting dark. We eat the last of the french fries. "A whole day's gone by since we found her," I say. "And there's no sign of him showing up."

Kris shakes his head. "No way. You said he'd come back. Maybe he couldn't make it today. The bastard might have a wife and kids and all that. Maybe he'll be here tomorrow. He'll come."

"Let's just call the police, we'll still be the heroes of the day 'cause it's us who found her."

"Maybe, but we'll be even bigger heroes if we catch the guy too," Kris says.

I'm not happy about this, especially since her smell has gotten stronger all day. If we let her lie until morning, how much worse will it get? I wonder. "Kris, we can't just keep standing here, waiting for someone who might not even come back. She's not getting any prettier to look at."

"The man's a psychopath, maybe it's what turns him on."

"Okay, but if he's a psychopath there's not a lot we can do . . ." There must be something I can say to convince him.

"Just leave it to me," he responds, and suddenly he pulls a knife out from the inside pocket of his coat.

"Fuck! Kris, goddamn! What are you . . . Fuck!"

"Take it easy, I'm not about to kill anybody or anything. We just need to scare him, maybe cut him a little."

"Kris, no, fuck it, we're calling the police." I pull my phone out, and I'm about to punch numbers when I get hit hard. Kris falls on me. His hands are on my shoulders, pushing them down, holding me against the cold ground. I can't see the knife. I try to catch my breath.

"Kris, goddamn. Get off, you're crushing me."

He leans over and looks me right in the eye. "You're not calling the police!"

"Get off me, goddamnit." There's a branch or something under me, he's pressing my backbone into it.

"I said, you're not calling the police. Right?" He presses my shoulders even harder. I can't get the bastard off me.

"Okay, okay. I'm not calling the police."

"Promise?"

"Yes."

"You promise?"

"YES, GODDAMNIT! I promise."

He lets go, and slowly I get to my feet. The tree limb has poked a hole in my coat, down at my lower ribs. My phone is halfway down the slope. Even from here I can see the number *1* on the display. That's as far as I got. Kris offers a hand, and I shove it away. I can get up by myself. I just have to catch my breath.

"Kris, you fat bastard!" I stick a hand in under my sweater. My back is sore, but it's not any worse than that. Fucking asshole.

"He'll come back," he says, and looks away.

I can smell her long before I reach her. It hasn't left me, the smell, it followed me yesterday when Kris and I left her. I tried washing it off but it was still there. My mother didn't seem to notice anything, maybe it was just me. When I got up this morning it was still there. It was worse on my coat. The hole in the back is bigger than I thought at first, or else it's ripped out more, but it's the only coat I have. I put an extra sweater on to keep warm.

I meet Kris on the lawn by the booster station. We haven't planned to meet here. We didn't make any plans at all after yesterday. He's smiling strangely. Both his hands are in his pockets. I can practically see from his look that the knife is back in his inside pocket. "Morning," he says, and smiles.

I say nothing, just walk past him, farther up toward the booster station and the railroad behind it. Why is he so happy? He follows, I hear him a few meters behind me. We keep moving along the path. He says nothing, but I can feel his smile knifing me in the back. Why is he smiling this way? He would have said if the killer had been here. I could ask him, but I don't want to. I don't turn, I just keep walking. And he follows a few meters behind.

"Get the hell out of here!" I yell, while I run toward the crow with a rock in my hand. I don't even come close to hitting it, but it's enough to scare the crow. It flies over to the other side of the body for cover. I pick up another rock. The crow takes off again. This time it lands on the edge of the barrier. It looks down at us. Kris plods along over to me, his hands in his pockets. He doesn't seem especially surprised. He's not smiling anymore, but he's not mad or all worked up.

"Shhh," he says abruptly. "People can hear you when you yell that way."

"Yeah? Fuck them. How many people you think yell 'Get the hell out' in one day in Valby?"

He shrugs and plods on, over to the body. The smell is much worse now. It feels warmer too. That, or else it's because I'm wearing an extra sweater. The crow still sits there. I throw the rock, but it sees it coming. It flies up and away, disappears between the trees. If it has found her, other crows will for sure be coming along too. I look up. There are a few dark spots high up in the gray sky. But they fly away.

"Fuck! Look at this!" Kris is standing at the body. I stand beside him and look down. Her eyes, which had been staring at us before, staring at nothing, are punctured and almost gone.

My hand flies up to cover my own eyes, but I lower it immediately. It still smells like death here. The dark spots up in the sky are back. How well *do* crows see? Can they smell her from up there?

"Kris," I say slowly, afraid that my voice is shaking.

"We're not calling yet," he says. "First he's got to come, we'll grab him, then we call."

"Kris, if we let her lay here much longer, there won't be anything left. Those crows are coming back as soon as we leave."

"This was your idea. We find the killer and we're heroes. It was your idea."

"I know it. But fuck it, hey, I was wrong. If he doesn't come back now, he's not coming back."

"No way. He'll be back. It's like you said. He's got to get off one more time."

I don't know why he keeps going on about what I said. He doesn't usually do that. But I don't dare say anything more. Not after yesterday. Instead I bend over, and without looking too closely at her messed-up face I grab the blanket and wrap it around her head. Close and tight. I don't want to take chances.

"What are you doing?" Kris asks. Again, that nice and easy voice.

"I'm covering her up. He doesn't have to get as far as taking his dick out or anything. We just need to get him, right? It doesn't really matter about her. If she lays here much longer, the crows will eat her. If we get the guy, the police or their fucking CSI team or whatever will take care of the rest. Okay? You'll still get to be the hero."

Kris doesn't answer, and I take that to mean it's okay. I feel him staring at me while I wrap the blanket around her. The blanket isn't nearly big enough, and after I've wrapped her head up I notice her legs sticking out from the knees down. I think about starting over, but I leave her like she is. Protecting her head is the most important thing right now. Protect the open wounds. Crows' beaks aren't strong enough to rip holes in skin. Only eagles and vultures and that kind of bird can. Crows need an open wound. Or an eye.

I take three steps away and throw up. Kris laughs at me. I squat down, lean against the barrier. Stay sitting, stare up at the sky. At the black spots. They disappear after a while. A train goes by. We hide behind the barrier. The slope is slippery. I kick the branch away. The one I landed on yesterday. Kris laughs again. Something is wrong about this. Something deeply, deeply wrong. I don't say anything. We wait. We listen. Trains pass by. Cars drive along down on the road. Buses. Kris goes for food. He hands me a burger. I don't eat it. I'm not hungry. I wait and listen. Stay crouched down with the burger in my hands. Kris takes a look. It's getting dark, getting dark fast. I did a good job with the blanket. The crows don't come back. The guy doesn't either.

I go home. Kris stays behind. "See you tomorrow," he says. "Get a good night's sleep and come back ready to go." The smell sticks to me. My clothes. My hair, my skin. I breathe through my mouth, but I can taste it on my tongue.

I don't eat dinner. Take a long bath, but the smell is still there. I go right to bed. I see her half-eaten eyes in the dark. There is something deeply, deeply wrong here.

I breathe icy air, and it hurts all the way inside my chest, but I keep going. I don't know if anyone at home saw me run out, and I don't care either. I run, slip on the ice a few times, fall, and brush myself off with my hands. It hurts, but it's not that bad.

I'm thinking: crows and their fucking beaks, they can't

do what eagles and vultures can, but what about foxes? What about fucking foxes and their teeth?

From where I live it's easiest to get up on the tracks from Vigerslev Allé. From the station. There's nobody on the street this time of night anyway. I fly up the steps, onto the platform, and down to the tracks.

There. Right there. I see two, maybe three, before I trip over a crosstie. They look up at me. "Hey, goddamnit!" I throw a rock. They run off, flee. I go down to the girl. They've been eating her.

They've been eating her. Her foot. Feet. They've eaten her feet. Her legs. All the way up to her thighs. Big chunks of meat bitten off. I start to cry. I can't help it. The tears stream out.

"I'm sorry," I say. "Sorry, I didn't know. I got here as fast as I could. I'm sorry, sorry." I wrap the blanket around her legs as tightly as I can. Just like I did with her head yesterday.

The foxes, they're still here. They're waiting at a distance, quiet. They're staring at us. At me and the girl. What should I do? I realize I left my phone at home. I can't leave her here. The foxes will be back on her as soon as I leave.

"Hey," I say. "We can't stay sitting out here." The blanket is wrapped tight around her. It's cold and wet and heavy, and my fingers hurt, but I can't stop now. I can't leave her here. "You're safe now," I say, and lift her up on my shoulder. "Nothing's going to happen to you. Not anymore. I'm going to take care of you."

At first it's surprisingly easy to carry her, but slowly I feel the weight of her dead body. The first time I slip on a crosstie she almost falls. I can't carry her all the way to the street. It's too far. But I can't leave her here, either.

The community gardens, the cottages. There's a hole in the fence there somewhere, I know there is.

The foxes keep their distance. More have shown up, but they stay away. I slip on the slope, fall backward, and hit my head on the barrier. Lose her when I fall. I look around. She's lying at the bottom of the slope, by the fence. I crawl down to her on all fours. No more falling. If something happens to me, who will save the girl?

I manage to get her through the hole in the fence and carry her down a gravel path, alongside hedges and past garden gates. Which cottage is it? The little green one. I look back at the slope to judge just where we are. A fox stands there staring at us. Fucking shitty animals.

I turn around. The cottage must be right along here on the left. Up a wide garden walk. I grab the doorknob. Locked. Try the potted plants. One after the other. At first I put them back carefully, but it gets to be too difficult with the girl on my shoulder. So I kick the pots over with my foot, one by one. Finally. The key. It's under the fifth or sixth one. I unlock the door and glance back quickly. No one in sight. Nobody has followed us. No foxes. No sex murderer.

I carry the girl inside and close the door behind us. Lay her on a small sofa, farthest back in the room to the left. I sit on the floor beside her. "I just need to rest a little," I say, to the air. "I just need to catch my breath, then I'll go out and call the police. I just need a break."

I open my eyes and immediately begin to shiver. The cottage is like ice. It's getting light outside. I must have slept, I feel stiff all over. I stand up slowly and look at the girl on the sofa. She's lying there like some kind of gift, wrapped up tightly in a much-too-short blanket. The bite marks on her legs stand out. They've taken quite a bit of her calves.

I turn and step over to the door. Through the window I

see Kris standing up on the slope, looking out over the community gardens. No doubt about it, he's looking for us. I open the door, but he's already disappeared again behind the noise barrier. I run down the walk. My legs hurt. Through the hole in the fence and up the slope. I run around the barrier. And smack into Kris.

I fall over. He looks at me for a moment, puzzled, then recognizes me. "She's gone. He's been here and took her." I can see he's been crying.

"No. She's down in the community gardens," I say, getting back to my feet.

"You moved her?"

"Yeah, the foxes—"

"You moved her. How are we going to catch him now?"

"Kris, it's too late. He's not coming back anymore."

He takes a step closer. His fists are clenched, and he nearly snarls at me. "How are we going to catch him now? How are we going to—" He doesn't finish his sentence. Instead he attacks me. I hit the ground hard, it knocks the breath out of me. He straddles me and shakes me by the collar.

"We were supposed to wait for him!" he screams. "That was the deal we made. Don't you remember?"

I'm hurting. Really bad. All over my body. My legs. My hands. My head. I can't take anymore. I moan: "She's down in the house. She's safe." But he can't hear me. He's crying, it's flooding out of him, his words come in short bursts. How I'd promised that the murderer would show up again, that we would be heroes. Tears drip down on my face, and I try to push him away. His hands press down on my throat.

Kris, stop!

Not a sound gets past my lips. I try to push him off but he's way too heavy. My hands reach around for something, anything. I get hold of a rock and hit him with it, but it glances off his arm and gets knocked out of my hand.

I can't breathe.

My fingers close around something long. A handle. The hammer. The one I lost that first day. It's heavy, but I lift it and swing it at Kris. Hit him in the temple.

Kris loosens his grip. He looks at me through his tears, surprised.

I swing at him once more, hit the same spot, harder this time. He lets go and holds his temple, gapes at me. He crawls away.

"Are you okay?" I gasp. Cough, spit mucus out.

"We just had to wait one more day," I hear him say as he moves off on his hands and knees. "Just one more day, he's on his way now, for sure."

Slowly I get to my feet, the hammer in one hand, rubbing my throat with the other.

"He's coming," he murmurs, and sits back against the barrier. "He's coming. Wait and see. He's coming."

"Okay," I say. "Okay, goddamnit. We'll wait for him. I've had enough of your goddamn shit, but okay. We'll wait for him. We'll wait till afternoon, then we call the police. Okay?"

Kris nods. He's still holding a hand against his temple. "Yeah. He's coming. Just wait."

I walk over and sit beside Kris, lean against the barrier. Even though it's cold, it feels nice to rest. I've been on the go for too long. Too tired right now to continue. I lift the hammer and dry the blood and hair off on my pants, and then we start waiting for the man.

THE GREAT ACTOR

BY BENN Q. HOLM

Frederiksberg Allé

I walked down the stairs. It was over. Utterly and completely over. I was tired. The red carpet muffled the sound of my footsteps. He lived on the fourth floor, and I finally made it all the way down and out to the portal, dark and cold as a sepulchre. You could hear the wind whistling outside on Frederiksberg Allé.

The old allé was completely deserted, it was four, four-thirty in the morning. I walked through the ironlike cold under the naked trees, past the cars covered with frost, got in the Mercedes, grabbed the thermos from the glove compartment. Dregs of lukewarm coffee with a few drops of aquavit. What the hell, I could still feel the shots of whiskey. I fished a cigarette out of his pack, only two left, shit. I could smoke a whole tobacco farm, drink an entire barroom. My hands shook, my body. The brief, blazing explosion of fire and light, smoke deep in my lungs. Soon I'll start the car, disappear.

Normally I wouldn't dream of taking a shift on that particular Sunday in February, when the film industry holds its big annual awards program. But I was broke, and several of the other drivers were down with the flu. All evening I had avoided the area around Vesterport Station and the Imperial Theater, stayed near the airport. Fortune smiled upon me: I picked up an elderly suntanned couple just in from the Grand Canaries, dropped them off in Helsingør, about as far from the awards gala as I could get. After I'd driven for over nine hours, my back ached, and it was a little past midnight when I dropped two stewed Chinese off at the SAS Hotel. Time to call it a day, at last. The red, castlelike main station, Hovedbanegård, hugged itself behind the sooted moat of railway cutting. It was as if the city was coated with a thin membrane of gray-white frost; a few frozen souls hurried by. The neon ads blinked uselessly. In twenty minutes I would be back home in Rødovre, popping open a beer, smoking a cigarette, watching some TV. I'd go to bed, sleep. I switched the meter off and felt deeply relieved.

Because of some late-night streetwork on Vesterbrogade I spotted too late, I had to turn up Trommesalen. Suddenly I was perilously close to Imperial. Damn. And sure enough: the rest of the city was empty, but here the slick sidewalks looked like a veritable penguin march on inland ice. The big party had just ended. Cars and people shot out. Couples in evening dress waved in the bitter cold; had my taxi been stuffed with customers, with a pink elephant tied to the top, they would have hailed me anyway, that's how it goes. I ignored the no-left-turn sign, found a nonexistent gap in the traffic, bounded over an island, and swung past the crowded slipstream, away from Imperial, continuing at a snail's pace past Hotel Scandic, which the old Sheraton was now called, and there in the windswept space between the concrete high-rise and Sct. Jørgens Lake, I saw him.

Involuntarily I slowed down even more, my curiosity simply overwhelmed me. Was it really him? Erik Rützou himself, the pompous ass? My archenemy. Yes, it was.

He walked slightly stooped, fighting off the gale that tugged open his black overcoat, exposing his tux underneath. It looked as if he was poling his way forward in a boat. The moment he caught sight of my taxi he eagerly began flagging me. A long whitish thingy shimmered at the end of his raised arm; a torch, it looked like, but it had to be a Bodil statuette. It could hardly be less, in Erik Rützou's case. I cursed the streetwork, my curiosity, and was about to floor it when a bicycler without lights swung out on the street. Against my will I stomped on the brakes.

Knock-knock.

Rützou pounded on the window, chalk-white knuckles, a cuff link blinked, he stared inside the taxi, his clenched fist reminding me of a baby's skull impatiently banging the glass; his slight overbite, which in some odd way served only to reinforce his beautiful, aristocratic face, and his black overcoat made him look like a drunken Count Dracula. Our eyes met, and time stood still. Erik Rützou's gaze wandered, but he didn't seem surprised to see me. In fact, he showed no sign of recognizing me. All he showed was that during the course of the evening he had consumed a considerable amount of alcohol, which in all likelihood he hadn't been obliged to pay for. Champagne and tall drinks in steady streams, served by stunning, blue-eyed blondes. He had sat there in the enormous warm-hearted movie theater in one of the first rows, together with the other luminaries from the film's cast and their spouses or "good friends," clips from the nominees had been shown, the entire theater had applauded, the entire theater had held its collective breath while some highly paid stand-up comic convincingly fumbled with the envelope and finally screamed "ERIK RÜTZOU!!" and an avalanche of enthusiastic applause rang throughout the theater, Scandinavia's largest, it felt as if the roof lifted like some gigantic manhole cover and he rose in feigned surprise, walked up on stage, gave a brief, incisive thank-you speech with a few jokes and wisecracks worked in, thanked the director and the rest of the crew, thanked his old private tutor who was sitting up in heaven drinking port, walked down off the stage, was cheek-kissed along the way by divine women and hugged by male colleagues, and sat down, beaming. Some people are simply born lucky.

All these stupid thoughts led to my not activating the central lock—he had already flung the door open, sunk down in the passenger seat, and said: "Frederiksberg Allé."

I mumbled lamely: "I'm not working."

"It will only take five minutes," he growled arrogantly. "Are you aware of just how goddamn cold it is!? We'll do it off the meter."

A car behind me honked. I took off automatically, as if I was in a trance, and wheeled past the thick cylinders of the Planetarium.

Erik Rützou sat preoccupied, fingering his Bodil, presumably received for Best Male Actor. During the Christmas season the entire metropolitan area had been plastered with billboards and posters for the film. We hadn't seen each other for at least fifteen years, maybe more—when time starts flying nothing can stop it—but I saw him constantly: on TV, on the front pages. On the side of a bus at a red light somewhere. He looked like himself, apparently I didn't. Otherwise he would have recognized me immediately. I mean, we'd acted together, goddamnit. Had been in the same circles for a while.

We drove in silence, or so I thought, but then, through the buzz of my humiliation, I realized that Rützou was sitting there humming. Was he completely sloshed?

Down narrow Værnedamsvej to Osbornehjørnet and the knife-sharp border of Vesterbro, then I blasted up majestic Frederiksberg Allé as if my ass was on fire, Rützou still saying nothing, just humming low, the heavy German cab steamrolling the paving stones on Skt. Thomas Plads, the large, round, eerily deserted square. The grand old buildings slumbered, unworried behind the double row of lindens and the allé's outer lanes, crowded with parked cars. We passed Café Promenaden, where I hadn't dared show my face for years; it was still illuminated inside with a yellowish light, a few customers hanging on the bar, I noticed thirstily, and then we were already there: Rützou silently pointed out his destination. I turned and slowly rolled down the narrow lane between the broad sidewalk and the allé itself. We had just glanced off the corner of Vesterbro and all of its pushers, kebab shops, rowdy late-night bars, and porn shops: here, everything radiated peace and quiet and safety. Cars were bigger in this neighborhood, the apartments too, not to mention the gigantic old villas on the side streets, hidden behind high walls. But it was also a lie. A myth. Because suddenly you'd see auto garages, dreary apartment buildings. And though I tried to appear calm and unaffected by the situation, I was a smoldering, gloomy apartment building myself, an ocean of domestic disturbances. I was a lie too. Because I was scared. Scared, yes. Not of him, but of myself.

Take it easy, Klaus, I told myself, it will be over in a few moments, you're not going to prison for murder here, you'll drive home to Rødovre and drink a beer, maybe two, have a goodnight smoke, maybe two, and then you'll go to bed. And if you can't sleep, no matter how tired and burned out you are, you'll take a sleeping pill, maybe two. If that doesn't help, you'll put on a movie, or call for some company. Most of all I wanted to sleep, drive out into a new day tomorrow evening. The only thing I was any good at. Driving. Up and down deserted roads, snaking in and out of traffic jams, flying across side streets while blind-drunk students disgorged alcohol in the backseat, drive and drive, pick people up, drive far and long, through the city, day after day, but mostly at night. I had become a night person, and I liked winters, the long dense dark. Autumn was my spring, the sublime overture of darkness.

Meanwhile, Rützou had begun frisking himself, hesitatingly, halfheartedly. The bum. Turned his pockets inside out, but all he found was a silver Dunhill lighter and a small set of keys. The damp, well-tailored smile almost turned serious. He was and is hopeless. He was and is a great performer. Our greatest living actor, according to the papers I tried not to read.

"Damnit, I left without my wallet."

"Old habits . . . ?" I couldn't help it. So often in the past I had seen him bumming cigarettes off unpaid gofers or underpaid stagehands. He wasn't actually stingy, he was just thoughtless. One time, many years ago, he'd asked if I had a smoke on me. "I've only got one left," I answered, and showed him the pack to prove I wasn't lying. "That's all right." He grabbed the pack out of my hand, asked for a light, slapped me on the shoulder, and went back to the shot. Strange, the memories you drag around with you.

He hadn't heard me, it looked as though he was struggling to remember something. He was several years older than me, fast closing in on fifty, the bohemian, longish dark hair was salt-and-pepper in spots. A handsome man, as I've said, but much smaller in person. In photos he always looked like some tall, half-decadent aristocrat, but he was only five-seven. At least I had him there, I was almost six-three.

"Give me the lighter while you run up."

Erik Rützou gaped at me, lifted the marble-white Bodil statuette. "You think I'll run off on you? Do you not have *any* idea who I am!?" He fell over, laughing. "You can have this fucking statuette, I already have at least ten others. What do you say?" Light from the streetlamp fell across his face, cutting it in half to resemble a black-and-white mask. He was actually quite pale, I noticed. As if he had seen a ghost. But apparently he hadn't. "Then you could brag that you won a Bodil. Tell the kids about the time you won the Bodil. Ha!"

As far as my children went, they'd probably prefer that their mother got the child support I owed her. It kept adding up.

"The lighter," I repeated.

"How do I know *you* won't run off!?"

"So a stupid lighter means more than this . . ." I couldn't bring myself to utter the word "Bodil." It was ridiculous, but I was a bit sensitive about the matter.

"Why don't you come up with me? Have a shot. And get your money." He already had the door open, his patent-leather shoes dangling out of the car, as if he was carefully testing the water's temperature. We could drown in this dark, cold river.

"I can't park here." I rolled on further; the side door was still open, the cold rushed in, the parked cars were bumper to bumper, I ended up parking halfway up on the sidewalk in front of a classy little shop that sold homemade chocolate.

We walked back through a large passageway and up a neat, well-kept, red-carpeted stairway.

On one floor Rützou cast a knowing glance at the nameplate. "The old prime minister, you know."

I didn't answer, for I was wondering why he hadn't brought some little sweet thing home with him. That wasn't like him, but maybe someone was up there warming his bed. Moreover, he looked even smaller than what I remembered, as if he had shrunk. He gasped for breath. Finally we reached his floor. My breathing wasn't normal, either. Winded, he pushed the door open and showed me into his entry, or hallway, where the ceiling was high, stuccoed everywhere. Rützou set his Bodil down distractedly on an antique bureau, as if it were his daily mail, ads.

An umbrella stand lay overturned, a large gold-framed mirror hung crooked, and a massive floor vase had been knocked over in the next room; the tall, shriveled, reedlike flowers looked like spears or enormous pickup sticks, and I spotted something on the wall that looked like blood but was just red wine, of course, a flowing stain with a delta of thin blue-red vessels. Lights on everywhere, as if he'd left abruptly. On a low table between two mahogany chairs, though most of the pieces had fallen on the floor, a few pawns and a bishop still stood, lonely and confused on a chessboard.

"A damn mess in here." Instead of lifting the floor vase back up, he stepped over it and crossed immediately to the bar, also dark mahogany. I had been expecting that he'd surrounded himself with Arne Jacobsen furniture and contemporary design, that cool, consistent Scandinavian style, but the rooms mostly resembled some English manor; all they lacked was a pair of cocker spaniels and a portrait of the family patriarch, the old major, above the mantel. Maybe that's what living in conservative Frederiksberg does to you. Back then he was a real left-winger.

"Whiskey? Cognac? Or . . . ?"

"Just whiskey, straight, thanks."

He pushed a thick little glass over to me, flung his arms out, irritated.

"Stupid bitch. Well, it's over now." Oddly enough, he looked thoroughly happy at the thought. "Are you married, uh . . . ?"

I hesitated, it was as if he'd been about to say something more. My name, maybe.

"I have a girlfriend." Yes, I did. The problem was that she'd just gotten a job in Greenland as a social worker. They were badly needed up there. But I needed her too.

"I'm finished with women." Rützou finally righted the floor vase, and with a simple, delicate operation arranged the dried flowers or whatever they were, took a pillow that for reasons unknown had ended up on a windowsill, and tossed it over on one of the large, plush sofas. I sipped my whiskey, stood over in the window bay, glanced down at the boulevard, the leafless trees. A single car lurched off, moments later a taxi shot by.

"This is a nice place here," I said, not even trying to hide my sarcasm, "with the theaters and the cafés and the park up the street. Quiet. The perfect place for the perfect solitary life."

"You think? Well."

"And it's only a ten-minute walk to Vesterbro. If a person needs drugs or sex."

He laughed shortly. Drank. "Are you insinuating that I'm the type who beats off in a booth at the Hawaii Bio?"

"They have booths in there?"

"I wouldn't know."

"Really? Because we were in there together once, Erik." Short pause, the famous theatrical pause. "After filming a scene."

Boozily, half-focused, he stared at me.

I swore silently. The words had just jumped out of my mouth. I hadn't meant to reveal myself, but the situation had gripped me, it was almost like standing on stage again, or in front of the whirring cameras. With a firm grip on the role. But the feeling was short-lived and empty. I drank greedily, as if I could somehow swallow the words back again.

"We were? Sorry, but I know a million people. And vice versa," he added, not without a certain satisfaction.

I seethed.

"After filming, you say? Are you a soundman or something? Give me a hint . . ."

"Forget it," I mumble.

"Okay, let's forget it. Such are the times, and the people. Forgetful, and I must pee." He stood up, brushed back his dark mane, more from old habit, I thought, sent me one of his impish smiles, and then I heard his steps dwindling down an apparently endless hallway.

I don't know. I could have taken off. He was gone a long time. I could have grabbed his Bodil and smashed everything in sight and continued through the double doors into the dining room, I could . . . Instead I finished off the whiskey and poured another. I spotted a pack of Marlboros on the coffee table, mine were all gone, I fished one out, stuck the pack in my inside pocket; when I thought about how many he had bummed from me in his time, he'd survive . . .

Finally I heard the thin sound of a toilet flushing far away, a door slamming open, steps approaching. More steps.

I stuck my head out in the long hallway.

"Did you see where I put that idiotic Bodil?" he blustered, from somewhere. The kitchen, I thought.

"Out in the entryway. The hallway."

"That's right."

He tottered out from a doorway, floundered past me, came back.

I sat down in the living room in a wing-back chair, sniffed the whiskey, drank. Could already make out the bottom.

"It could be I do remember you. Faintly. Søren, isn't it? I remember being out on a drinking binge with a soundman once after a shoot. Think we ended up at a hooker bar in Vesterbro. Was that you?"

"Yeah, let's say that."

"And now you drive a cab?"

"You got it."

"Do you recall us fucking any women that night, Søren?"

"Till they couldn't walk."

"Which is how it should be. Let's drink to that."

"But . . . now you're finished with women?"

Rützou hesitated a moment, then smiled modestly. "Absolutely finished, you can never be; they're standing in line. But this woman here," he cast one of his knowing glances around the room, "I am thoroughly finished with."

"Yeah," I said, "luckily new women keep showing up, new roles. I mean, for someone like you . . ."

He coughed. "Sorry?"

I repeated what I had said, word for word. As if I were learning it again. Acting. For it may have been half an eternity since we had seen each other, since we, well, had acted together. Together from morning to night at rehearsals. Hit the town together, bent some arms, chased women. All of that. But if he really couldn't remember me, he'd have had to be suffering from advanced Alzheimer's. And despite everything, that didn't appear to be the case. But something was wrong. He seemed to be a shadow of himself. We actually resembled each other. Again.

"Pouring in," came the delayed response, as if he didn't really care to tune into the conversation's wavelength.

"But maybe it's dangerous when a guy thinks he can walk on water," I said softly.

"What do you mean by that, Søren?"

"Cut the Søren shit. I nearly fell for it, but . . . how stupid do you think I am?"

"I wouldn't know. But you look like a half-brained overweight cab driver, I can see that much."

"And you look like a sick cream puff. But I'm disappointed in you, Erik. Overplaying this way. Even if I've put on a few pounds since back then."

"What *could* he be babbling about?" he emoted, speaking to the stucco rosette on the ceiling, hamming it up. Then breaking out in a horse laugh, bending over, slapping his knee. "Of course, Klaus, damnit. It's you. Now I remember you! But I thought you were dead and gone . . ."

"You recognized me the first second. And you still didn't say a thing . . ."

"Let's say that, then."

"Yeah, let's."

"Listen, my friend. That girl who biked right in front of you. I just wanted to get home. I couldn't get a cab, I didn't want to go into town with the others. Tap on the window, see a middle-aged fat guy who looks familiar. What's his name? I'm thinking. But I meet people all the goddamn time. I'm sorry, Klaus, but you've been out of the picture for fucking twenty *years*!"

"Fifteen," I replied childishly. "And now I'm the one who has to piss."

Along the way I took the opportunity to explore the apartment, the rooms. The bedroom was no exception to the strange sense of disintegration that filled the apartment: clothes were scattered all over, shirts, suit jackets, wardrobe doors stood wide open revealing rows of suits, the big double bed was unmade. A large ceiling fan whirled around for no reason, weekly magazines and pages of dialogue lay on the floor. The office was a cave of relics from a long, successful life. A big framed film poster from one of his most famous roles, a few small paintings from a wild, well-known Danish artist, and high shelves, completely filled up. But the shelves held more than books: photo albums, piles of gossip mags, scrapbooks, a pith helmet, bits of kinky eroticism, including an enormous phallus. In one corner, a southern French village of wine in unopened gift boxes and solid wooden crates. A desk globe inside of which I envisioned a cosmos of liquor bottles, a brand-new set of golf clubs parked against an easy chair. A couple more Bodils stood in a window-sill. Despite everything, it hadn't amounted to more than that. A gigantic desk with a laptop. Along with a horde of photos framed behind glass of Rützou alongside diverse beauties and famous colleagues, the desk was flooded with manuscripts, in-vitations, bank statements. I picked up a random letter from the bank—he was loaded, the bastard. Then I found another letter. The sender's official name and logo was up in the corner. I picked it up . . .

When I returned, he abruptly said: "It's your fault that I'm sitting here. In a tux and bow tie."

"Really?"

"I preferred the stage. Sensing the audience in the theater, sitting in the dressing room, going out for a beer afterward with everyone. Film felt very lonesome to me. No, not lonesome, fragmented, you might say. You know: you show up, say your lines, walk off, and that's it. You might meet with the actors at the premiere." He inspected his well-groomed hands, the whis-key glass he had set down the chess table, a short and stout rook, golden brown. "But then you simply vanished that time, called in sick or whatever it was that happened . . ."

"When?"

"Playing the innocent, are we? That leading role in the Carlsen film was yours. Have you repressed that, man? You must think I'm senile. You disappeared off the face of the earth, so they called me instead." Rützou flung out his arms again, theatrically, and there was nothing else he needed to say: that film was his breakthrough, the roles started pouring in afterward.

"You've performed at the Royal Theater between all the films, I know that much, Erik. Even at Kronborg! I think I've

seen you in commercials too. And some really bad family films."
The kids loved them.

"Everything except the old bawdy films," he laughed. "They
were before my time. But you're right." He stifled a belch. "But
anyway."

"You raked in the roles and the money, man."

"I have." He nodded solemnly. "I have," he repeated. "And
ladies." He tasted the word, stretched it out, lay-deeze. "But . . .
what happened, really, back then?"

"Uh . . . yeah." Another cigarette. "It was . . . it was nerves,"
I admitted, after a second. I had nothing to lose. Maybe I even
needed to talk about it; I had never told this to anyone, not
even my wife back then, definitely not the kids. "The pressure
was too much. I couldn't handle it. The thought of playing that
part, I couldn't wait for it to start, I was so happy, and I was
dying of fright. Not just performance anxiety, but real anxiety.
The long and short of it is, I crashed."

"And when you finally got up again, it wasn't so easy to find
parts," he added sympathetically; that is, malevolently.

"No, it was easy enough, at first. Certain bit parts. Like the
deranged bar type, and the disgusting apartment caretaker. Always halfway drunk. The guy nobody likes."

"Oh yeah," Rützou said. "It's so tiresome playing yourself
all the time. Don't misunderstand me. It's why I have always
taken various parts. Hamlet one day, beer commercials the
next. But listen, Klaus. You could have worked your way back,
slowly. But you gave up."

"Yeah, I did. It wasn't fun anymore. And I couldn't bring in
enough to make a go of it, financially."

"Financially! Bah! I have a good friend, a well-known writer.
He's not exactly swimming in money but he writes anyway. Because he can, won't do anything else."

"Does he have a rich wife?"

"No, Klaus. He's got balls!"

I finished off the whiskey, hissed: "I'm groveling at your feet, Erik. You *are* the greatest. And the ride's on me." I got ready to stand up. "Thanks for the drink."

"Plural, if I may say. You have put away two very serious drinks. Downed them. Doubt you can drive. You want to destroy your glorious taxi career too?"

"I was close to a Bodil for best off-meter driving, right?"

"Ooh, I had forgotten how screamingly funny you can be. Listen: you can still get it, Klaus." He reached for the bottle of whiskey on the chess table between us, some expensive brand I'd never heard of. The Bodil stood there too, tall and elegant, as if it was silently listening. "Stay for a while, let's have a nightcap."

I sank down in the chair, held my empty glass out like some beggar. He had hit my weak spot. I've never been good at saying no. If I lost my driver's license, then . . . Usually I drank only after work and on off-days. Except for the few drops of aquavit in my thermos.

"What can I still get?" I said, mad at myself.

"The lady here." He stuck the statuette up in my face. I pushed his hand away, but he kept sitting there waving it around. "A special-award Bodil. For all you could have accomplished . . ."

Of course I wanted to smack him, but I had driven a cab for so long and met so many extremely drunk people or just plain brain-dead types that I had learned to control myself. People had vomited all over my gearshift and my clothes, they had put a stranglehold on me from the backseat, they had tried to run from the fare, even that stoned-out floozy from Skovlunde without any money who invited me up, yeah, I hadn't even smacked her when she screamed that I'd raped her when her boyfriend suddenly appeared in the apartment, a big dude. I hit him, sure, but in self-defense. The judge couldn't understand what I was doing in her apartment, and my wife couldn't either.

Rützou fenced with the Bodil as if it were a sword or a scepter, right at the tip of my nose. I grabbed it and held it threateningly above him.

"What the hell are you doing, Erik?" Now it was me doing the acting.

"Getting you to wake up. You still have it in you. You are not a big zero. All this could have been yours. But you were an amateur. You blew it all. And look at yourself now, what you've become: a beer gut in a cheap leather jacket. It looks like something you bought on the black market in Moldavia. All that's missing is the mustache. And by the way," he added off-handedly, "you should do something about your eyebrows, they look like two goddamn bushes."

He sat close to me now, leaning forward, a scruffy birdlike figure in a tux.

"What happened with your girlfriend?" I asked.

"Fuck her."

"You threw her out, didn't you? You're throwing everything out, aren't you? Cleaning house." I laughed, pointed to the chaos in the room. "If you can call this cleaning house."

"You blew it all, Klaus. When you pull out of here, I'm calling the police, you'll be nailed for drunk driving. Fired, out of work. Maybe you can find a cleaning job."

I sat the glass down carefully. I didn't pity him, or only very little.

"It's terminal, isn't it? Where at? Lungs? Throat? Lymph nodes?"

"Life is terminal. Did you read the profile of me they published? Nobody will write about you, will they? You're dead and buried. The papers haven't been interested in you for a hundred years. I've even looked once in a while. Usually people show up in these 'Where are they now' type columns, but no. You are just a goddamn moving man driving humans around in an old diesel car. Meaningful work, eh? Challenging."

"How long do you have left? Three months, six months?"

"I have a full calendar, Klaus. Lars von Trier calls me constantly, begging me. They call from Hollywood, goddamnit!"

"Yeah, I'm sure. But before long you won't be able to answer the phone. You're sick. You're dying." I threw the letter from the hospital in front of him, but he ignored it.

"Who calls you, eh? They call from offices and bars, say, 'Yeah, hello, can we get a cab to Amagerbrogade, name's Jensen.'"

I had put my glass down, but I still sat there with his Bodil. His idea was that I would use it to smash in his skull. That was his plan, however and whenever it had come to him. Invite me up, provoke me, humiliate me. Something like that. I set it on the chess table, and yes, he was still a great actor, for he didn't bat an eye.

"I don't know, Erik," I drawled, because an idea had come to me. I stood up. My head buzzed a bit, too much whiskey in too short a time. But I was used to it. It would be all right. If he went for it, the revenge would be more than sweet. "Do you really want me to kill you, Erik? Just like that, without getting anything in return?"

For a long time he said nothing.

Then he cleared his throat and spoke with a surprisingly calm voice: "All right. I have a lot of cash on me. You can take some of the antiques. All the silver. Nobody saw us. You drove with the meter off. Nobody needs to know a thing. All you have to do is do it." A crooked smile. "For once in your life just do it, Klaus."

"Okay," I said.

Surprised, Rützou stared at me.

After another moment of silence, I was afraid he was getting cold feet, but then, in the same composed, toneless voice as before, he said: "Do what you will, just do it quick. Goddamn quick. Understood?"

I nodded politely.

"One second." He disappeared down the hall, rustled around in his office, and came back with a thick envelope that, excited now, he handed to me.

I looked. Nothing but large bills, lots of them. I stuck the envelope in my pocket and put the gloves on that I'd pulled out of my leather jacket.

Rützou had poured himself an extra large whiskey, and he drank so it ran down his chin and throat and stained the elegant white shirt under his tux.

"Let's get it over with, goddamnit," he gasped.

I started right in. Before any regrets came along. It's not nearly as easy to strangle someone as you might think. It requires a lot of strength and grisly patience. But that I had! Rützou's eyes started to bulge, the whites popped out, he gurgled and, I couldn't believe it, turned an even more ghostly white than before. He put up a little resistance, but most likely that was a natural reflex. For the bastard really wanted to die. Though he wouldn't be getting his wish, not yet.

"Shhoke harr-er, gaw-dammuh!" he babbled.

"Can you say please?"

"Puh-eeeze."

His blue tongue hung halfway out of the preposterous, already putrefied chasm of his mouth, his eyes had shifted from white to violently bloodshot, life slowly faded from them; it was a fantastic sight, he hissed and gasped and drooled like a god-damn snake, and then I abruptly dropped my stranglehold.

"Did you really think I'd do it, you idiot?"

Rützou tumbled backward, grabbed his throat, and gasped deeply for breath. He stood and swayed in his ridiculous patent-leather shoes, completely groggy; he'd pissed his pants, I noticed, and I was already celebrating my little stunt when he suddenly threw himself upon me in a rage and bombarded my face with rock-hard punches, his anger apparently increasing his strength because I was starting to see black. Now it was me on the edge of being knocked unconscious. I had no choice but to hit back. I slugged him straight on the chin.

Rützou fell his entire length and banged his head on the sharp corner of the coffee table. It sounded ugly. My knuckles ached in my gloves. Rützou was on the floor, lifeless. I prayed that he was only unconscious, when I saw a thin trickle of blood appear. More of it came, and more, until it was a small, dark lake.

Desperate, I fell to my knees and shook him, but there was no doubt.

Rützou was dead.

The asshole had tricked me after all.

For several minutes I sat and stared into space, unable to think or act. Then I downed a shot and began removing all traces of my fingerprints: I was on file. One of the last things I did before leaving the apartment was to empty my glass and wash it carefully. It was like being in a film, or no, a grainy documentary . . .

Then I left.

Down the stairs, the wide, red stairs.

* * *

And there I sat. It was still pitch dark and incredibly cold. I took my gloves off and fumbled around for the pack of cigarettes, only two left. The moment the flame rose from the lighter, I saw a flash of my gaunt and battered face in the rearview mirror. It was the stupidest possible thing I could do, to sit here smoking; someone might see me. But I really needed that cigarette. The money in the envelope, I'd completely forgotten about it. What had I done with it? Yeah, the money was safe and sound in my pocket, and in a moment I would be gone, headed for the hills, nobody would connect me with his death. I stuck the key in the ignition.

But then another thought hit me, harder than Rützou's fist. His girlfriend! They'd had a fierce fight earlier that evening. There were conspicuous signs of strangulation on his neck, anyone could see that he hadn't just fallen down drunk. Suspicion would immediately fall on her. Maybe she had an alibi, maybe not. And if she didn't, what would I do?

It was her or me. This would never end. Except for the one who was dead.

LAST TRAIN FROM CENTRAL STATION

BY GUNNAR STAALESEN

Central Station

(Originally written in Norwegian)

I stedgade lay like a painted corpse as I emerged from Central Station late in the afternoon one Friday in November, the year the U.S.A. elected its first black president and the world immediately looked much brighter than it had the previous eight years.

For a long time, Europe has begun for most Norwegians in Copenhagen, and Central Station is the gateway to the rest of the continent. There you can buy an aquavit in the cafe at eight in the morning, even on Sunday, and you realize at once that you have arrived in another world.

Norway's capital was located in Denmark for four hundred years. The despotic Danish sovereigns ruled from Copenhagen with an iron hand. At the beginning of the 1700s, a young man traveled from Norway to Denmark and became the first modern Nordic writer: Ludvig Holberg. Danes claim him for their own, Norway says he is Norwegian, but we in Bergen don't take the debate all that seriously. We know exactly where he came from. The Danish encyclopedias also put it quite correctly: Danish writer, born in Bergen.

I had followed in Holberg's footsteps many times myself, not in the pursuit of happiness, but usually to search for some young person who had run away from home. Copenhagen was also the most natural place for those on the run to hide out. It wasn't so difficult to get there, but still you felt you were far away from home.

After the regular ferry route between Oslo and Copenhagen had developed into a floating orgy of alcohol and the night train from Oslo had been discontinued, most traveled by air to Kastrup, Copenhagen's airport. Generally I had taken the train. Now the only train ride was the one from the airport, but Central Station was still the customary place to get off. You took the escalator up from the platform to the main hall, where the big city's noise and commotion hit you immediately. Arrivals and departures were announced over the speakers at regular intervals. Travelers of all nationalities and age groups passed by, some with backpacks, others with heavy suitcases that rolled on nifty little wheels, everyone on their way somewhere, even when waiting impatiently in groups. A railway station of this caliber is like a monument to the restlessness of the times, partings and farewells, greetings and embraces, teary smiles and sparkling laughter, noisy outbreaks of anger and murmured, intense confessions. All types of figures meet here, from the poorest beggar with outstretched hands to the richest businessman with the world's fattest cigar clenched between his teeth like a lighthouse.

As for me, I didn't stand out in any particular way. From the moment I walked into the hall, my gaze wandered from face to face, without much hope of finding the right one. After all, I hadn't seen her for twenty-three years.

Heidi Davik was her name in 1985, and Heidi Davik was her name still. In the years between she had been married and divorced and changed her name back and forth. But both times it was her father who had given me the assignment.

The first thing he asked when he came to my office on that

Thursday in November was if I remembered him. He was short, white-haired, and not too dissimilar from the candidate who had lost the American presidential election. But he was probably a few years younger, in his late sixties, I guessed. He was well-dressed, in a double-breasted suit.

"Faintly," I answered.

"Thor Davik. You were in Copenhagen and found my daughter Heidi in the spring of 1985." He opened the briefcase he'd brought with him and pulled out an old photo, yellowed and worn at the edges. "I gave you this shot back then."

He handed me the photo, and I looked down and nodded. I recognized her. Back then she had been a sweet little girl, sixteen, with long, dark hair, a self-conscious gaze, and a nice smile. I had found her in Christiania, the free state, where she was living in the back room of what resembled a ceramics workshop, with a Dane two years older than her who had even longer hair and a short, scruffy beard, reddish-blond. There had been wailing and gnashing of teeth when I convinced her to accompany me back to Bergen, but it didn't come to blows when she had to part with her soulmate. He looked rather miserable when I escorted Heidi out to Pusher Street and through the gateway of what had once been an abandoned military area, but which was still Scandinavia's most popular hippie colony, though it had aged somewhat, just like the hippies.

"She doesn't look like this now, I assume?"

"No, I just wanted to . . . Here!" He handed me a much more recent photo of an adult Heidi. I recognized her look and smile, but her hair was cut very short and bleached in blond streaks.

"So what's the story?"

He gave me the short version. After returning home from Copenhagen, things had gone well for her. She studied to be a physical therapist, got a full-time job, married a colleague, and after seven years of marriage without children, she got a divorce. "Her name was Lorentzen when she was married, but she took her maiden name back after the divorce."

"And what brings you here today?"

His gaze wavered. "It sounds almost like a bad remake of some film, but . . . she's back in Copenhagen. She's been there for fourteen days, and she doesn't answer her phone. We don't know where she's staying, either. I . . . her mother is very worried."

"But she's an adult now." I made a quick calculation. "Close to forty, if I'm not mistaken."

"So what?" He seemed aggravated. "Your children are your children, all their lives."

"And you won't go down and try to find her yourself?"

"No. It's impossible. She blames us for everything that's gone wrong."

"Everything that's gone wrong? You've just described a more or less normal life."

"Yes, well, except that we forced her to come home back then. She has never been able to forgive us for that."

"The young man she was staying with down there . . . did she ever hear from him again?"

He scrunched his lips together. "We don't know. But . . . we found this, among her papers, after she moved back in with us following her divorce. A small apartment in the basement. We can come and go . . ."

I realized he was trying to make excuses as best he could, and I held out my hand. He gave me a tourist postcard, conventional, with a photo of Tivoli on the front. I turned it over. There wasn't much written: *I'll meet you here, as planned. If problems, call this number. Your Christian.* Below it he had written a telephone number that began with 45, the country code for Denmark.

I looked at the more recent photo again. "Christian—and a phone number. Have you tried calling him?"

"Yes, but he said I must have the wrong number."

"I see."

"And we don't have the strength for it. I want you to go to Copenhagen and see this man, Veum. We want to know what has happened to our daughter. Why she doesn't answer us . . ."

I took the job, got on the Internet, and reserved a plane ticket for the next day. Meanwhile, I searched for the name and number and found what I was after: Christian Mogensen, with an address on Wesselsgade, which according to my well-worn map of Copenhagen lay right next to Sortedams Sø, one of the city's lakes.

I thought about calling him before I left Bergen but decided that it would probably be more effective to wait until I was a short taxi ride from where he lived.

It worked. The man who answered the phone sounded flustered when I introduced myself as a private investigator from Bergen, but he admitted that he was indeed Christian Mogensen and that he had sent a card to an old girlfriend in Bergen. I said that if he didn't provide information that would lead me to Heidi Davik, I would be at his door like some crazy Viking faster than he could say "three mackerels."

He hesitated a few seconds, but when I added "or like a bulldog gone berserk," he gave me an address on Lille Istedgade and said that's where I would find her, if she was at home.

"Lille Istedgade?" I said, and he took my tone of voice in such a way that he quickly added, "Yes, but Istedgade isn't like it used to be."

"No?"

"Not at all."

In many ways he was right. True, the street still had a porno shop or two, and a few of the girls strolling the sidewalk in what seemed to be a casual manner wore conspiculously short skirts for November. The long look I got from one of them told me that I could warm myself up with her if I was cold.

Nonetheless, there was a shined-up look to the street that hadn't been there in 1985, and when I got to the address Christian Mogensen had given me, a side street to Sønder Boulevard, the building proved to be newly renovated, the stairway nice and clean, and the list of tenants in the vestibule indicated that it was an apartment building. The left-hand apartment on the fourth floor—the one Mogensen had told me to go to—was apparently unoccupied. At least there was no name on the list.

On the way up I met a couple descending the stairs. The woman was blond, with hair pulled back severely and gathered in a knot. She wore an elegant dark-blue coat and carried a small black envelope purse in her gloved hand. She stared straight ahead, not looking in my direction. Her companion did, however: a broad-shouldered man with short dark hair, in a black winter coat and dark pants. The look he sent me was angry and hostile, as if he were saying: *Try taking her away from me, if you dare . . .*

For a moment or two I considered whether the building might be something other than what it seemed, perhaps a refuge for sadomasochists or some other crazy group. Then they passed by me, leaving behind only the reek of her strong perfume. I assumed it was hers, but you can never be sure. Not nowadays.

No one opened when I rang at the fourth-floor door that had no tenant name. I tried several times, and the doorbell could be heard all the way out in the hall, but there was no reaction from inside. I studied the door. It was made of solid, heavy wood, and the lock seemed secure, not one you could work open with a hairpin and a credit card.

I grabbed my phone, called Mogensen again, and gave him my sob story.

"Well, she's just out somewhere," he said.

"Then I'll pay you a visit instead."

"No, no. Wait right there, Veum, I'll come to you."

"And how long will that take?"

"Less than a half hour. Get a cup of coffee in the meantime."

I walked back to Istedgade, found a café on a corner, noticed the woman with the encouraging look at one of the tables but didn't accept the invitation this time, either. I sat at the bar on a stool high enough to keep an eye on the entrance to the building I had just left, and I ordered a cup of black coffee and a Brøndums aquavit, the closest I could come to a Simers Taffel south of the Skagerrak.

After twenty-five minutes a black Mercedes pulled up and a man got out. He was tall and somewhat rangy, with red-blond hair and a beard. He looked around before crossing the street and entering the building.

I emptied my glass, nodded at the waitress, and followed him.

I stood in the hallway and listened. At first I heard nothing. Then a door slammed, followed by hurried footsteps down the stairs.

When he reached bottom he met my gaze. Now I recognized him. His hair was shorter, beard neat and well-trimmed, and he was distinctly better-dressed than the last time we'd met. But it was the same man I had found her with in Christiania twenty-three years earlier.

His voice shook when he said, "Veum?"

"That's me. What's going on?"

Before he could answer, his phone rang. He put it to his ear, and as he listened he gradually grew paler. "But . . . but you can't . . ." He glanced up the stairway, as if he expected someone to come after him any second. "Yeah . . . all right, I'm coming. Track seven."

Then he lowered the phone and looked at me again. His expression was darker than the night, it was as if someone had poured poison in his ear. "I have to go."

"I'm going with you."

He looked like he was going to object, but just shrugged his shoulders. We went out to the sidewalk. He walked past his car without a glance.

"Where are we going?" I asked.

"Central Station. Track seven."

"And what's going to happen?"

"We're going to meet them."

"Who?" Impatient, I grabbed his arm. "Heidi?"

He jerked loose from my grip and looked at me, his despair about to flow over. The darkness surrounding us had settled over Copenhagen. At the end of Istedgade rose Central Station, its steep gable like some heathen house of God. The wind that hit us came from frozen outposts. It was no merry evening in the King's Copenhagen—or was it the Queen's nowadays?

"No," he snapped. "Svanhild."

He rushed toward Central Station, and I did what I could to keep pace.

No more was said. At the street's end we walked directly in through the nearest entrance and bolted up the steps to the main hall, where Christian Mogensen made a beeline for the stairs to track seven. I followed.

The tracks at Copenhagen's Central Station lie in an excavated area underneath. On track seven, it was announced that an intercity train to Århus-Struer was arriving in five minutes. Mogensen ran down the steps as if the train was pulling out right in front of him. Without any hesitation I followed at his heels.

The platform was packed, but Mogensen shoved his way through until it thinned out in the crowd of travelers standing with suitcases and other luggage, ready to board as soon as the train pulled in.

They stood waiting for us at the far end of the platform, the blond woman and the broad-shouldered man I had met in the hallway an hour earlier. Mogensen stopped a few meters from them and stood with arms hanging, gasping for air. I stayed behind but off to one side of him for a clear view.

A few tracks away, an S train was headed out to the suburbs, maybe up to what Copenhageners called the "whiskey belt." No one here on the platform at track seven was indulging in whiskey. But the looks they exchanged were as cold as ice cubes.

The woman I gathered to be Svanhild twisted her lips into the sourest smile I'd seen since Maggie Thatcher. "What's wrong, darling?" she said to Mogensen.

"You're both crazy! Was he the one who did it?"

The broad-shouldered man took a few steps to the side and raised his arm like a gunman before the last shootout. He nodded in my direction. "Who's this clown?"

Mogensen turned halfway around, as if he'd forgotten that I had followed him. Then he pulled out his cell phone and held it in front of them. "I'm calling the police! I am—right now!"

"Remember to give them your confession," Svanhild said, with an evil smile. "They'll find your DNA when they test the sperm in her vagina. You gave me a nice-sized quantity of it this morning, have you forgotten? You didn't say no, even when the gorgeous love of your life was waiting on Lille Istedgade—"

"You don't mean—"

"A trip to the bathroom and a quick drain into a little bottle. That's all it took. But we also grabbed a few hairs from your brush just to be safe and laid them on her pillow."

I had a sinking feeling in my stomach. "What are we talking about here? You're not saying that—"

Mogensen turned to me again, his face as white as a sheet. "They killed her. That woman there—that evil woman, my wife—she couldn't let me live with another woman. The one I've wanted so much all these years." He turned back to Svanhild. "Why didn't you take me instead?"

I was inclined to believe him. Her smile was more evil than that of the queen in *Snow White and the Seven Dwarves*.

"It wouldn't have hurt enough, darling. Not long enough."

"And he helped you! My partner, your lover, Frederik Vesterlund."

"It was a sheer pleasure. For him too. He raped her while I held her down. But don't worry. He didn't come. Only you did."

I could hardly believe my ears. Christian and Frederik stood staring at each other, two kings on the same platform. Like some fake arbitrator I walked between them. "But you're forgetting one thing," I said.

"What the hell is this Norwegian doing here?" Vesterlund bellowed.

"He's the crown witness for the prosecution," I said. "I can testify that I saw you two leave the building before Mogensen arrived. And when he came, he wasn't in there long enough to have done any of these things at the scene of the crime that you're babbling about."

The train for Århus and Struer whistled in the tunnel behind us.

It all happened within a few seconds.

Svanhild pointed at me, and as if she was commanding a dog, said: "Frederik, get him!"

Frederik Vesterlund lunged at me, but Mogensen stepped in before he reached me. Vesterlund swung at him, but Mogensen stepped to the side, grabbed his arm, and pushed him along. They stumbled toward the edge of the platform, and in the moments before the train was about to thunder past, they tottered at the very edge. The people behind us screamed in terror, the brakes screeched, and with a violent shove Christian Mogensen took Frederik Vesterlund with him down onto the track, where a fraction of a second later they disappeared under the massive train. Then it got quiet. Completely quiet.

Svanhild Mogensen stood like a limestone pillar in the middle of the platform. Then she began moving, slowly and studiously. She opened her handbag, found a pack of cigarettes, stuck one between her lips, and lit it with a gold lighter. She gazed at me through the blue smoke with the look of a cobra just before it strikes.

She walked toward me, her hips swinging discretely. As she passed, she blew a lungful of smoke in my direction. "Oh well," she murmured. "I had no use for either one of them any longer."

I stood and watched her leave. Several railroad employees passed. One of them stopped in front of me.

"Did you see what happened?"

"I saw the whole thing."

"We have to call the police."

"Do it."

* * *

After I had given my statement to the police, they insisted I follow them down to Lille Istedgade.

They broke the lock, and I walked into the apartment. We found Heidi where they had left her. Lying in bed, naked and dead, with a blue and yellow necktie tight around her throat and a dead man's sperm inside her.

Her face was blue-gray, her eyes empty and lips distorted in a grimace that showed she hadn't left this world voluntarily. Someone had pushed her over the edge and let her dangle. It wasn't a pretty sight, even for a hardened detective.

I said to myself: What if I hadn't found her back in 1985? Would she be lying here now? Or would life have been entirely different for both her and Christian Mogensen?

I told the police the whole story, and I saw their skepticism grow with every word I spoke. "How the hell are we supposed to prove that?" groaned the policeman leading the interrogation.

"You have to bring her in for questioning."

"We already are. She's on her way."

"If you need a witness, I'm more than willing to come back to Copenhagen."

"You're not too scared?"

"Not yet."

The last hours before I left for the airport I spent at Jern-banecafe on Reventlowsgade, close to Central Station, where the service was first-class. I ordered a Tuborg Classic and so many Brøndums that I finally lost count. A small model rail-road ran back and forth under the ceiling. I sat and followed it with my eyes to be sure. But no one threw himself in front of it. Not a single person.

It wasn't pleasant news I brought back home with me to Ber-gen. No one put their arms around me when I told them what had happened, though I'm not exactly used to having that happen.

Several weeks later I stumbled onto a Danish paper at a kiosk in the park. A teaser on the front page piqued my curiosity. I flipped through to a spread inside the paper. There was a beautiful photo of Svanhild Mogensen, smiling cooly at the photographer. The short article explained that after the tragic death of her husband at Central Station earlier in the month, she reported that she intended to continue their successful Amager business and would lead it forward as its new director. Nothing was mentioned about any regrets she might have had; no doubt she didn't have any.

It's said that crime doesn't pay. And who said this, I'd like to know? More on target was the man who said that hidden behind every great fortune is a crime.

I sent her a card with my name on it. But I never got an answer. She surely had better things to do. And so did I, for that matter.

ABOUT THE CONTRIBUTORS

NAJA MARIE AIDT (b. 1963) is one of Denmark's most acclaimed lyricists and short story writers; her latest collection, *Bavian* (2006), received the Critics' Award and the Nordic Council's Literature Prize. In 2008, Aidt moved from Copenhagen to Brooklyn, New York.

JONAS T. BENGTSSON (b. 1976) published his debut novel *Amina's Letters* in 2005, and has since written a novel about brothers, *Submarino* (a 2010 film by Thomas Vinterberg), which like his story in this volume takes place partly in the Northwest district, Bengtsson's home ground for many years.

CHRISTIAN DORPH (b. 1966) and **SIMON PASTERNAK** (b. 1971) have attracted considerable attention in the Danish crime fiction community with their novels *In a Moment in Heaven* (2005), *The Edge of the Abyss* (2007), and *I'm Not Here* (2010), which have been translated into six languages.

AGNETE FRIIS (b. 1975) and **LENE KAABERBØL** (b. 1960) debuted in Danish crime fiction with *The Suitcase Boy* (2008)—the first book in a series featuring the Red Cross nurse Nina Borg. Kaaberbøl has been for many years an internationally best-selling fantasy writer. Friis is a journalist and also a fantasy writer.

HELLE HELLE (b. 1965) is the author of various short stories and novels, including the acclaimed novels *Down to the Dogs* (2008) and *Rødby-Puttgarden* (2005). The latter won the Critics' Prize. Helle Helle lived in Vanløse from 1988–1993 while employed at Bakken (an amusement park north of Copenhagen) as an information girl clad in a green uniform with shoulder padding; later she attended Copenhagen's Writer's School.

BENN Q. HOLM (b. 1962) is a Copenhagen writer best known for the novels *Hafnia Punk* (1998), *Album* (2005, adapted into a TV series in 2008), and *Copenhagen's Mysteries* (2008).

GRETELISE HOLM (b. 1946), author and national commentator, has in recent years achieved much success as a writer of crime fiction, inside and outside of Denmark.

LENE KAABERBØL (b. 1960) and **AGNETE FRIIS** (b. 1975) debuted in Danish crime fiction with *The Suitcase Boy* (2008)—the first book in a series featuring the Red Cross nurse Nina Borg. Kaaberbøl has been for many years an internationally best-selling fantasy writer. Friis is a journalist and also a fantasy writer.

MARK KLINE (b. 1952) has translated the fiction and poetry of a number of contemporary Danish writers. He has had many short stories published, and for years he has been a bluegrass musician in Denmark. He and his wife live in the South Harbor section of Copenhagen.

KRISTIAN LUNDBERG (b. 1966) is a lyricist and writer from *over there*—Sweden—where he has gained notoriety with his crossover and extremely experimental crime series about his hometown, Malmø, a city on the edge of dissolution as an axis for borderless crime in the new Europe. Policeman Nils Forsberg is at the center of the books, which include *Eldätaren (The Fire-Eater,* 2004), *Grindväktaren (The Gate-keeper,* 2005) and *Malmømannen (The Malmø Man,* 2009).

BO TAO MICHAËLIS (b. 1948) received his master's degree in comparative literature and classical culture from the University of Copenhagen, where he now teaches. He is a cultural critic at the Danish newspaper *Politiken*, and has written books on crime fiction, Raymond Chandler, and Ernest Hemingway; and papers about Dashiell Hammett, Paul Auster, and several other American writers.

SEYIT ÖZTÜRK (b. 1980) won second prize in a writing contest for "new Danes," for his short story "Where I'm Sitting Now," which appeared in the anthology *New Voices* (2007). Öztürk is of Turkish descent, and has lived most of his life in Valby, more recently moving to Nørrebro.

SIMON PASTERNAK (b. 1971) and **CHRISTIAN DORPH** (b. 1966) have attracted considerable attention in the Danish crime fiction community with their novels *In a Moment in Heaven* (2005), *The Edge of the Abyss* (2007), and *I'm Not Here* (2010), which have been translated into six languages.

KLAUS RIFBJERG (b. 1931) has been a major fixture in Danish literature over the past fifty years. He was born and raised in Amager, in Eberts Villaby.

GUNNAR STAALESEN (b. 1947), a Norwegian author residing in Bergen, is known and loved for his Bergen trilogy *(First Blush of Dawn, High Noon,* and *Evening Song)* and several volumes of crime fiction starring private detective Varg Veum.

SUSANNE STAUN (b. 1957) has made a name for herself in the Danish crime fiction scene with her books about the profiling expert Fanny Fiske, the latest of which is *My Girls* (2008).

KRISTINA STOLTZ (b. 1975) has written three volumes of poetry, books for children, and the novel *The Tourist Hotel* (2006). Her second novel, *Human Track,* will be published in 2011. She has lived in bohemian Nørrebro most of her adult life.

GEORG URSIN (b. 1934), a former public servant, had his literary debut at the age of seventy-one with the Kafka-esque crime novel *Cherlein and Schmidt* (2005). He has since written four more crime novels, the latest of which is *Murder at the Museum* (2009), all of them highly acclaimed. The Danish Crime Writers Academy honored Ursin in 2008 for *The Anonymous Movement.*